Jase turned back to the soft click of the other door handle.
The creature that emerged struck him dumb. Literally. He could not have formed a coherent word and spoken at that instant even if the fate of the free world hung in the balance. His body instantaneously warmed and his stomach did a slow, hard roll, then another. Her sultry musky scent infiltrated his senses and attacked him like a lethal virus. His mouth went dry.

Holy Mother.

Big jade-colored eyes that slanted upward at the corners reminded him of a feral cat. A sleek, black feral cat. Boldly, she stared unwaveringly at him. Her cool indifference was unsettling. Straight hair so black it almost looked blue hung like a veil around her heart-shaped face. The delicate nostrils of her short aquiline nose flared, and her ruby red lips parted just enough to reveal brilliant white teeth.

Jase couldn't help it. His eyes traveled from her ethereal face down that long slender neck to breasts so full and creamy they reminded him of caramel apples. He bet they were fake. They had to be. She wasn't wearing a bra, her nipples stiffened as he stared, and he knew for tits that perfect to sit up that firm and that high they had to have had some help.

She extended a slender hand, the nails perfectly manicured and real, not those fake red claw jobs the hookers favored.

"Sergeant Vaughn? Jade Devereaux, proprietress of Callahan's. How many I help you?"

You can help me by relieving this boner.

ALSO BY KARIN TABKE

JADED

KARIN TABKE

POCKET BOOKS
New York   London   Toronto   Sydney

Pocket Books
A Division of Simon & Schuster, Inc.
1230 Avenue of the Americas
New York, NY 10020

First Pocket Books trade paperback edition June 2008

POCKET and colophon are registered trademarks of Simon & Schuster, Inc.

For information about special discounts for bulk purchases,
please contact Simon & Schuster Special Sales
at 1-800-456-6798 or business@simonandschuster.com.

Designed by Carla Jayne Little

Manufactured in the United States of America

10 9 8 7 6 5 4 3 2 1

Library of Congress Cataloging-in-Publication Data

Tabke, Karin.
   Jaded / by Karin Tabke.
      p. cm.
   I. Title.
PS3620.A255J33 2008
813'.6—dc22

ISBN-13: 978-1-4165-6444-7
ISBN-10:   1-4165-6444-6

To Jeff. You are in my heart always. Don't ever forget it.

ACKNOWLEDGMENTS

Right off the bat I'd like to thank Sergeant Jim Conley for being a gentleman, friend, and a great homicide detective source to tap into. You went beyond the call of duty to answer my many questions, and I cannot thank you enough. To his wife, Patty: thanks a million for lending me your hubby. Dinner is at our place next time!

To my friend Liz Iannacone, for her insight and expertise in child psychology. My bad guy is sufficiently twisted because of you.

To Megan McKeever, thank you for "getting" Jase and Jade. And thank you for making *Jaded* stronger.

And always, to my husband, thank you so much for all of those times in the past when I asked, "Honey, what would a cop do in this situation?" or "What is the procedure for . . . ?" And thank you in advance for the many more cop questions that you will undoubtedly take time out of your day to answer for me. I love you.

Saturday, 11:32 p.m.
Callahan's

"Touch me again, Mr. Townsend, and I'll cut your balls off and shove them so far down your throat you'll choke to death."

"My lovely Jade, is that any way for a lady to talk to a gentleman?" Townsend asked.

Jade smiled, the gesture not true enough to part her lips. She cocked her head back and to the side. Andrew Townsend's glassy eyes dropped to her chest. Though the smooth fabric of her sapphire-colored Chanel sheath dress covered her from neck to knees, the jersey hugged her curves like a taut second skin, detailing in sexy silhouette exactly what lay beneath. Its sole purpose was to tease. And Townsend was worthy prey. From the moment he picked her up at the club earlier that evening, his eyes, and hands, had strayed. She'd been hard-pressed to keep his groping at bay and her composure intact.

For the first time in many years, she felt the urge to turn around and walk out the double teakwood doors of the club—and keep walking. But that was impossible. Instead she swept her eyelids low and maintained her even breathing pattern.

"Mr. Townsend, you are not my definition of a gentleman."

He grabbed her elbow in a quick movement that surprised her. With the amount of scotch he'd consumed she doubted he had it in him. He was not a nice man sober, but lit up as he was now, he was downright belligerent. She'd parried her fair share of rudeness from men in her day, but Townsend was driven by something more than the alcohol tonight. A man used to naming his price for whatever commodity he fancied at the moment was not getting his way, and as his kind often did, he resorted to bullying tactics.

"I don't know what your definition is, honey, and it doesn't matter." He yanked her against his chest, his scotch-soaked breath mingling with the garlic of their dinner earlier that evening. "I've paid for you lock, stock, and barrel, now I want what's coming to me."

Her back stiffened. Not wanting to create a scene that could ultimately cost her other exclusive members, Jade relaxed against him, giving him a taste of what he so desperately craved, and would never get. It was fair play in her mind, and she was not one to not exact a little revenge. Besides, if Townsend didn't come back in the hopes of one day landing her in bed, she'd failed in her job. In his heated pursuit he would return again, and again. She pressed her full breasts to the fine cotton of his tailored shirt. "You've paid my price—for dinner and conversation, Mr. Townsend. There are no fringe benefits."

"You're a prick tease."

Jade laughed slow, the sound low and husky. She knew from experience the sound poured over a man like warm honey over a fresh-baked biscuit. A laugh she had been told could wheedle a priest from the pulpit. As intended, it garnered an immediate result. She felt him rise against her hip, his minimal package jabbing into her like a boning knife.

Men were so easily distracted and so easily led. And she was eternally grateful for that fact. Were it not true she would no doubt be working much harder for far less pay than what she garnered here at Callahan's. When she thought of the consequences of a nine-to-five job she reined in her temper. "I resent that remark, sir. I explained the nature of our date. If I remember correctly, you were rather intrigued to *not* go beyond my boundaries. You said, 'Why should I have to pay for something my wife gives me for free?'"

His dark eyes morphed into a hard glare. "I lied."

Jade pressed her hips against his erection, smiled wider, and then pulled her arm from his grasp and stepped back. "I didn't. Now, please excuse me."

"You'll regret this!" he called to her retreating back.

Jade didn't hesitate in her long sanguine stroll to her small office just past the long bar, the hidden door resembling another polished wooden panel. She smiled graciously at the couples whose heads turned at Townsend's outburst, as if it were a normal annoying occurrence.

"Mr. Townsend, a Glenlivet on the house," Mac, her bar manager, said. He'd no doubt witnessed the entire ugly exchange. Mac was a good man. He stood quiet sentry over the bar, and on the very few and very unpleasant occasions when a member became unmanageable, he maneuvered them as seamlessly as he uncorked one of the vintage bottles of wine for which Callahan's was known. He was their guardian angel.

Jade made a mental note to reward Mac once again for his ability to redirect a man's desires.

In these days and times it was becoming increasingly difficult to keep her "dates" in the neutral zone she had constructed around herself. The private nature of Callahan's was becoming less private.

It was rumored that Jack Morton, the new owner, was strapped for cash, and so instead of culling the applicants who had the necessary funds to buy in but lacked the pedigree, he ballooned the application fee, as well as the annual membership dues, and rewarded the mongrel's thirst for social status with a provisional membership. Andrew Townsend was one such member. The man inherited several car dealerships from his father, and spent the profits like a sailor on leave.

And because it was Andrew Townsend, and because he only understood one language, she had been more than willing to tell him exactly, in words he understood, what she would do if he pursued her.

Yes, times were changing at Callahan's. And armed with that knowledge, Jade consoled herself. She could roll with the change. Once a chameleon always a chameleon. She'd always been able to adjust her color to any palette. It's what kept her alive.

And if her time ran out here? She'd pull out and make stake somewhere else.

"Jade," a soft voice asked from the darkened corner next to her office door.

Jade's demeanor instantly softened, and she smiled at Genevieve, a girl not much older than her little sister, Tina. "Do you need something, sweetie?" she asked.

Genny nodded, her thick golden blonde hair bobbing under the low lights. "I need to ask you a favor. Can we—"

"Well, now, look at Goldilocks," Townsend slurred as he stepped between the two women. He turned dark eyes on Jade, then looked at Genny. "I bet *you* like to show your appreciation, doncha, honey pie?"

"Mr. Townsend, in your current state, I don't think—"

"It's okay, Jade," Genny interrupted. She bestowed a huge smile on the drunk, linking her arm with his. "Jade has told me all about you, Mr. Townsend. I think I remember her telling me you were an avid football fan. I *love* football."

Jade made a motion to stop Genny, but was warned off with a sharp nod from the girl. Jade held back, and not for the first time. She could control what happened in the club, but what members and employees did on their own time? That she had no control of.

Several hours later, tired and feeling uncharacteristically lonely, Jade made her way to the private parking lot behind Callahan's. Her feet were sore, her patience drawn as taut as a trip wire, and her sudden fatigue settled deep in her bones. She wanted to sleep for a month, putting her life on hold. She sighed. She'd have to settle for a soak in her tub with the spa jets full blast on her back.

Holding the keys to her BMW, she clicked the lock fob, the sound of the popping locks sounding strange in the empty lot. The headlights glowed eerily. She shivered, the seclusion unnerving, and looked up to see several spotlights out near her car. She made a mental note to call Ernesto, her maintenance man, when she got in later that night.

"Are you too busy for me now, *Miss* Jade?"

The fine hair on the back of her neck spiked. Warning bells shrilled. Turning slowly around, her back to the driver-side door, her left arm at her side, Jade maneuvered the key in her hand and pressed a button on the small black handle attached to the chain. A four-inch blade popped out.

"Mr. Townsend? I thought you and Genevieve had a date."

He stood a good four inches taller than she, which said a lot about his height. In her heels she stood six feet tall. "Yeah, we did. But she ain't you."

He closed in and pressed the length of his body against hers, the heavy odor of scotch mixing with the stale gas fumes in the cloying air of the lot.

She'd survived far worse than anything Andrew Townsend could dish out. Jade notched her head back and looked him square in the eye. "You have an awfully short memory, Mr. Townsend."

He laughed, the sound full of self-importance. His blood-shot eyes dipped to her lips. "You have the poutiest lips I ever saw. So full, and lush, and red. Do you know how many times I've dreamed of them locked around my dick?"

His hands rested against her hips and for such a blundering drunk, almost reverently he slid them up her waist. Her skin flinched beneath his touch. Claustrophobia closed in. Her chest tightened. Old memories, memories she'd buried long ago, reared their ugly heads. Spots blurred her vision. Her hands shook.

"I can be gentle, Jade. I can be whatever you want." He dipped his head to her hair and inhaled. "You smell so fuck-able."

Townsend's voice yanked her back to the present. A surreal sense of relief flooded her. She could handle Townsend.

He was just a horny, drunk, middle-aged man. Jade took a deep cleansing breath. She was safe from the ghosts of her past. She'd been too careful.

Her vision cleared and Jade looked straight at him and smiled. Townsend's eyes pleaded with her for relief. She'd seen it a hundred times on as many men. Her reaction was always the same. Cool disdain. And no desire for any physical interaction. On any level.

Softly, so as not to arouse him further, Jade pushed against his chest with her right hand. "Mr. Townsend. I can't be bought."

His eyes glittered under the low light. Townsend withdrew his hands from her waist and stepped back. Tenuous relief flooded her. Until he retook his step and jammed his fingers into her hair at the temples, digging deep into her scalp. Pain prickled. Her back arched. And her past came crashing into her present. Her fingers wrapped tighter around the key fob. He yanked her hard against him.

"Then I guess I'll take what I want for free."

CHAPTER

1

"Looks like somebody didn't like this guy much," Jase Vaughn said, then sipped a fresh cup of coffee. He closed his eyes, savoring the rich taste of the brew. He didn't know where Abu at the Drive By got his beans, and he didn't really care. He was just grateful for the fact that every single time he walked into that dive of a gas station the coffee was hot and it was fresh.

"Ya think?" Vangie Duncan, the crime-scene tech assigned to the scene, said.

Jase opened his eyes and looked up from his squatting position next to the trussed-up body over to the little blonde tech. "I can see why you graduated top in your class." He bestowed his most dazzling grin on her and watched the color rise in her cheeks. Maybe later he'd take her out for a beer and see what developed.

He looked around for a place to set his coffee cup but realized he couldn't. Instead, he frowned. Fire had done their usual bang-up job decimating a crime scene. Jase took another sip of his coffee. Good thing rigor had set in; otherwise, they'd have left all their shit lying around after they ran a line, cluttering up his scene even more. As it was, they'd left enough debris on the blood-soaked asphalt to fill a small trash bag. Who the hell knew what evidence they'd tracked off.

He grinned. Payback was a beautiful bitch. Fire didn't much like standing by for the techs to scrape their boot bottoms for trace evidence.

Jase looked over his shoulder to the beat cop who'd discovered the body, widening the perimeter. He was chatting with the watch commander, who'd gladly relinquished control of the scene to Jase, now the lead detective, when he'd arrived.

He'd get to questioning the uniform shortly. He glanced at his watch and noted the time. His partner would be arriving soon. He looked back at the stiff. It looked like they had their work cut out for them.

Jase took a closer look at the victim. White male, approximate age forty-five, naked, hog-tied—hands to feet behind his back—and recently entered the life, or as in this case, death, of a eunuch. Jase cringed. The guy's balls had been whacked, and from what he could tell it looked like the killer used them to shut him up. From the bloodstain under the vic's hips, it was obvious the mutilation happened on the spot. Whoever did it contained the scene, making it nice and neat.

A wad of clothes, the vic's, he presumed, lay in a heap several feet from the body. The only other visible wound from Jase's angle was a puncture wound under the rib cage on his right side. Maybe a little torture but probably not the wound that killed him. But until the ME had a chance to go over the body, they wouldn't know for sure. The stiff's dark eyes had the hard cloudy look of a marble, but even with the dullness of death, petechiae was evident. Jase's guess was asphyxiation. He stood and shook his head. What a way to go, choking on your own balls. Dayum. Talk about payback.

He squinted at the late-morning sun, then back to the body, then across it to the tech. "We've let the heroes stew long enough. Go get what you can off of Fire's boots, then get back here."

Vangie nodded and stood.

"And be careful where you walk," Jase instructed.

She gave him a look that said, "Do I have 'stupid' stamped on my forehead?"

Jase just grinned. He stood and stretched his long legs. It was near noon on this fine Sunday morning, and while he'd resented the initial phone call interrupting his gym time, now he was grateful. He glanced down at the poor slob trussed up like a holiday pig. Whoever did the guy had a grudge. Jase's blood warmed to the challenge. He loved to put puzzle pieces together.

He glanced over at the uniform who was just finishing his admirable tape job. Several other cops milled along the perimeter, keeping the small crowd from the scene.

"Officer?" Jase called.

The kid looked over and hurried to him. "Yes, Sergeant?"

Jase stepped away from the body, set his cup on the top of the nearby Dumpster, and pulled his spiral notepad from the inside of his sports jacket. "Who called it in?"

"No one. I came across the body."

"So you were first on scene?"

"Yes, sir, this is my beat."

"Anyone loitering?"

"Nope, this part of town is quiet on Sunday mornings."

"You're day?"

"Yes, came on at eight, stumbled across the body at nine forty-five."

Jase looked up and down the isolated alley. The Dumpster the body lay next to obscured its view from the street. Yet the body wasn't concealed. "Looks to me like whoever did this wanted the body to be found fairly quickly." He jotted notes down and looked over at the cop. "What made you come down this alley on such a fine Sunday morning?"

The color in the cop's face rose just enough to be detected. "I was going to catch up on paper." He looked over at the stiff. "Instead, I got more."

Jase nodded. Couldn't blame the guy for wanting to take what would normally be a slow time of day and catch up on reports. "Any heads-up in lineup? Any reports of abduction, screams, disturbances?"

The kid shook his head. Jase pulled his radio from his belt. "Detective Seventeen to Dispatch."

"Go ahead, Detective."

"Any calls overnight in Boy beat? Loud noise, maybe screaming? Anything?"

"Stand by, Seventeen, while I check the mids' log."

Jase scanned the perimeter of the yellow crime-scene tape. Almost two dozen people had assembled, along with the usual vultures from the local news stations.

His gaze continued along the trendy buildings on Forty-eighth Street. Montrose, an upper-middle-class suburb of Silicon Valley, catered to the well-to-do. Mostly financial and high-tech, although it had its share of crime. But homicide, especially this type of homicide, was uncommon. It's why he put in for this unit. For too many years, UC had taken too much away from him. He was ready to get back to basic police work.

"Detective Seventeen?"

"Go ahead."

"The only thing I show is an anonymous call at oh three thirty-five regarding an injured party several blocks from there. However, the beat officer cleared it UTL."

Unable to locate. "Dispatch, let me have that twenty, please."

"5150 Thirty-ninth Street at Bayside. The caller indicated the parking lot in the back of the building."

The uniform whistled as Jase jotted down the address.

"Ten-four." He looked at the cop. "What's so significant about this address?"

"Bayside and Thirty-ninth? The two-story white brick building? No street number, just a brass plaque that says 'private' on it at the front door?" The officer wagged his eyebrows. "Ring any bells?"

Jase scowled. "Cut to the chase."

"Callahan's. It's some *shee-shee* men's club."

"'Shee-shee' as in high-priced call girls?"

"Yeah, something like that, but as long as I've worked this beat we haven't had any trouble from them. We don't bother them either. I've heard Congressman Kosa and even one or two police chiefs like to throw back a few there now and then."

Jase wondered what else they threw back there. He made a note to go visit the lot, and of course the "men's club."

"So we get a call at almost four this morning, an anon saying someone was hurt in the private parking lot. Cops show up, can't find a body, you show up six hours later and find a stiff less than a mile from where the caller said the body was?"

The uniform nodded. "That about sums it up."

Jase's eyes narrowed. "You could see rigor had set in, why'd you let Fire in?"

The uniform grinned and shook his head. "Sergeant, you've been undercover too long. In this town Fire comes through and does whatever the hell they want. I told them the stiff was stiff. They pushed past and started doing their thing until it occurred to them the guy had no line. But I got pictures of the original position before they came and fucked it up. They wanted to untruss him, but I convinced them not to."

Jase nodded and addressed the officer by his name tag. "Good job, Martinez. I want those pics ASAP. Go ahead and take pictures of the alley and street, get pictures of the crowd. Have another uniform chat it up with the spectators. I want info cards on everyone here who isn't a cop. My partner, Ricco Maza, should be on scene shortly, send him over to me, and if there's anything the tech needs, help her out."

Jase walked back to the body, careful not to step on any evidence. It would be hours before the coroner arrived and he didn't have that kind of time to wait.

He caught Vangie's eye as she finished up with the last fireman, and inclined his head toward the pile of clothes near the body.

As she approached he said, "See if there's anything in his pockets."

"Sir, we have to wait—"

"I'll accept full responsibility."

"But—"

Jase stuck out his hand, palm up and open. "Give me the damn gloves and I'll do it myself!"

"I'll do it."

"Andrew Hard Townsend," Vangie said, opening the wallet she'd pulled from the back pants pocket of what looked like tailored slacks. Being a man who appreciated nice threads, Jase recognized the scuffed loafers as custom Italian. If his wardrobe was any indicator, the guy was loaded. Wonder if he was married. Jase's eyes returned to the body resting on its left side. "I bet he's wearing a wedding band. Once you have enough pictures, let's roll him over."

Vangie gave him a sharp glare.

"Listen, Duncan, I'm in charge of the crime scene *and* this case. Either do what I tell you, or I'll call in a tech who will."

"It's just, well, sir, protocol states—"

Again, Jase held out his hand impatiently for gloves. She sighed and handed him a pair, but said, "I'll do it, but I'll need help turning him over."

Jase nodded and put the gloves on.

When they rolled the body slightly to the right to expose the left hand, Jase nodded, satisfied. "I guess Mrs. Townsend is as good a place to start as any." He jotted down the address on the driver's license. "See if there's a cell phone."

Vangie rummaged through the pile of garments, finally shaking her head no.

"Interesting, the killer leaves everything but the cell phone."

"How do you know he had a cell phone?"

Jase shrugged and jotted notes down as he spoke. "The wallet has over seven hundred cash in it, all of his credit cards seem to be there, no empty slots, and his ID. What person under the age of sixty do you know who doesn't have a cell phone on them at all times?" Jase bent down and turned the slacks over. "See? An empty clip on the belt."

Vangie nodded. "I would have caught that."

His mood tightened. "Sure you would." He stood, and just as quickly his mood lightened. Montrose's rendition of Hollywood Cop came striding on scene. Vangie followed Jase's gaze and he heard her breath catch.

Jase grinned as he caught the stares of every female in sight, as well as several males behind the yellow tape. Despite Ricco's swagger, dark good looks, designer threads, and million-dollar smile, he was a damn good cop.

"Jase, *amigo, qué pasa*?"

Vangie popped up from her position near the body and extended her hand. "I'm Evangeline."

Ricco stopped in his long stride and bestowed a smile on the little tech that almost made Jase gag. "Forgive me, *precia*, I didn't see you. How could I miss such a beautiful lady?"

He took her hand and instead of shaking it like a normal man, he brought it to his lips and kissed it. Vangie looked like she was ready to swoon.

"Knock it off, Maza. We have a homicide, in case you haven't noticed."

Chapter

2

As Jase pulled up in front of the multistory mock–Italian villa he shook his head. He wasn't loaded but he'd been smart with his investments and had used his hazard pay on some fairly risky business ventures, and despite the rocky market he'd done well, *really* well. Even with his small fortune he would never dump it all into such a behemoth of a place as this. It stood out like a bald man at a wig convention. The new-money stench hit him at the curb. The Atherton neighborhood was old money, so the neighbors must have cringed when Townsend moved in.

The only thing missing was pink flamingos. He pulled up into the wide circular drive, the one with several fountains of naked women, as well as men at full mast.

He sighed and glanced at his watch. It was nearly two. He'd never liked giving a death notice, and liked it less now. The guy probably had kids. He knocked on the door. A voice called out from deep inside the house. The sound of a child's laughter, then a high-pitched scream, followed by more laughter drifted through the door to Jase. Shit, at least two kids.

"Ingrid, *la puerta*!"

The door suddenly opened and a round ruffled Latina in her late fifties gasped as she looked up at him.

"*Buenos tardes,* señorita."

She blushed and giggled. "Señor."

Jase laid on the charm. "*Soy* Sergeant Vaughn, *con* Montrose *policía.* Is Mrs. Townsend available?"

Ingrid's eyes widened. "Señora!" she called, then backed into the vast entryway, motioning him inside. Two little girls poked their heads out from around a large urn, their brown eyes bright, mischief dancing in them.

Ingrid shooed them away. "Ingrid, who is—" Mrs. Townsend, he presumed, as the voice materialized into a person. Younger than he thought, midthirties, trim, dressed to the nines on a Sunday afternoon.

"*El policía,* señora," Ingrid said, doom lacing her tone.

Mrs. Townsend cocked her head and half smiled. She knew—something.

"What did he do?"

"Mrs. Townsend, I'm Jason Vaughn, Sergeant Vaughn, Montrose PD. Is there somewhere we can go and speak privately?"

The sudden set of her jaw spoke volumes. She shooed the kids away and waved Ingrid to take them.

Jase followed her into a large overappointed room. The heavy brocades and ornate furniture did not complement the architecture of the house. After giving the room a cursory look, he gestured to the chair. "Please, sit down, Mrs. Townsend."

"My name is Natalie and I'd prefer to stand. What has my husband done?"

"Mrs. Townsend—" She opened her mouth to protest. "Ah, Natalie, I'm afraid I have bad news."

"*What* did he do?"

"Earlier this morning your husband's body was found—"

Her face paled and she reached back for the arm of the chair. Jase moved to her and gently guided her into the seat.

"'Body found'? Is he—okay?"

"No, ma'am, he's dead. The apparent victim of a homicide."

"Oh my god!" She crumpled into the chair.

"I'm sorry, is there something I can get you or someone I can call for you?"

"No, no, I—he—I don't believe you!"

"I'm very sorry, I know this is a shock to you, but I need to ask you a couple of questions."

Stunned, she just stared at him.

"When was the last time you saw Mr. Townsend?"

"He, oh my god, the girls, *the girls*."

"Mrs. Townsend, please, I know this is a shock, but the sooner you can give me information, the sooner we can find out who killed him."

Her brown eyes turned up to his and narrowed, her shock momentarily evaporating. "How did he die?"

The question shouldn't have caught him off guard, but it did. The vision of Townsend trussed up like a pig with his shaved-off balls shoved down his throat flashed before him.

"I'm sorry, I won't know that until I read the coroner's report." Even if he did, the details would be something only he and the killer would know.

She sunk her face in her hands and shook her head. As shocked as she was, there were no tears. She looked up at him. "Hazard a guess?"

Jase's eyes widened. "Come again?"

She stood and walked over to an inlaid box sitting on a table. She flipped the lid and picked up a cigarette, grabbed the crystal lighter that looked like a mini sculpture of David, and lit up. Blowing a long stream of blue smoke his way, Natalie Townsend faced Jase with her free hand on her hip. "Well, let me guess. Did some irate husband shoot his dick off?"

Jase started taking copious notes. "Why do you ask that?"

"Because my husband was as addicted to sex as I am to these damn cigarettes!" She poked it at him in accusation.

"Do you know any of these men by name?"

"I can give you a list as long as your arm."

"I'd appreciate that. Can you tell me when you last saw your husband?"

She took a long drag of the cigarette, then blew out a longer stream of smoke. "Friday night, he was off to his 'club,' he said he'd be home, but called me later that night and said he was going to head down to Pebble with a few of the guys for the weekend."

"Did he come home for his clubs?"

Her head shot up and her eyes narrowed. "My husband has everything he needs here and at his office in San Jose. One stash for each of his lives."

"What is this 'club' he belongs to?"

"I'm not sure. He never talked about it, but Sissy Trianfo, of Trianfo Vineyards, told me about it. Her husband, Eddie, belongs. I don't know what it's called or where it is, but he had a woman there. Hell, he had them everywhere."

"Mrs. Townsend, where were you last night?"

She laughed, viciously ground the cigarette out in the crystal ashtray, then pulled another from the box and lit it in an irritated gesture. "Home. Here with my children. Ingrid will vouch for me."

"I'd like your husband's cell phone number."

"Which one?"

"All of them."

She took a piece of paper from the desk drawer, along with a pen, and wrote them down. She handed Jase the paper.

"Mrs. Townsend, if you have immediate plans for travel outside of the state, please cancel them."

"Am I a suspect, Detective?"

Jase smiled. "You are a person of interest in that you have intimate knowledge of the deceased." He looked around. "I'd like to speak to Ingrid."

"She only speaks Spanish."

Jase smiled again. "No problem."

She frowned, but went to the intercom on the wall and pressed a button to call Ingrid.

Several minutes later the chubby maid walked into the room, her eyes downcast. She gave her employer a quick nervous glance, but Natalie nodded.

"*Por favor*, Ingrid *el* detective wishes to speak with you. Tell him I—"

"Thank you, Mrs. Townsend, I can speak for myself," he interrupted. Then added, "Please, leave us alone." Natalie scowled, shot Ingrid a glare, then exited the room.

Jase gestured to the chair. "*Siéntese, por favor*." Wide-eyed, Ingrid sat on the edge of the chair. He wondered if it was because she was nervous or because she'd get drilled for sitting on the missus's furniture. Probably both.

"Where were you last night?"

"*Aqui*."

Jase smiled. "Now that I know you understand English, señora, let's stop playing ignorant illegal. Okay?"

Ingrid gasped, putting both of her hands to her mouth. Her big brown eyes widened and instantly tears welled. Jase fought the urge to roll his eyes.

"I'm not *la migra*, I'm a detective investigating Mr. Townsend's death. Help me; I help you."

Ingrid stared down at her shoes.

"Señora?" he prodded.

Hesitantly, Ingrid looked up at Jase and nodded. "Okay, Señor Detective."

Jase gave her a reassuring smile. "Where were you last night?"

"I am here."

"All night?"

She bobbed her head. "*Sí, con las*—with the little girls."

"And where was Señora Townsend?"

"Here also."

"For how long?"

"I think she here all night."

"Do you live here?"

"*Sí*, Detective."

"Does Señora Townsend ever leave the house at night when everyone is asleep?"

Ingrid looked up, and Jase saw the fear in her eyes. "The truth, Ingrid."

"I do not know. At eleben, *la* señora likes to watch the news in her room. Ebery night, I say good night to her and go to my room."

"Where is your room in proximity to hers?"

"She is upstairs. I am downstairs and in de back. I hab two rooms. A bedroom and my own little libing room."

"Did she leave after you went to bed?"

"I don't know. I watch *las dibas*. I fall asleep."

"So if she left the house, you wouldn't know it?"

Ingrid nodded, and he knew it cost her to admit the truth.

"*Pero*, Señor Detective, *la* señora? She would neber leave *las hijas*. Neber! She would wake me up if she leabes the house."

"Maybe, Ingrid." But what if she were out to kill? Natalie Townsend didn't strike him as dumb. Knowing her kids were safely tucked in and their nanny only one floor down, even the most ardent of mothers could leave the house feeling confident their children were in good hands. Especially if one were only going to be gone for an hour or two in the middle of the night.

It was almost a half-hour drive from the Townsends' front door to the crime scene. Take twenty minutes or so to whack the old man, jump back into the car, and presto, you're home and in bed before one of the kids has a chance to wake up.

Jase nodded to himself and made notes.

Satisfied, for now, he didn't push. If he needed more info he had his trump card, and Ingrid knew it.

As the nanny exited the room, Natalie Townsend breezed in but not before she bestowed a huge smile on Ingrid. Completely recovered from the "shock" of her husband's death, the formidable widow faced Jase and handed him a piece of paper. "The names you requested. Now, if there isn't anything else, Detective, please see your way out."

"I'd like to speak to your children."

"Not on your life."

He snapped his notebook shut. "As I said, don't leave the state."

As Jase drove around the circular drive, he called Ricco and gave him the cell phone numbers. They'd have info in a matter of hours.

"What's your read on the wealthy widow?" Ricco asked.

"Genuinely shocked and after that wore off, genuinely glad to be rid of the bastard. Apparently, Andrew Townsend had a hard time keeping it in his pants."

Ricco chuckled. "An even harder time now."

"No shit. Whoever killed him had a grudge. It doesn't get more personal than chopping a guy's balls off and stuffing them down his throat, then watching him choke to death."

"I'd think that would put the widow at the top of the list, especially if she knew about his dog tendencies."

"Normally I would, too, but she was genuinely shocked. That said, she's definitely in the suspect pool. I may have just witnessed an Oscar-winning performance. I'm going over to the parking lot where the anon caller said there was an injured person, see if I can find anything."

Twenty minutes later Jase stood at the far end of the back parking lot of Callahan's. He called dispatch and had them replay the recording:

"Nine-one-one, what is your emergency?"

"I—there's a man, he's hurt in the parking lot behind Callahan's," a husky female voice said. It was obvious the owner of the voice was trying to alter it. There was a faint accent, one he couldn't quite put his finger on. She seemed rushed, out of breath. Afraid.

"Ma'am, what is—" The line went dead.

Jase asked dispatch to play it again, then again, each time hoping to pick something up. Each time it was the same: a rushed female voice, the call from a telephone booth three miles away. If the person was so concerned, why not use her cell phone? Or a closer pay phone? He deduced the reason for that was the person who did the crime didn't want to do the time. Most criminals didn't.

Despite the sunny late afternoon, Jase pulled a flashlight from the trunk of his car and turned it on. He wanted maximum visibility. From the back door, methodically he walked every inch of the lot, his light to the ground, cutting slowly back and forth. After almost thirty minutes he stopped. There on the freshly painted traffic paint designating the parking stalls—one dark drop with slight splatter around it. He squatted down and resisted the urge to touch it.

Definitely blood splatter. He set the flashlight down a foot away and pulled out the gloves he'd taken from Vangie's box, along with an evidence bag. He pulled the swab from the bag and dabbed at the spot. Dry. He took what he could of the sample and slid the swab in the bag and sealed it.

He looked up and squinted in the afternoon sunlight. On a plaque on the privacy fence in front of the stall were the initials *JD*. It was the only designated spot in the parking lot. He looked up at the ten-foot fence line and smiled. A camera.

Jase pulled his cell out and dialed Ricco.

"Maza."

"You still on scene?"

"Just getting ready to go."

"Get over to the phone booth at the Quick Stop at Diles and Essanay Boulevard. It's where the nine-one-one came from this morning. Look for cameras. I want Duncan to dust for prints over there but I want her over here first. I'm at the back lot on Thirty-ninth, Callahan's. We might get real lucky,

Ricco my man. There's a camera mounted on the fence. Let's hope it has film. And, I have blood."

"You're a good man."

"As soon as Duncan gets here, I'm going to pay the infamous club a visit."

"I want in. I hear the women in there are American versions of geishas."

Jase grinned. "What do you know about the place?"

"I have an uncle who belongs, or used to. You need a pedigree and scratch to even apply."

"Townsend strikes me as a mutt."

"He is, but he's got grit, and friends."

Jase nodded. "What's life without friends?"

Jase was going to find out just how good Townsend's friends were.

After Vangie collected the bloodstain and a few fibers he'd isolated, Jase tried the back door to the building. As he expected, it was locked. There had been no traffic into or out of the lot in the hour he'd been there. Walking around to the front of the building, he tried the door. Locked. He pressed the discreet doorbell several times, the distant chime of the bell clear. It didn't seem to go deep into the building. Probably didn't want the dudes disturbed. When there was no response from the other side of the door, Jase headed back to his car.

His stomach growled. He had plenty to occupy his time while he grabbed a bite, and waited.

CHAPTER

3

"May I help you, sir?"

Jase flashed his badge under the nose of the Ichabod Crane lookalike who spoke with a British accent and had opened the innocuous front door to Callahan's, and who also barred Jase from crossing the threshold.

The Brit eyed Jase's badge with an uninterested glance. "Am I supposed to be impressed . . ." The Brit looked at Jase and cocked a plucked brow. "Sergeant Vaughn?"

Jase flipped the wallet closed and slipped it into the breast pocket of his Armani jacket. "You're supposed to be a good doorman, and let me in."

"I'm sorry, Sergeant, this is a private club and only members are permitted beyond this point."

"I'm here on official business, I'd like to speak with— what does a private club have? A manager? Specifically, the one with the initials *JD*."

"I'm afraid without an appointment that isn't possible."

"I'm afraid, then, Ichabod old man, I'll call a black-and-white to park out front of your *private* club until the manager calls the cops, at which time *I* will arrive."

The man stood rigid, his long narrow nose twitching in distaste. "One moment, *sir*."

Jase smirked as the door closed and he heard the lock turn from the inside. "Prick."

Several minutes later, the stuffed shirt ushered Jase into a large, round, wood-paneled vestibule. Black-and-gold granite floors with heavy polished-brass pots overflowing with exotic greenery filled the room. Two matching brass-studded black leather settees sat flush against two of the walls. The scent of fine tobacco wafted in the air. Heavy crystal ashtrays sat on engraved rosewood end tables. Fine artwork adorned the walls. The smell of old money permeated the thick wooden walls.

Jase was impressed. He wasn't a stranger to the finer things in life. With no family to provide for, he could retire tomorrow and live a very comfortable life. His few extravagances weren't limited to fine clothing, wine, and a good cigar. He liked fine women. He'd dated more than his share of debutantes over the years, and while he had a penchant for what money could buy, he had no desire to settle down with any of them, even if it meant digging into Daddy's millions.

Jase grinned. Nope, he wasn't known as "Hit and Run" for nothing. He liked the ladies and he liked his freedom, and more than that, he liked the control he had over his life and emotions, with no desire to propagate. Scratch that, he lived for the act of propagation, just not the end result. He made sure years ago there would be no heat-of-the-moment mistakes running around with his DNA. He was clean and he was snipped, and if he ever had a daddy pang, he'd get a puppy.

The minutes ticked by. If Ichabod was jacking him around he wasn't going to like the consequences. The first twenty-four hours were crucial to a case and his time was running out. Jase was just about to try the brass handle to the door Ichabod went through when it opened and the Brit appeared. "Miss Devereaux will be right out."

Ah, so there is the *D* half of the infamous *JD*. A woman managing this place? Interesting. She must be a bruiser. One of those old washed-up women who'd seen the prettier side of life way back when, then when the looks and body took a dive resorted to the other side of the sheets. Management.

Jase nodded to the doorman, who closed the door and walked stiffly past him to the front door, where he stood like a wooden soldier. *What a shitty job.*

Jase turned back to the soft click of the other door handle.

The creature that emerged struck him dumb. Literally. He could not have formed a coherent word and spoken at that instant even if the fate of the free world hung in the balance. His body instantaneously warmed and his stomach did a slow, hard roll, then another. Her sultry musky scent infiltrated his senses and attacked him like a lethal virus. His mouth went dry.

Holy Mother.

Big jade-colored eyes that slanted upward at the corners reminded him of a feral cat. A sleek, black feral cat. Boldly, she stared unwaveringly at him. Her cool indifference was unsettling. Straight hair so black it almost looked blue hung like a veil around her heart-shaped face. The delicate nostrils of her short aquiline nose flared, and her ruby red lips parted just enough to reveal brilliant white teeth.

Jase couldn't help it. His eyes traveled from her ethereal face down that long slender neck to breasts so full and creamy they reminded him of caramel apples. He bet they were fake. They had to be. She wasn't wearing a bra, her nipples stiffened as he stared, and he knew for tits that perfect to sit up that firm and that high they had to have had some help.

She extended a slender hand, the nails perfectly manicured and real, not those fake red claw jobs the hookers favored.

"Sergeant Vaughn? Jade Devereaux, proprietress of Callahan's. How may I help you?"

You can help me by relieving this boner.

Jase took her hand. The current of electricity that sparked between them startled him. The jolt went straight to his dick. His eyes narrowed, and hers widened. She tried to pull her hand from his. His fingers tightened. Her warmth surprised him. It shouldn't have. He bet she was a tiger in bed.

His eyes raked her long lithe form, the silky black halter dress she wore doing nothing to quell his imagination. In that moment, as he envisioned her long legs wrapped around his waist as he thrust deep into her, and that red pouty mouth of hers open, panting, begging him to fuck her harder, he knew the vision would become a reality.

"I can think of several ways."

She yanked her hand from his, her eyes cooling to stone. Retreating a step, she said, "State your business."

Taking his time while enjoying the sight, Jase pulled his notepad from the breast pocket of his jacket. He flipped it open, ignored the throb in his dick, and wished he could ignore the woman standing no more than three feet from him. She was damn distracting.

"I'm here regarding Andrew Townsend. Was he here last night?"

"I'm afraid, Sergeant, I cannot divulge that type of information."

"Why not?"

"The names of our members are not for publication."

"So you're saying he was a member?"

"I'm saying, if he were, we would not divulge the information. It's privileged."

"Answer me this, then: Do you personally know Andrew Townsend?"

"I choose not to answer your question."

"Do you know he was murdered not far from here last night?"

Jade gasped. "How—?" Then she quickly collected herself. "I'm sorry for anyone's death, Sergeant Vaughn."

He watched her closely. Her nostrils flared and her left hand trembled. He noticed a Band-Aid on her left ring finger. "What happened?" he asked, pointing to her hand. She quickly covered it with her other hand before releasing it. She looked him straight in the eye. "I cut myself shaving."

Jase grinned. "Honey, a girl like you doesn't shave. I bet you've had every annoying strand of hair on that lovely body of yours plucked, waxed, or lasered."

Jade stepped back. "Sergeant, I'm afraid if you would like any further information you'll need a search warrant. Now, please excuse me."

"One moment, Miss Devereaux."

Jade turned those mesmerizing green eyes on him. Her long black lashes hovered over them like the wings of a raven. Her full lips pursed. Another day and another time and he'd pursue those lips until they were his. But business first.

"We can do this the easy way. You tell me: one, if Townsend was a member here; two, if he was here last night; and three, allow me to question everyone who had contact with him, or we can do this the hard way. I get a warrant and go public."

He watched the play of her expressions. While to the average Joe she managed to appear disinterested, Jase was an expert at reading body language. And once he got past the lushness of her he could read her as easily as the Sunday paper. She knew Townsend, all right, and she was lying about her finger, and she was weighing the pros and cons of his proposal.

"One moment please," she softly said before disappearing through the door from which she had entered. Jase glanced over to catch the wooden soldier eyeing him with what could only be described as contempt.

Jase shrugged it off. He'd been dissed by worse than that guy. The soft click of the door behind him sent a jolt of desire straight to his dick. *Damn.*

He turned expecting Miss Devereaux, but instead a rather portly older gent in a fine gray suit opened the door wider. "Sergeant Vaughn, my name is Thomas Proctor, Miss Devereaux's majordomo. She has instructed me to show you to her office."

Jase nodded and followed the man. "Were you here last night, Mr. Proctor?" Jase asked to the retreating back. As if he hadn't heard the question, Proctor didn't respond. Jase knew better. "If you were, don't go anywhere. When I'm done with Miss Devereaux, I want to talk to you about a member, Andrew Townsend."

Jade sat rigidly behind her desk, the force of her strained muscles starting an ache at the base of her spine. Andrew was dead! And, god help her, she'd killed him! Swallowing hard, she flinched when the discerning detective spoke.

"I'd like to see the tape from the camera out back."

"It was disconnected last month."

"Why?"

"I'm not at liberty to say."

"Did you see Andrew Townsend last night?"

A myriad of thoughts flashed through Jade's mind. If she went to jail, what would happen to Tina? If she told the truth, that she was defending herself against a man who would have raped her, would it matter?

No, she decided, nothing would matter if the cops found out the truth about her. She shivered despite the warmth of her office. Andrew Townsend might be dead, but she felt justified in her defense of herself. She raised her chin, her gaze clashing with the handsome detective's.

She smiled, her confidence restored. "Naïve" was a word she knew how to disrespect. Long ago she made the decision to never again be the whim of any man, and she wasn't going to break her cardinal rule, not even for this righteous cop standing so arrogantly before her. Let him come at her. She had money, she had the connections, and she had the righteous belief that she'd acted in self-defense. But more than that, she believed in her innocence. This time.

"If I did, I'm not at liberty to say."

Jase's aquamarine-colored eyes squinted beneath long black lashes. Their intensity managed to keep Jade more off balance than aligned. He was, she decided, probably one of the most handsome men she had the good fortune, or in this case misfortune, to meet. The planes and angles of his face met in fluid symmetry, even the small scar on his chin just below his full bottom lip did nothing to mar his sensual visage. Quite the opposite. It gave him the rugged look of a man who didn't mind getting his hands dirty.

She looked down to his hands. Big hands, with long thick fingers. Square fingernails and blunt fingertips. Hands she instantly knew could kill, and most likely had, but just as easily those hands could give pleasure. She trembled. Jade's instincts screamed that this man was a predator in every sense of the word. And for the briefest of seconds, fear flirted with her confidence. Her instincts, finely tuned and never wrong, tagged him from the moment she laid eyes on him as dangerous on every level.

"Miss Devereaux, let me clarify why I'm here. A man was murdered. That's against the law. It's my job to find out who did it."

"Don't be condescending with me, Detective."

"Don't play hard to get with me. I don't have the time or the patience."

Jade smiled and stood. She hadn't missed the way his eyes had raked her from head to toe when she'd walked into the vestibule. Or the way they'd kept returning to her chest and legs. While she might have no need for a man other than for monetary reasons, she knew the impact her physical assets had on the opposite sex. And she had no qualms in using them to get what she wanted. But what every man who had the misfortune to cross her path found out too late was that her greatest asset was her brain.

She warmed at the thought of playing cat and mouse with this man. If he sniffed too close to the truth, she may just have to pull out all the stops. Would he rise to the bait of her body?

Jade's thoughts grinded to a halt. The last time she had willingly allowed a man to touch her, had actually wanted it, she had been used and lied to. Her cheeks flamed in remembered shame. Her heart broke that day into a million tiny pieces. Not once had she looked back or down to pick one of them up in any attempt to mend her heart.

It was a lesson learned young and well. Men wanted one thing from her, and if there was ever going to be another time, it would be on her terms and her terms only.

Jade watched the handsome detective from beneath lowered lashes. Her belly did a slow roll, the odd sensation one she'd long forgotten. It occurred to her at that moment that she wanted the man standing so close to her to reach out and touch her. She wanted . . . to feel again.

Jase stepped closer. The scent of the woman who stood so close was damn distracting. "Was he a member here?" he softly asked.

"How did he die?" She looked straight at him, her big green eyes open wide, unwavering. Call it gut instinct, but Jase knew at that very instant there were more layers to Jade Devereaux than a giant onion.

"Did he hurt you?"

Jade blinked and her cheeks drained of color.

"Townsend, did he hurt you?"

Jase caught the rush of relief in her eyes. Who did she think he meant?

"How did he die?" she asked again.

"I'll ask the questions, Miss Devereaux."

Jade blinked and her eyes refocused to hard.

"I think, Sergeant Vaughn, I've said enough. If you'll excuse me."

She turned to go, but Jase grabbed her arm. She whirled around, her speed and ferocity surprising him. Now her green eyes blazed like smelted emeralds. He put his hands up and backed up a step. No harm, no foul.

Effortlessly and instinctively, he changed strategy and

attacked from a different angle. "We can do this the easy way, Miss Devereaux: You can tell me all about Andrew Townsend. Or I can get a warrant and open this entire place up and expose your members and their privacy. It's up to you."

"You and I both know for a judge to sign off on a warrant you need stiff probable cause."

He grinned. "You're as smart as you are beautiful." He stepped closer, but she held her ground. "My techs lifted a blood sample from your parking lot this afternoon, and I'll bet you dinner it matches Mr. Townsend's."

"I'll bet you it doesn't."

He extended his hand. "I'll take that bet."

She hesitated before she extended her hand. He was sure the hesitation was not because she was afraid of losing the bet, but because she feared his touch. He looked closer. Someone had damaged this woman. Damaged her bad. For all of her bravado, he understood her resistance to intimacy at its most basic level. Slowly, he wrapped his fingers around her hand. He felt a tremor zip through her body. But he played to win, and if he had to unwrap her slowly, layer by layer until he got to the vulnerable core of her, he'd do it. He pulled her closer. She was so close now he could see the pulse of the black striations surrounding her irises. "If you win?"

"Then you leave me and my club alone."

"How did you cut your hand?"

She withdrew her hand. "None of your business."

"How much does it cost to join your little club?"

She smiled, her eyes dancing. "If you have to ask, you can't afford it."

He may not be able to afford it, but he could always back-door his way in. He handed her a card. "If your memory suddenly comes back, give me a call. Or when I win, I'll be calling you."

Jade laughed, the sound low, thick, and throaty. His dick flinched. Dammit, the woman was potent. "I always win, Detective." She moved past him to the door and opened it.

"I'm not done with you yet, Miss Devereaux. I'm going to go hang out in the lounge area for a while. I suggest you call the owner and get his permission to speak to me. I really don't want to drag you downtown for questioning."

"Legally you can't, and you know it, so don't threaten me with it."

Jase grinned and his blood revved. "You are one smart lady." He moved to the door and opened it, his grin nearly splitting his face. "But I'm smarter."

Jase saw himself out as far as the main lounge and called Ricco to come on down. Two sets of eyes in this joint would be better than one. And he knew Mr. Hollywood Cop could get any woman to sing any tune, in any octave, when he turned up that Latino magic of his. Jase shook his head. He'd never had a problem in the female department, but dayum, if they didn't fall out of trees around Ricco.

Putting thoughts of his partner aside, Jase casually took mental notes of each person in the club. At the moment that included the wooden soldier of a doorman; the majordomo, Thomas Proctor; the brawny bartender; and a stock boy. He'd caught a glimpse of a few men in black slacks and tuxedo shirts. Probably servers.

Jase strode to the vestibule door and walked through. He surmised that when the club opened for the evening's festivities, the "guests" would come through a gauntlet. First, the front door manned by Ichabod. Once past that Rottweiler, they'd have to get by the scrutinous Thomas Proctor, the brute of a majordomo bouncer, before they would no doubt be welcomed into the large circular bar and lounge by Jade. He doubted she would be the first female face. She was management and, while he would expect her to mingle, it made more sense for the "working girls" to hustle up to the men as they came in. Hmm, kind of like a cat house.

Jase scowled. For a gentlemen's club, at that moment not one drop of estrogen filled the room. Maybe they made an entrance? He walked back into the lounge and caught Proctor's glacial gaze as he discreetly talked on a cell phone.

Jase smiled inwardly. If that guy thought he was going to back down because of a few glares, he was mistaken. He sure as hell wasn't going anywhere soon. His police business aside, Jase's male curiosity got the better of him. It would take a SWAT team to pry his ass out of Callahan's tonight.

Despite the lack of female companionship at the moment, the lounge was a gig he could get accustomed to real quick. It reeked of old money, fine brandy, and cigars. Subtle, delectable scents wafted in from the dining room he guessed was off one of the many doors that lined the back portion of the circular room. An impressive black-and-gold–veined marble fireplace nearly took up one wall. Brass-studded chairs and settees similar to the ones in the waiting room were casually grouped around the fireplace. About half a dozen smaller cherrywood tables with chairs wide enough to seat two, for those interested in a more intimate conversation, were tucked into a handful of private alcoves. Bold paintings in robust colors depicting several amorous scenes hung subtly lighted. Lush potted plants finished off the classic comfort of the room. Jase nodded. Well done, and very interesting.

Though the main attraction proved scarce at the moment, Jase was certain when the women made their appearance, the term "gentlemen's club" would take on its full meaning. He glanced at his watch. It was still early. He glanced at the gleaming bar. Fine brandies lined the beveled glass shelves, along with every other high-end alcohol imaginable. The big man behind the bar polishing the slate bar top flashed him a less than friendly look. A kid nearly flattened him as he hurried around the end of the bar with a box in his hands.

The bartender broke a smile and rubbed the kid's carrot top after setting the case on the bar top. "Perfect, Rusty. Now, go ask Miss Jade which brandy she wants to feature tonight." The kid smiled and shuffled past Jase.

Jase observed the kid's hesitant step before he took several direct strides toward the office. Rusty seemed to have a hard time making up his mind. Was it out of fear or was he slow? Could he have whacked Townsend's balls and hog-tied him? Jase doubted it. The person who did Townsend had a methodical motive. The kid could barely look him in the eye and could hardly haul the case of wine up onto the counter. Townsend was a big man who worked out regularly. No way.

But that didn't keep the kid or anyone else in the place off the suspect list. Everyone was a suspect until they were unequivocally ruled out. And even then, mistakes were made, oversights happened, so even for those removed from the list there was always option B: to go back on it.

So even if Rusty looked physically incapable? Maybe he had help. Of course, without motive . . .

Jase's gaze turned back to the big bartender. He could have done the deed with his little finger. Maybe he wanted Jade for himself, and thought Townsend was getting too demanding. Maybe it was another member who got a jealous hair up his ass. Hell, maybe a bunch of the girls had had enough of the drunken Lothario's groping and took matters into their own hands. His eyes traveled to the closed door at the end of the hall. Maybe Jade snapped. And just maybe Proctor or the Rottweiler helped. They seemed hell-bent on shielding Jade from him. Why?

The possibilities were wide open.

Hesitantly, Rusty knocked on Jade's office door.

"Come in," Jade's deep, husky voice called. Jase's blood shot south. He moved closer to the open door.

"Hello, Rusty." Her voice was pure, warm honey. Jase watched the kid's body twitch. Jase felt the same damn thing.

"Um, Mac told me to ask you which brandy you wanted featured tonight."

"Hmm, how about the Napoléon?"

Rusty bobbed his head and backed out of the room, slamming into Jase. He didn't look up but scrambled out of the way.

Jase caught Jade's gaze across the space that separated them. For a long moment Jase let the sizzle in his blood simmer. He felt things in his body he hadn't felt since he was fourteen and about to get his cherry popped by a very wise and very curvy twenty-three-year-old.

Jade stood and walked to the door; slowly, she closed it. He heard the lock click from the other side and with that sound the spell was broken. Jase physically shook himself. That woman was dangerous.

"Nice place," Ricco said from behind Jase. He let out a long breath and turned, more than grateful for the interruption. He needed to focus his big head.

"Buddy, you are in for a treat tonight," Jase said to his partner. "And I hope you have your dick strapped to your leg because if the proprietress, Jade Devereaux, is any indication of the ladies this place puts out, we're in trouble."

Ricco laughed and slapped Jase on the back. "I love my job! Now, tell me where we are."

Jase brought Ricco up to speed and set him off to interview the servers, who were lurking along the fringes, and to take a crack at the surly doorman.

"I'm going to go back and see if the lady of the house has had a change of heart."

Ricco grinned. "Maybe you should allow the master to take a crack at her."

Jase scowled. The thought of Jade responding to his friend disturbed him. And what bugged him more was that it bugged him in the first place. Jase almost stepped aside and gave Ricco his blessing, but he didn't. He glanced at the closed door. No, Jade Devereaux was a nut he would crack. Alone.

"Thanks, buddy, but I think I'll tackle this one solo." He stalked past Ricco toward Jade's office. Mac cut in front of him, blocking Jase's way.

"She's busy."

Eye to eye, not more than two feet separated them. Jase smiled. He had no intention of making Mac his adversary, but damn if he was going to allow this guy to impede his investigation. "You know," Jase started, "we can do this one of two ways. I'll leave it up to you how you want to play it."

Mac's eyes narrowed to slits. "Jade plays tough, but she isn't. Rough her up and you'll have me to deal with afterward."

"Are you threatening me?"

Mac nodded. "Yes."

Jase's smile, which had waned, sprung back up. "I'll leave her in one piece."

Grudgingly, Mac stepped aside.

Jase moved past him and knocked on the door. A long moment later he heard the lock click and the door opened. Her scent wafted around his senses in a slow sensual swirl and Jase felt like if someone nudged him, he'd be on his knees. The potency of the woman standing angrily in front of him jarred him.

"What is it now, Detective?"

"I have more questions."

Jade stepped back and opened the door wider. She moved to her desk and turned to face him.

"I'm glad you changed your mind," Jase said, closing the door behind him, then stepping closer into the small tidy office. For the second time that night he observed every non-descript item. Instead of sexy and exotic like the woman sitting behind the desk, he found the room cool, aloof, with no hint to her personality, family, or preferences. It seemed staged to him, as if the owner didn't want to give away any clues to her personal life.

White desk, white walls, white accessories.

"I didn't change my mind. I was finally able to get through to the owner, Mr. Morton, and he advised me to cooperate with you—to a point."

"What's his first name? And where is he?"

"Jack. Jack Morton, and currently he's in Milan."

"When did he leave?"

"Two weeks ago."

"So you run the place?"

She nodded. The elegant curve of her neck reminded

him of a swan. A dark, solitary, exotic swan. He wondered who'd hurt her so bad.

"I'm the proprietress."

"What is the scope of your duties?"

"Is that pertinent?"

"It is."

"I run the daily club operations. We have a restaurant, lounge, and billiard room upstairs."

"How does a place like this work?"

She sighed as if impatient. "Callahan's is a gentlemen-only club. After strict screening, if an applicant is chosen, there is a membership fee, as well as an initial processing fee. The membership gives you the privilege of dining and/or socializing here with the other members, or with one of the ladies who are employed by Callahan's."

"As in high-class whores?"

Jade stood, the force so hard her chair hit the wall behind her desk. "Hardly. The women here are educated, hard-working, honest young ladies. While our members may purchase a date for an outside dinner or a social function, there is no sexual exchange. We are *not* a brothel, Sergeant." She pointed to the door. "If you insist on insulting me, leave."

"Lighten up, Miss Devereaux. I call them as I see them and right now I've got a dead guy who is known to hang out at this *gentlemen's club* run by some ghost who is currently in Italy and at every turn in this place, I'm turned away by some moody brute, and you, the lady in charge, is giving me crumbs. So excuse me if I'm just a tad bit suspicious. Now, what time do the doors of your *gentlemen's club* open for business?"

Jade sat down in her chair, the effort smooth and sleek. Languidly, she crossed her legs and looked up at the detective. She'd have to be blind not to see the way the detective's eyes flickered downward every time she moved. The dress she wore was discreetly deceptive. It gave a man the hope that with the wrong move, one or both of her breasts would pop out. She took great pains to make sure no more than necessary was revealed.

"I'll tell you what, Detective Vaughn. Feel free to talk to any employee here, on their time, not mine. I have a business to run, and I don't like blips."

Jase grinned, the gesture startling. He had straight white teeth, his canines just a smidge longer than average. He looked like a big, bad, hungry wolf. She shivered, and understood that the man standing in front of her was not one who liked to play games for which he didn't make the rules.

She smiled. That was okay; she relished knocking men off their balance beams. They all deserved to want, but not to touch.

Jase flipped his notebook closed and slipped it into the breast pocket of his tailored black suit. For a cop he had excellent taste in clothes.

"I'll make myself invisible out there, pretend like I'm a guest." Jade opened her mouth to protest, but Jase halted her with his hand open in a stop position. "I give you my word, my partner and I will be discreet. Either allow me free rein out there or I call Vice and make it ugly for everyone."

He had her between a rock and a hard place. Jade slid the chair back and slowly stood. In a slow unhurried gesture she flung her hair over her shoulder, straightening her shoulders. Disappointment lurked when Jase's gaze didn't drop to her chest. Instead he held her gaze in an unwavering stare.

"I'm sure Miguel would not take kindly to that."

Jase cocked a brow. "Miguel?"

"Velasquez, your current chief of police. He stops by at least once a week."

Not breaking his gaze, Jase laughed low and moved around the desk, stopping no more than a foot from her. His spicy manly scent tickled her nostrils. "I don't back down from empty threats, Miss Devereaux."

Jade played her hand. She stepped in closer to him, so close that if she took a deep breath her nipples would brush his chest. She didn't dare. But he did. Jase's blue eyes danced as he moved incrementally against her. Her body jerked at the contact. Her eyes widened, and heat flushed her skin.

"Be careful, Miss Jade. I bite."

Jade didn't flinch. "So do I, and I draw blood."

Jase smirked and stepped back from her. "We'll see about that." Then he simply walked out of her office, softly closing the door behind him. Jade sank into her chair, her knees suddenly unsteady. What the hell had just happened?

And dear lord, why? She was the cat in the cat and mouse game. *Always*, she held the control. She used her body and the promise of it to lure men into opening their wallets wider. It's what kept them coming back. But this man, Jase Vaughn, knocked her off her game as effortlessly as if he were flicking a piece of lint off his thousand-dollar suit.

She shook her head and composed herself. It was a fluke. She'd been too long without a man. Her body stiffened. Eleven years to be exact, and the reason why was as vivid in her brain today as it was all those years ago.

Shame engulfed her.

It would be another eleven years before she allowed a man to touch her again, and maybe another eleven after that.

CHAPTER

4

Jase made himself right at home in the club, despite Jade's protests. Quietly he observed his surroundings, careful not to draw too much attention to himself than he already had. Ricco was seated in a discreet alcove with one of the servers. Always prepared, Jase turned on the envelope-thin minirecorder he always carried with him.

It became painfully apparent some time later that despite his skillful yet subtle interrogative tactics, the staff, while chatty, was just as tight-lipped with actual info to both Ricco and Jase as Jade had been. At first he thought they were just shy, but as he questioned one person after another, he observed every last one of them glance toward Jade's office at least once during his questioning and usually several times.

Where they afraid of her or protecting her?

Jase needed a drink. He glanced across the lounge to Mac, and ambled over good-naturedly. He'd see what he could get out of the big man. His overprotectiveness intrigued Jase.

Was he Jade's lover? He acted like a possessive boyfriend. Had he killed Townsend out of anger? While Jade didn't strike him as the type to mix relations with employees, anything was possible. He'd made bad reads before. And had learned from those few mistakes never to count anyone out of the equation.

And if he'd ever come up against a hard read, it was Jade Devereaux. Cool, calm, and collected on the surface, she burned hot under that mask of hers. He could see the heat in her eyes. Even if it was anger. He grinned. Where there was smoke, there was fire.

Jase made himself at home on a cushioned leather barstool. He made eye contact with Mac. The big man walked slowly toward him. "What can I do for you this evening, sir?"

"Coffee."

Silently, Mac turned and went to the other end of the bar, where he poured coffee from a silver urn.

Mac set the steaming cup down and brought cream and sugar. Jase nodded his thanks and sipped it black. "Excellent. Blue Mountain?"

Mac nodded, his eyes suspicious, not sold on Jase. Jase set the cup down and leaned forward. "Look, I'm not here to break your balls. I'm investigating a murder. Help me out."

Mac leaned into the bar. His scowl softened, but his dark eyes watched Jase with suspicion. Casually, he took a towel from behind the bar and began to rub the gleaming surface.

"What do you want to know?"

"What happened between Jade and Townsend last night?"

Mac quirked a brow at Jase and continued to wipe the bar

in front of him. If he kept at it, he'd rub a hole in it. "Who told you she had a problem?"

Bingo. Jase smiled and leaned an arm on the bar. "Does it matter?"

Mac shrugged. "Jade runs a tight ship, she's honest, and has a heart. If her and Townsend got into it, it's because he was asking for it. She never loses her temper, and she always makes sure the guests are taken care of."

"Just how taken care of?"

Mac snorted. "I can see why she keeps to herself. Men are pigs."

"How does she keep to herself in this place?"

"She just does."

"Does she socialize with the employees? Away from the club?"

Mac tossed the towel under the bar and, hands balled in fists, he placed them against the edge of the bar and glared at Jase. "Look, this place is run as clean and smooth as a naval station. If these ladies want to leave with a guest, then that's their own private business. The members only pay for their time here, or for an escort to an event. Nothing more and nothing less. Stop trying to make them into whores."

"How often does Jade leave with a guest?"

"Never."

"How often does she 'date'?"

"Rarely."

"Miss Jade said you needed more cab?" The redheaded kid asked.

Mac nodded to Rusty. The kid gave Jase a quick glance, followed by a shy smile. Jase smiled back.

"Bring me up a case of the '91 Opus."

The kid nodded and started to turn, but Jase put his

hand out and stopped him. "After you bring the case up, let's talk."

Rusty shrugged and said, "Okay." Then he scampered away.

Jase turned questioning eyes back to Mac. "What is your full name?"

He scowled and refilled Jase's cup. "William Trent Mac-Donald. Most people call me Mac, here they call me Mr. Mac-Donald."

"Who's the kid?"

"A stray. Rusty Daniels."

"A stray?"

"Yeah, Jade has a penchant for them. He showed up one day looking for a handout. Jade gave him a job. So far he's worked out."

"So tell me what Jade and Townsend did last night."

Mac shrugged again. "Dinner, I think, not here, though. But they came in around ten. Date over."

"So she rarely dates but has dinner with that lowlife?"

"Probably a favor."

"For who?"

"You'd have to ask Jade."

"What was Townsend's condition?"

"He'd had a few scotches."

"In your opinion, was he under the influence?"

Mac nodded. "I'd say he shouldn't have been driving."

"When did he leave?"

"Not sure exactly, maybe around midnight."

"Did he leave alone?"

Mac scowled again. "He left with Genevieve."

"Genevieve?"

"Yeah, she's new."

"I thought he just came off a date with Jade."

"Jade likes to keep things clean and separate."

"So, Townsend was looking for some extracurricular action, Jade shot him down, he got pissed and settled for the new girl, Genevieve?"

Mac ignored the question and stepped to the end of the bar, taking the case from Rusty, who found the floor more interesting than his surroundings.

"Rusty, I'm Detective Vaughn, I'd like to ask you a few questions about last night."

The kid looked to Mac, who nodded.

It was obvious to Jase the boy, or more accurately the young man, was a few lightbulbs shy of a full fixture. He wrung his hands and shuffled his feet under Jase's scrutiny.

Jase reached out a hand and clasped the younger man's shoulder. "I'd just like a few answers. So just take a deep breath and relax."

Rusty took Jase at his word. He took a big deep breath and composed himself. He even smiled. Jase squeezed his shoulder, then released him.

"Did you see Mr. Townsend here last night?"

The kid nodded.

"Did you see him with Miss Jade?"

The kid made an odd sound similar to a cat's meow. His right foot moved back and forth.

"It's okay, Rusty, just tell the truth," Mac offered.

Rusty looked up and his eyes narrowed. "Miss Jade had a drink with him."

"Did they argue?"

Rusty's eyes dropped to the floor. "I don't know."

"Did you see who Mr. Townsend left with?"

Rusty glanced up at Mac, then the floor, then finally back to Jase. "He left alone."

Mac cleared his throat. "Don't you remember he left with Genny?"

Rusty stepped back, shaking his head. "No, Genny left first."

"Do you remember what time that was?" Jase asked.

Rusty nodded and closed his eyes, his brows furrowing. He looked to be in pain.

"He gets migraines when he gets confused or upset," Mac explained.

"I'm sorry, Rusty, I didn't mean to upset you. I just want to find out what happened to Mr. Townsend. What time did he leave?"

"It was late. I think after midnight."

"Did you see him again?"

"No."

"What time did Miss Jade leave last night?"

Rusty pursed his lips. "I don't know. I left around one and she was still in her office."

Jase took a card from his breast pocket and handed it to Rusty. "My number is on the back. Call me if you remember anything, okay?"

Rusty smiled and slipped the card into his back pocket. "Okay." He scurried off and Jase looked up to find Mac watching him.

"He's a good kid."

Just as Jase was about to settle back into the barstool and pump Mac some more, Ricco came up behind him.

"Jase my man, we need to talk."

Jase excused himself and the two moved over to a small table near the immense fireplace.

"I just got off the phone with Tawny," Ricco began. "I had her run Townsend's cell phone numbers. I have names, numbers, and times. It appears our boy Townsend was a playah, and a juggler to boot."

"Let's start with his calls yesterday and last night."

Ricco flipped open his notepad. "Okay, of the three phones, two were active yesterday. One has only incoming calls, and voicemails, but the other one, I think this was his booty call. That phone has several voicemails, mostly from women looking for him. I have the list of names here. There was also an outgoing call at one this morning to a cell phone that called him at seven last night. The call at seven lasted three minutes. The one at one this a.m. was only seventeen seconds."

"Who is the cell listed to?"

"A Jade Devereaux."

Jase's skin warmed. He *knew* she was hiding something.

"Did you get film on the phone booth?"

"Nope. Nada. The one camera at the Quick Stop was too far away. Dumb-ass owner said it hasn't worked for months. I told him to take care of it or I'd come back and give him a ticket. On a more positive note, we dusted the booth for prints."

Jase shook his head. "Damn, I was really hoping for a visual. The camera here has been disabled. We could've wrapped this case up nice and neat tonight. I'm positive the nine-one-one call was made by Miss Devereaux."

"But do you think she did him?"

Jase's gut told him no, but maybe his dick was doing some thinking for him. "I'd say right now she is definitely a person of interest, and if she whacked Townsend, she had help." As Jase looked around the room, several employees avoided his gaze. "And I'll lay odds that person is in this club tonight."

Ricco smiled. "Well, this is one tight-lipped group. What did you manage to get?"

"Devereaux runs Callahan's. Townsend was here last night, and they had dinner. Who he left with at the end of the night is debatable, but several accounts place him leaving around midnight. I have a feeling our Miss Devereaux had more than dinner with this guy."

"You really don't think the wife had anything to do with it? From what you told me, she had the MMO."

Jase was quick to answer. "My hunch is Miss Devereaux has the answers. She had opportunity, she had means if she had help, now all we need is motive."

"All right, brother, I'll have Tawny get on these other numbers. The coroner said she'd have something for us by midweek." Ricco flipped his notepad closed and stood. Jase followed him. As they walked to the bar, Ricco asked, "So when can I meet the mysterious Jade Devereaux?"

Jase opened his mouth to tell him to be patient, but his words jammed in his throat.

At that moment the door at the end of the short hallway near the bar opened. Jase settled his hip against the bar chair and watched in quiet fascination the way her body moved when she walked. It was poetry in motion. Long fluid strides, her hips swaying ever so slightly, her long hair following behind her like a gossamer veil.

"*Santa María, Madre de Dios,*" Ricco breathed.

Jase's blood warmed. His sentiments exactly. And for the third time that day Jase was struck dumb by Jade's sensuality. He could honestly say, over all of the years and of all the women he'd known, not one of them was as naturally sensuous as the woman across the room. He knew full well she was very cognizant of her power, but he also knew, even if she didn't accentuate it, her sex appeal would still slap a man in the face with its raw appeal. He'd hate to be the guy married to her.

As Jade's gaze traced across the room, she passed over him as if he were nothing more than a stick of furniture. His pulse pounded against his veins. She was one long, cool drink of water, and if he weren't careful he'd find himself drowning in her icy current. Her eyes rested on Ricco standing rigid beside Jase before they continued around the room.

"She could unseat a saint, Jase."

No shit.

Jase asked himself why she hadn't told him she was with Townsend last night. The answer was Detective 101: She had something to hide. And he very much looked forward to prying that information from her.

Dragging his gaze from her body, Jase did his own cursory recon of the intimate setting. His interest was instantly heightened.

Several women, each rivaling the next in beauty, had slipped in. They looked like Victoria's Secret models. Beautiful girls next door. There were blondes, brunettes, a redhead, and two of the most gorgeous African American and Asian women he'd ever seen. They were clean, coiffed, and he bet they cost a fortune to maintain.

"Amigo, I hear my name being called," Ricco said and took off toward the mass of feminine pulchritude.

Jase could easily understand how a man could lose his mind, and a lot of money, in this place. He was in playboy heaven! No wonder guys broke the bank to join. Jase grinned as several women lit up like Roman candles when Ricco swaggered into the flock.

Jase's gaze swept back to Jade, whose eyes were riveted

on him. She raised a dark brow in quiet question. He smiled slowly and raised his brow in return.

He watched her make her way toward him, stopping to chat with a few of the ladies. He had the impression from her light touches and earthly smiles that she made every person she chose to grace with her attention feel as if they were the only person on earth. But her haughty reserve didn't fool him. She was a skilled actress. He wondered what it would be like to have her genuine attention.

And he wanted her attention. Her *undivided* attention.

"Well, Detective, did you dig up all of our dirty little secrets?"

Jase stood to his full height. In her strappy high heels, she stood almost nose to nose with him. She smiled and cocked her head to the side. In a fluid sweeping gesture she pushed her wave of black hair behind her shoulders. "What are you thinking, Detective?"

Jase grinned wider. "I was just thinking how good those heels would feel digging into my back."

He had to hand it to her. She didn't flinch. She was a cool one. Instead, she trailed a fingertip down the front of his fitted black shirt and pressed close to him. The tips of her breasts brushed ever so lightly against the linen of his shirt. The contact sent a shot of blood to his dick. He curbed the impulse to slip his arm around her waist and draw her closer to him. Not to ravish, but to savor. She smelled so damn hot, and her skin he knew was on the searing side of warm. He bet she would melt beneath him.

"Detective, isn't it inappropriate for a police officer to proposition a suspect?"

He leaned in closer, and her nipples dug into his chest. "I never said you were a suspect."

"No, you didn't, but I can see the wheels turning in that cop head of yours." She reached up on her tiptoes and pressed her face close to his. In a quick move, she nipped at his bottom lip. "It's too bad, Officer."

When she retreated, Jase's hand slid around her waist, just as he had wanted to do moments before. Her body stiffened. He yanked her against him. "If you can dish it out, my little prick tease, be prepared for some payback." He swept his lips across hers in a hard kiss before letting her go. She grabbed the chairback next to her. Her wide eyes spoke the truth. He'd shocked her. He grinned, and swept her with a hot gaze, his eyes settling on her hard nipples. He'd stake his retirement it had been a long time since she'd had a man. His body heated up at the prospect of being the one to tune her up. But caution cooled his blood. She was, at this juncture of his investigation, shaping up to be his prime suspect.

Jase followed her gaze to the silent room. Every eye, from Mac's to Ricco's to the other girls', was open in naked surprise.

Her warm body trembled and she quickly changed tact. "Detective Vaughn, touch me again and I'll break your hand."

Jase raised a brow, amused. His gaze raked her tall curvy form. "It would be worth it."

She opened her mouth to retort but another female of a very determined kind slipped effortlessly between them. Jase's body, being every bit male and on sensory overload as it was, responded to the hand that slid down his thigh. A warm floral scent enveloped him. He like it, a lot, but if he had to choose, he'd pick the scent of the other woman, the one who stood several feet away from him, looking as if she would reduce him to a eunuch on the spot.

"Jason Vaughn, you never called me back," a soft, purring, vaguely familiar voice whispered in his ear. Full breasts pressed against his arm. He ran his hands down soft warm skin and pulled slightly away. Warm whiskey-colored eyes smiled up at him and full pink lips pouted. "You hurt my feelings."

Holy shit! A vague memory of a bender two years ago after he'd come out of a deep-cover operation sprung into his head. "Shannon?"

She smiled. "I'm Dominique here."

Jase glanced at Jade, who continued to watch with interest. "I like the name. It fits. What brings you here, *Dominique*?"

"Stanford Law isn't cheap. I work here two nights a week."

"Oh, really? Were you here last night?"

She slid her right arm through his left arm and tugged him away from Jade. "Buy me a drink and we can catch up."

"I'd be happy to." Without giving Jade another look, Jase steered Dominique to the bar, where Mac stood with a perplexed expression on his face. "What's with him?" Jase asked. "Mac have it for Jade?"

Dominique stiffened just enough for Jase to detect. "Every man in this place has it for her. You'd think she had buried treasure between her legs."

Jase squeezed her hand and smiled. "Jealous?"

Dominique pouted. She had great lips, but he'd seen better. Just a few moments ago, in fact. "Not like you think. I have a one-hundred-and-eighty-thousand-dollar student loan to repay, and she cramps my style. I try to work the nights she isn't here, but those are few and far between."

"Do you normally work Saturday nights?"

"Not usually, but I'd heard Jade was going to take a couple of days off, so I came in."

Jase gave Mac a nod and asked Dominique, "What would you like to drink?"

She smiled and nuzzled into his chest. She'd never been shy and from what he remembered of her in bed she was quite the contortionist. "Don't you remember?"

Jase pursed his lips and slowly shook his head. Those were soon-forgotten details. And if the truth be known, their brief but intense affair lasted less than a week. And it was several years ago. How was he supposed to remember what she liked to drink?

"It's been a long time, Shan—ah, Dominique."

She pouted more profusely, then turned to Mac. "I'll have my usual, Mac."

He nodded and proceeded to make her a lemon drop. And he went real easy on the Grey Goose. Jase suspected that while the ladies encouraged the gents to throw down and consume alcohol, they kept their wits about them. After all, it was easier to seduce a drunk man than a sober one.

"I'll have another coffee, Mac," Jase said. He nodded, not looking up from squeezing a fresh lemon.

Several minutes later, drinks in hand, Dominique led Jase into one of the alcoves just off the main lounge.

Dominique slid intimately up against Jase and sipped her martini. "So, are you still chasing bad guys through the badlands of California?"

"Yep." Jase sipped his coffee and set the cup down on the table. He turned and faced his companion. "I need answers about last night."

Dominique smiled and sipped her drink again. "I'll give you more than answers."

She slid her hand along his thigh. His skin tingled. But when the sensation hit him it wasn't the sexy blonde glued to him he thought of. He clenched his jaw and slid his hand over hers, halting her groping. "Shannon, I'm on the clock."

She giggled. "So am I. But when I get off later tonight, I'd really like to pick up where we left off."

Jase put her hand in her lap and moved slightly away. He didn't want to upset her, he just wanted information.

"Did you see Jade with Andrew Townsend last night?"

"I did."

"And? What were they doing? How were they acting? Did you see or overhear anything unusual?"

"Why are you so interested in Jade and Mr. Townsend?"

"You don't know?"

"Know what?"

"Townsend was found dead this morning, several blocks from here."

Dominique's hand shook as she set her glass down on the table. "I'd heard something."

"Something? I figured everyone here would be talking about it."

"Jade doesn't like us to gossip."

"It's not gossip when it's a fact. What else doesn't Jade like?"

"She didn't like Mr. Townsend."

"Did she tell you that?"

Dominique shook her head and reached for her drink, this time her hand was steady. It seemed the women in Townsend's life were shocked to hear about his death but recovered fast. "She didn't have to. Jade doesn't like *any* man."

"Why do you suppose that is?"

Dominique shrugged. "Us girls have our ideas."

Jase smiled and leaned in closer to her. "Care to share?"

Dominique squinted her eyes but smiled. "Why? So you can use it against me and get me fired?"

Jase frowned and put his hands over his heart. "That hurts, Shannon. It's not how I roll. You know that."

Her face softened and she leaned into him, running her hand up between his thighs, then stopping at the hard juncture, she pressed into him. His little head responded. "I remember exactly how you roll. And I haven't had a roll like that since. Come to my place later."

"Tell me why your boss hates men."

Shannon moved away and eyed him with a glare, then shook it off. "She's frigid and hates to be touched. We think she was raped or something. You'd think we had the clap or something, the way she keeps herself away from human contact."

An unexpected jab of anger caught Jase off guard. He knew she'd been damaged. Her body language screamed it. But frigid? No way. Heat burned beneath her icy veneer. "Did she like Townsend less than the average guy?"

Shannon shrugged and sipped her drink. "God, I'd give my right arm right now for a real drink." She set the glass down and looked Jase straight in the eye. "He wanted more from her, just like every other cock in this henhouse. She wasn't interested. They fought. He left."

"A verbal fight, or did he put his hands on her?"

"I was a wee bit occupied myself, but now that I think about it, he did grab her."

"Why didn't Mac come to the rescue?"

Shannon laughed. "Jase, if that gorilla jumped across the bar every time a guy came on strong with one of us, he'd be a damn rabbit. We *are* trained professionals." She smiled and moved in closer. "We know just how to diffuse a man's sexual tension."

"Is that what Jade did? 'Diffused his sexual tension'?"

Shannon laughed out loud. "I told you, she doesn't let a man that close. She probably talked to him with that honey voice of hers, and calmed him down enough to not cause more of a scene. Had he pushed, Mac or Thomas would have handled him."

"Tell me about Genevieve."

Dominique pouted. Jase had to admit, her full pink lips were a distraction. "She's new, she's blonde, she's stacked."

"Does she like her job?"

Dominique had the audacity to look affronted. "We *all* love our job!"

"Really? You like coming on to men for a living?"

"We're not prostitutes, Jase. And in case you haven't noticed, I happen to like men. A lot. I get paid to meet some fabulous movers and shakers. Don't knock what I do."

Jase sat back and chewed on her answer. The fact that she enjoyed what she did didn't soften his view of it. His mother and sister liked it, too, all that male attention, but at the end of the day these women used their bodies for gain, just like his mother and sister had all his life, and he had a problem with that on a basic level.

The thought of subjecting himself to another human being, and allowing them to touch him because they purchased the right to do it, made him feel like he needed a shower. He could think of a lot of other ways to earn an income than getting paid to be groped, or, as he suspected of these women, for straight-up sex.

"When did you become a prude, Jase?"

He shook his head. "I'm not a prude."

She smiled and tossed the rest of her drink down. "Okay, poor choice of words. How about, don't judge me until you've walked a mile in my shoes?"

He focused on her and nodded. "Did you see Townsend leave with anyone?"

"I don't know if he left with anyone. I can ask around."

Jase sipped his coffee and frowned. Cold. "I'd really appreciate that, Shannon."

"Can I see you later?"

He smiled and squeezed her hand. "When this case is wrapped up, we'll talk about it."

She pouted prettily and called to his retreating back. "I want to do more than talk."

Jase smiled, then walked out of the room, glad for fresher air, when he collided with something warm and soft. He reached out to catch the body he nearly flattened, and looked down into two flashing green eyes. Instead of taunting her by keeping his hands on her, Jase righted Jade and released her. "Are you all right?" he asked, wanting to touch her again.

Her brief perplexed expression puzzled him. "Did you get what you wanted out of Dominique?"

Jase grinned. "And then some."

In a smooth, effortless gesture, Jade brushed her long hair over her shoulders. "Then she is up to her usual stellar work ethic."

Jase moved in closer, careful not to touch. "I thought you said this place wasn't a brothel."

"Did you offer Dominique money for sex?"

"No."

"Did she offer you sex for money?"

"No."

"Then why ask me that question? I told you, Detective: What my employees do after hours in the privacy of their own homes is none of my concern."

"Maybe there is an unspoken perk that comes with the inflated membership fee you charge?"

"Prove it."

"I intend to."

"I'm sure you will try, Detective. Now, while you're busy at your job, please allow me to do mine."

Chapter

5

A calm commotion caught their attention. Jade's eyes looked over Jase's shoulder and a smile flashed across her face. He thought it looked artificial, but to the average eye it looked genuine enough. He turned and followed her gaze. Jade swept past him, her perfume wafting around his senses. As if a string attached him to her, he followed.

"Mr. Hiro," Jade said, her voice light and airy. She bowed deeply, showing her respect and no doubt giving her guest a nice shot of her tits.

Jase focused on the man. He looked familiar. When Jade spoke again, this time in animated Japanese, Hiro grinned. Returning the banter, the man took Jade's hand and kissed it. Jase could almost feel her body stiffen. Her features tightened. Politely, Jade withdrew her hand.

Jase wasn't sure which action he was more surprised by: Hiro's public display of affection to a woman or the fact that Jade allowed him to take her hand and kiss it.

Hiro looked perplexed. "Have . . . I offended you, Jade?"

Her smile could have melted snow in the arctic. And so the show continued.

"Your girl is just full of surprises, isn't she?" Ricco asked from behind Jase.

"I think I'm in lust," Jase answered and watched, fascinated, as Jade morphed from the cool package she had been with him to a smooth, sultry siren with the other man. Touching his shoulder with her fingertips, Jade walked the businessman over to an intimate grouping of chairs in the corner near the blazing fireplace.

"Be careful you don't fall into the crack, brother," Ricco warned, as he strode past Jase and closer to the women.

Jase didn't give Ricco's words much credence. He'd been attracted to a lot of suspects, and he'd never lost sight of his case. He wasn't about to lose it here.

Magically, drinks arrived and Jase watched Jade lean toward Hiro and say something. It must have been a toast because they raised their glasses and clinked them. Irritation rose and Jase looked around the room. In the space of only a few minutes several more men arrived. He glanced at his watch: 8:03.

They must have been fighting one another to gain entrance at the front door. He understood all too well. He found release in the soft hotness of women. And he liked smart, classy women. Here they abounded. Sure beat bar-hopping. Not that he did much of that. Like Ricco, women seemed to fall from trees around him.

His gaze swept back across the large inviting room. He was relieved to see Shannon attempting to entertain one of the two newcomers who hovered around Jade and Mr. Hiro.

A redhead clung like a vine to Ricco, who didn't seem to mind much.

Sure reminded him of a high-class brothel.

"They can't resist her," Mac said as Jase sat at the bar. "She's like a bright light and when those moths get too close, they get their wings burned."

Jase took the bourbon Mac offered. "How about you, Mac? Have you ever wanted in on the action?"

Mac's face darkened. "A woman like Jade Devereaux doesn't notice a man like me."

"Did she burn Townsend?"

Mac stepped back from the bar. "Andrew Townsend isn't our typical member." He uncorked a bottle of the vintage Opus and began to decant it. "What happened to him, anyway?"

"Someone killed him."

Mac scowled. "I heard that part. How?"

"Coroner's working on it."

"I get it, you can't divulge details only the killer would know."

"Something like that."

Jase sipped his drink. The smooth liquid gold of the single-barrel bourbon caressed his tongue like warm velvet. "Nice." He raised his glass toward Mac.

"Blanton's, my compliments."

He glanced back across the room and scowled. Nearly a dozen men in the salon had gravitated toward Jade. For someone who was purportedly a man-hater, she maneuvered around them seamlessly.

"Do you think your boss hates men?"

"I think if you want the answer you need to ask the right person."

"Did Jade date Townsend?"

"Yeah. Once or twice."

"For such a man-hater, was that unusual?"

Mac laughed, inclining his head toward the salon where Jade was nearly concealed by the group of men surrounding her. Her soft laughter wafted through the room like music. "Does that sound like a man-hater to you?"

"An act."

"Maybe. But like I said, she rarely dates these days and when she does, she goes for the passive men like Mr. Hiro there. Townsend was not passive."

Mac was contradicting himself. "You tell me Jade doesn't date, but she goes out with Townsend. You tell me she doesn't care for aggressive men, yet Townsend, from what I hear, thought he was god's gift to every female on the planet, and you also tell me Townsend wasn't the normal trade here. So what gives?"

Mac didn't speak for a moment, and when he did his words were low and measured.

"I hear the new owner is hard up for cash. Two months ago Townsend's type needed connections, a pedigree, *and* bank. Now all you need is bank." He shook his head. "Like I said, he isn't our usual clientele. Callahan's has always catered to old money, blue bloods and the dignitary type. Not the car salesmen."

"Do you know who opened the door, and why?"

"Not my job. Jade would know."

Jase made a mental note to ask her. The ever-benign majordomo Thomas escorted another man from the vestibule into the salon. "Looks like more fresh meat," Mac said. The scorn in his voice was not lost on Jase. He had to hand it to the barkeep. The guy had class and resented the likes of the new flash coming in. Jase took a double take at Mac. Just how much did he resent the new flash?

Like every other man in the place, this one was dressed in classic casual evening attire, and he strutted around as if he owned the place. Money did that to a lot of people, gave them false impressions of themselves.

Jase watched the newcomer scan the room. He didn't need to follow the stranger's gaze to understand his body language. His body stiffened, like a dog hitting on a bone. Jase watched with interest the color drain from the man's ruddy complexion, then slowly refill. The guy took a handkerchief from his pocket and dabbed his glistening brow. The room was not warm.

Jase glanced at Jade, who hadn't looked up from her conversation with a tall Latino gentleman, and walked toward the newcomer.

Thomas walked toward them. "Mr. MacDonald, I'd like to introduce Mr. Otis Thibodeaux."

Mac extended his hand and smiled. "Welcome to Callahan's, Mr. Thibodeaux. What's your pleasure this evening?"

The man's muddy eyes darted to Jade. Jase's followed, and just at that moment Jade looked up. Her eyes clashed with the man's next to him. He saw an expression cross her face so fast he wasn't sure he had witnessed it. Sheer terror. Just as quickly she recovered, and a veil of impassive acknowledgment glazed her eyes.

Jase's antennae hummed. She knew this guy.

Jade made polite noises to her gathered admirers and stood. In long seductive strides she crossed the room toward them.

While she smiled warmly at the newcomer and said, "Welcome to Callahan's," Jade did not extend her hand.

Thomas smiled and began the introduction. "Miss Devereaux, please make the acquaintance of Mr. Otis Thibodeaux. He is a special guest of Mr. Morton's."

She continued to smile, the gesture not lighting her face; instead, her cheeks looked stiff, as if the gesture was forced. "Again, welcome to Callahan's, Mr. Thibodeaux."

Thibodeaux grinned, grabbed her wrists, and yanked her close to him. Jade's body went so rigid so fast Jase thought she'd snap in half. "Suga, just like down in Lusiana, you can call me 'Big Daddy,'" he drawled.

Jase watched the color drain from Jade's cheeks, but other than that she remained as cool and gracious as a Southern morning. Except when she attempted to withdraw her hands. Thibodeaux's tightened. Her arms trembled.

"Mr. Thibodeaux," she softly suggested, "why don't you let Mac know what you'd like from the bar, one of the servers will bring it to you, and come join our little gathering in the corner. I'll be happy to introduce you."

Again, she attempted to pull her hands from his but he held them firm. Jase watched closely, more than intrigued. Thibodeaux moved in closer to Jade. "I don't want to meet anyone else. I want a private party, with you."

"I'm sorry, Mr. Thibodeaux—"

"Call me 'Daddy.'"

Jade looked perplexed. "Mr. Thibodeaux, I don't think I understand your request for a private party."

The good ol' boy moved closer and let go of her hand, but ran his fingertips up Jade's arm. Her skin flinched, and an imperceptible shudder ran through her. "C'mon now, suga, you know what I mean."

Jade stood stock-still, her back rigid, her color even. "I'm sure I don't."

Otis gave Mac and Jase a knowing smirk. "Excuse us, gentlemen."

He inclined his head away from them.

The two moved over to an alcove at the back of the room. Jade pulled a heavy velvet curtain, obscuring them from nosy eyes. Jase followed, determined to hear as much of their conversation as possible. Casually, he pressed up against the wall just outside the drawn curtain.

"Well, well, well, if the colonel could see you now, Ruby Leigh, he'd come back from the dead," Thibodeaux mocked.

"I'm sorry, Mr. Thibodeaux, but what are you talking about?"

He laughed low. "Still think you're better than everybody else, don't you?"

"I'm afraid I have no idea what you're talking about. Perhaps you have me confused with someone else?"

"You did a good job hiding, Ruby Leigh, but I've found you. Now, you got something I want, and I'm not leaving until you give it to me."

"Sir, I'm sorry, but—"

"Do you know what Sheriff Taylor dug up in that burned-out trailer of your mama's?"

"Mr. Thibodeaux, I assure you, you have me confused with someone else." Jade pulled back the curtain and her gaze clashed with Jase's.

She turned to Otis, who looked as if he were about to explode. "But allow me to buy you a drink. Your trip won't be for naught."

As she walked past Jase, Otis grabbed her and shook her. Something in Jase snapped. He grabbed Otis by the shoulder. "No touching the merchandise, man," Jase growled, his voice dark, low, and close. Otis jerked around.

"Bug off, man. I didn't come here to take no for an answer," Otis charged back.

In a quick subtle gesture, Jase clasped Otis around his thick neck with his right hand. He pulled the man's face toward his. Low and menacingly, he said, "No touching the lady. Do it again and I'll kick your ass all the way back to Lusiana, *Big Daddy*."

He released the miscreant, and Otis had the good sense to skulk off to a corner and lick his wounded pride. Jade stood rigid. The only clue to her mood was the rapid rise and fall of her chest. She pivoted on her heels and walked over to where Mr. Hiro watched with a concerned look on his brow.

Several minutes later, Jase watched Jade leave with the businessman. Jase caught Ricco's eye across the room and inclined his head toward the door.

When the men met, Jase said, "I'm following her, stick around and pump for more info."

A moment later he was out the door. He wasn't sold on the place not being a clearinghouse for high-priced whores. In fact, he was sure Jade had mastered the art of pulling the wool over the local PD's eyes. Maybe Townsend had threatened to expose her and the club? As motives for murder went, it sounded like a good one.

As Jase followed the large black stretch with Jade inside of it, he called in to the PD to get the paperwork for a GPS device started so he could watch Miss Jade's comings and goings from his laptop. The lady was hiding a lot behind those big green eyes and he was going to dig until her secrets were revealed.

The stretch rolled up in front of La Hacienda Rosa. He'd been there just a few weeks ago with . . . hell. Jase racked his memory. She was tall, buxom, and blonde, but damn if he could remember her name. The food wasn't bad, but he suspected what most people were paying for was the Barcelona villa ambiance. It was a nice place. And it had private dining rooms.

He smiled as Jade exited the limo, towering over Hiro. He watched the man's arm slip around Jade's waist as he guided her under the high arch of the entrance. For someone who didn't like to be touched, she didn't push his hand away. Once the stretch was gone, Jase pulled his unmarked to the curb, flashed his badge, and said to the attendant. "Don't move it."

Jase made his way into the first of three dining rooms. While there were many tables tucked into alcoves, none of them were occupied by his number one suspect or her "date." He came up empty in the second and third dining rooms.

Jase walked back to the maître d', who did his best to ignore him. He flashed his badge. "The Japanese gentleman and his date, where are they?"

"I'm sorry, Officer, but when our guests step into our house, their privacy is assured."

"How private is your resident status?"

The man's caramel-colored skin blanched to white.

"They are in a private dining room. I cannot allow you to interrupt them."

"I don't want to interrupt them, just—observe."

"As I said, it's private."

"Just show me where, I won't disturb the occupants."

Grudgingly, the man strode through the main dining

room and into a second atrium dining room, then turned down a short hallway that led to a wide arched entryway with a fountain in the middle like a courtyard. Surrounding the courtyard were four doors with hand-painted roses on them, each a different shade of red. "The couple you speak of is in the *rojo* dining room."

Jase glance up, and in the alcove above was a small balcony. "How do I get up there?"

The maître d' scowled and gave him directions.

Situating himself up in the alcove on a stool, Jase could see straight down into the courtyard, a perfect view without being seen.

He noted the time, 10:30 p.m., and sat back to wait. It wasn't long before Jade came out of the room. If he wasn't mistaken she looked a little—disheveled. He scowled at the implication. Looked liked the gent was getting his money's worth.

Jade hurried to the ladies' room, ignoring the elderly attendant, who stood when she entered. She stared at her smudged lipstick, and in an angry gesture she swiped the remaining color off, smearing it across her cheek, leaving a red wake.

Angrily, she washed her hands and took a cloth towel from the attendant, then worked on her cheek to remove the red slash. Opening her purse, she quickly got to the repairs. As she put a final touch to her lips, Jade stopped her movement.

In the space of twenty-four hours her house of cards had begun to crumble around her. Townsend was dead, that cop who disturbed her on a very primal level shows up at her doorstep, Otis Thibodeaux's rude assumptions, and now Mr.

Hiro wanted to call her hand. A call she was blindsided by. For three years the man had not touched her; tonight he couldn't keep his hands off her. She almost lost it when he unzipped his pants and set his small but burgeoning penis against her thigh, covering her mouth and forcing her hand to grasp him. It was the first time in eleven years she had touched a man like that. And the revulsion of doing so made her realize she hadn't missed a thing.

Her stomach rolled and she fought the urge to vomit in the brass sink.

"Señorita?" the ancient attendant said.

Jade glanced at the old woman's serene stare and smiled, and then looked back into the mirror. It didn't lie. Her haunted face stared back.

"*Estoy bien, gracias.*" She took the cool damp cloth the woman held out to her and pressed it against her cheeks. She wanted to go home, to get into her favorite pair of flannel PJs, and sleep for a week. Instead, she straightened her shoulders, dug for a few bills in her purse, and handed them to the attendant, then stalked out of the restroom.

Giving her dress a final readjustment before she entered the room, Jade looked up. The balcony used to seclude the musicians was empty, except—she narrowed her eyes—for the shadow of a man sitting quietly in the background. Probably management keeping an eye on the private rooms. Exhaling a deep breath, Jade stepped into the private dining room.

As she entered the room, Jade halted midstep, closing the door quickly behind her. She didn't know whether to laugh or cry. Lying naked and spread-eagle on the linen tabletop among the margaritas and their *camarones* cocktail was Katsuo Hiro. His four-inch penis pointed to the ceiling.

She'd seen worse. "Mr. Hiro, I'm afraid I'm not as hungry as I thought. I'd like to return to the club."

His dark eyes glittered, not in malice but mischief. He really was quite harmless. "Play geisha with me."

Slowly, she shook her head and as one would speak to a child, she said, "I told you, no more geisha."

Katsuo rolled over to his side and stroked himself, his eyes closed for a moment. Then he hissed in a breath, piercing her with a hard gaze. "I am not partial to begging for sex, Jade." He snapped his fingers and thrust his hips at her. "That is your dinner, whether you're hungry or not. You owe me for three years of patience."

Having gained control, nonplussed Jade smiled and strode into the room, stopping at the edge of the table. "Come, my lovely Jade," Hiro cajoled. "Open those beautiful lotus blossom lips, and wrap them around my samurai sword."

If the situation wasn't so lewd, she'd laugh. "I'm afraid, Mr. Hiro, you will have to find your lotus blossom lips elsewhere. I don't give blow jobs on command, and not for any payment, imagined or otherwise. Now, if you don't mind, I'll step out while you dress and we can finish—"

The door swung open. Jade cried out and whirled around. The server had been forbidden to enter, not even to knock. *No disturbances*, Mr. Hiro had mandated.

Jade's eyes widened as they clashed with the owner of the ocean blue ones. The detective's dark face scowled as he quickly surmised what was going on in the room.

"You almost had me believing you were as innocent as Snow White. Shame on me," he said, his gaze unwavering.

"This is a private dinner, sir! I demand you leave at once," Katsuo shrieked. He didn't bother getting up from the table nor, at the very least, did he cover himself with a napkin. Not that he needed one; a cocktail napkin would have sufficed.

Jade kept her cool. "All is not always as it seems, Detective. Are you going to arrest me?"

"I'm thinking about it."

"And what would be the charge, dining with a naked man?"

"Sir, I demand at once you leave us to our privacy!" Hiro insisted.

Jase ignored Hiro's demands and continued to hold Jade's gaze. Jade quirked an eyebrow. The detective looked like he wanted to strangle her.

"You looked a little rattled a few minutes ago, are you all right?"

She doubted his concern. He was hoping to catch her red-handed. "I'm fine. Please leave us."

Jase nodded. Then exited the room.

Hiro relaxed back down on the table, grabbed his receding erection, and wagged it at her. "Come, my sweet cherry blossom, open your mouth for *Papa-san*."

Jade sighed and grabbed her margarita. She took a long sip and thought how much she'd enjoy a shot of Patrón. "Mr. Hiro, zip up, I'll be waiting in the bar for you."

Jade exited the room amid Mr. Hiro's demands for her return. She wondered what she had done to make him think that after all these years she was his for the taking. Since Jack Morton took over two months ago, the status quo at Callahan's had steadily gone downhill. It was time for the meeting he kept avoiding.

Jade slid onto a smooth leather-backed barstool, and immediately the bartender moved in front of her. "Señorita? *Qué te gustaría ordenar?*"

"A new life?"

"*Qué?*"

"A shot of Patrón, *por favor,* and make it a double."

Instantly, two shotglasses materialized in front of her.

She felt his energy long before he spoke. And very unlike what Katsuo's presence did to her, a sudden heat emanated from inside of her, and the soft percussion of warm breath against her ear sent shivers coursing along her skin. She licked the salt on her hand, downed the shot, then sucked the lime wedge.

"I bet this happens once in a blue moon," Jase said from behind her.

Jade turned in the seat, refusing to back away when he leaned into her. Where Katsuo couldn't generate a reaction, Jase did, on many levels. Locking gazes with him, she licked her hand and threw back another shot.

When she sucked the lime, Jase smiled. "I had you pegged for Cristal all the way."

"Champagne has its place, Detective, but not here, not tonight."

"Then maybe some sake?"

"Hardly."

Jase didn't retaliate. For the small gift, she was grateful. She was tired of being on the defense with him.

"I was going to offer you a ride home."

"I have a ride." Not that she wanted it.

"Your date left."

Jade shrugged. "I'll call a cab."

"Why do women have to be so stubborn?"

"Why do men not understand the word 'no'?" Jade waved over to the bartender. "*Por favor,* a cab."

"Of course, señorita."

Jade moved a fifty-dollar bill across the bar, then slid off her chair on the opposite side of Jase. "Thanks, though, for the offer."

She didn't have to wait long. The cab pulled up and she slipped in, giving the driver the address.

The fact that the nosy detective followed her didn't bother her. The fact that Katsuo Hiro expected sex from her didn't bother her. Even the fact that Jack Morton had somehow conveyed to the members that sex was now a commodity didn't really bother her, not as much as it should; she could deal with men. No, what bothered her was the fact that she was pretty damn sure she'd killed Andrew Townsend.

Several hours later, Jase watched Jade's black BMW pull out of the back lot. As he hit the gas to pull up behind her, another car, a dark sedan, cut in front of him from across the street. Jase eased up on the gas and gave himself plenty of room behind Jade and the car following her. Since he already had her address he wasn't worried about losing her, but his concern rose. The sedan was hot on her tail. He called in the plate to Dispatch.

A rental.

Twenty minutes later, Jade pulled into her garage and the car following her pulled right up into her driveway behind her. Jase had a clear shot of the driver as he exited. Otis Thibodeaux.

By the time Jase parked across the street, Thibodeaux was inside. Jase hurried out of his car across the street to her front porch. The town house was nice, in an upscale yuppy neighborhood of Santa Clara. Jase knew they ran about six hundred K; he'd almost bought one himself a few years back when he was snatching up real estate. He'd run a title search and see who owned it. If it were Jade, that would explain a lot. Managing a gentlemen's club didn't pay *that* well.

He stepped closer to the front door and listened. Nothing. He looked through the beveled glass, being careful not to be seen. He saw Jade start up a winding stairway, Otis was right behind her. Disgust welled in him. He'd read her all wrong. And aside from the fact that it appeared he had lost his knack for reading people, he was furious she was nothing more than a high-priced whore. There was a part of him that wanted the beautiful, classy lady to be more than what he knew she was. While he was sure she couldn't have pulled off the hog-tieing murder of Townsend alone, she certainly could have been an accomplice.

He pressed his ear closer to the door and listened.

Jade turned and faced Otis, who had barged into her home. She never should have opened the door. "I'm sorry, I told you, I'm not this Ruby Leigh you keep saying I am."

Otis moved a step closer to her. "Then tell me why you let me in, Ruby Leigh."

Jade swallowed and lied. "I thought you were my twelve o'clock."

Otis smiled, the gesture ugly. "It's almost one."

Jade shrugged, trying to play it off. "I lost track of time tonight, I've been—engaged."

Otis moved another step closer. She backed up into the wall. "Well, since your twelve o'clock didn't show up or left coz you weren't here, I'll be happy to take his place."

Jade shook her head. "I'm sorry, all of my dates are

screened. Maybe another time." She moved past him toward the front door. Otis wasn't taking no for an answer. He headed her off and steered her down the hallway into the living room.

"You always did think you was better than the rest of us. Where's the pride in finding out your boyfriend got paid for screwing you?" He moved closer, pushing her against the wall.

The air thickened in her lungs. But she was adamant. "You have me confused with someone else."

He slapped her across the mouth and grabbed her breasts, squeezing hard. Jade bit back a scream as her world went black. Fear clouded her senses. Her chest tightened. The overwhelming urge to flee overcame her. Otis's hot, wet breath slammed against her cheek. "I've dreamed of these tits for years, Ruby Leigh." His fingers bit deeper into her skin. "It was me who wanted you up at the house. Daddy stole you right out from under me." He ground his hips against her, his erection jabbing into her hip bone. She swallowed hard, keeping her eyes squeezed shut.

Visions of Tina's sweet smiling face sprung up in her mind. She stiffened to steel herself, forcing herself to face her fear of this man. Jade's eyes flew open. "Please. Stop! I'm not your Ruby Leigh!" Adrenaline infused her with a burst of courage. She shoved off his bulk and stepped away from him into the hallway.

Otis wasn't deterred; he followed her step for step. "You got something else I want, Ruby, and I'm not leaving here until you agree to give it to me."

Jade shook her head, grasping for composure. She couldn't cave now. She wouldn't. Her life and the life of her sister hung on her remaining strong. "Please, Mr. Thibodeaux, Otis, I don't know you. I don't know who Ruby Leigh is. Please leave."

"The colonel left you money, Ruby Leigh. He left you money for fucking him all those years. Now I want it. And you're gonna give it to me." He dug papers out of the breast pocket of his jacket. "Sign these and give me my money."

Slapping the papers away from her, she moved down the hall toward the kitchen. She had a gun in the drawer near the sink. If she had to threaten him with it to get him out of her house, she would.

Otis picked the papers up from the floor and followed her into the kitchen. His eyes widened in surprise when he stared down the short barrel of the snub-nosed Colt Python she held in her hands. "I told you, Mr. Thibodeaux. I'm not Ruby Leigh. I'm Jade Devereaux. I was born and raised here in California, and if you don't leave my house right now, I'm going to shoot you dead, then call the cops and tell them you broke into my house and I shot you in fear for my life." She pulled the hammer back. "Now, you decide. Live or die."

In a lightning-quick motion she never expected, Otis backhanded her across the face. The gun skittered across the granite floor. Then he slapped her hard in the mouth. Grabbing a hank of her hair, he pulled her face close to his. "I'm going to give you twenty-four hours, Ruby Leigh. Twenty-four hours to come to your senses. If you don't, I go to the cops myself and tell them how you killed your mama then set her on fire."

Jade gasped in shock. Her heart constricted so tightly she thought it would never resume normal function. She couldn't breath. Blood drained from her face. Her cheeks chilled. With the violence of an earthquake, a hard shudder jolted through her body.

Otis smiled and thrust her from him. "I thought that might knock some sense into that trailer park head of yours."

Jade grabbed the nearest thing she could find, a ceramic fruit bowl complete with fruit, and hurled it at Otis. She clipped him in the side of the head. "Get out of my house and don't come around here again, you—*swamp rat*!"

The minute her mother's favorite term for the boys who came sniffing around the trailer left her mouth, Jade regretted it. .

Otis laughed. "Twenty-four hours, Ruby Leigh. Twenty-four hours."

A loud crash, followed by a scream, moved Jase into action. Not wasting any time, he tried the front door and it opened. He stepped through and nearly collided with Otis Thibodeaux.

The other man pushed past Jase with a sneer and said, "She's all yours, mister."

Jase reached out to stop him, but Jade's voice stayed his hand. "Let him go."

Against his better judgment, Jase allowed Otis to leave. He closed the door behind him, wanting to go after the bastard, but instead he moved down the hall.

The sound of running water led him to the kitchen. What he saw when he entered the room struck him speechless. Jade stood at the kitchen sink, her hair a wild mess around her shoulders, her dress ripped at the right shoulder, exposing the high curve of her breast. His gaze moved to her face and his blood heated. Her left eye swelled and she held a towel to her lip.

The cop in him wanted to go after Thibodeaux and kick

his ass before he arrested him. The man in him moved to Jade, wanting to comfort. To protect. Jase raised a hand to pull the fabric of her dress up to cover her chest. She flinched, a primal snarl escaping her lips. Part fury but mostly fear.

While he didn't make another move toward her, he wasn't deterred. She was like an abused kitten, hissing and spitting at any hand that sought to touch. Something deep inside him was moved at the sight of this proud wounded woman.

"I won't hurt you, Jade. Let me fix your dress."

Wild-eyed, she shook her head and stepped farther back until she could go no farther, the counter impeding her escape. Without breaking her stare, she used her free hand to pull up the shredded fabric. The minute she let go it slipped back down, this time exposing the edge of a rosy nipple. Jase growled this time. He stepped past her and pulled a towel off a hook next to the sink, opened it, then gently laid it across her chest.

She watched with haunted eyes. Her breathing increased and her breasts heaved as if she'd just run a marathon.

"I won't hurt you," he repeated, his voice soft, his tone soothing.

Slowly, he reached out and pulled the towel away from her mouth. "Son of a bitch!" Her lip was split and bleeding. "That asshole is mine," Jase said.

He turned to go after Otis, but Jade grabbed his arm. "Let him go," she said, her voice tired.

Jase turned back to her, his eyes narrowing. Her hands recoiled as if he'd burned her. "What the hell is going on here?"

Jade shook her head and pressed the towel tighter to her lip. She flinched under the pressure. "A misunderstanding. He thinks I'm someone I'm not."

"Ruby Leigh?"

"If you eavesdropped, why are you asking me?"

"I want the truth."

She stood silent, staring at him. Her face swelling.

Jase cursed and stepped over to the Sub-Zero fridge, grabbing a handful of ice from the ice bin. He took the towel from Jade and wrapped the ice in it, then handed it back to her. He made his way quickly around the kitchen for another towel and filled it with ice. Gently, he placed it against her eye. "You're going to look like a boxer after a knockout."

Jade jerked away from him and eyed him suspiciously. "Why are you here?"

"I heard your twelve o'clock canceled." She slapped him. Jase grabbed her hand but quickly let go of her. "What's the going rate for rough sex these days?"

"If you think your opinion means anything to me, Detective, you're sadly mistaken."

"It should. I could arrest you right now."

"For what?"

"Impeding an investigation."

"I'm impeding nothing. If you're going to arrest me, do it now so I can call my lawyer. Otherwise, leave."

Jase took another step back, giving her space. It was obvious, despite what she'd just been through, that she'd rebounded, and his intimidation tactics weren't working. As a man he didn't like using them on a woman, but as a cop he had no such compunction.

She was a fighter, he'd give her that. He looked closer at her face again and despite the swelling and the soon-to-be bruises, she was stunning. A stunningly beautiful hooker. In any other place he'd never guess it of her. Maybe a wayward princess or runaway debutante, but a hooker? No way. And it bothered him. A lot.

Hookers were at the bottom of his food chain when it came to women, and he had more respect for her than that. But he'd heard what he'd heard, and he was going to get her. His gaze swept the gourmet kitchen.

Casually, he leaned against the oak butcher block. "I have a few questions I'd like to ask you."

"I'll be happy to answer them with my lawyer present."

"Did you have a date with Townsend the night he was murdered?"

Jade's good eye narrowed. She was going to have a hell of a shiner in the morning. She didn't answer.

"I want the last three months of the parking lot surveillance tapes." Jade opened her mouth to speak, but he put a hand up, stopping her. "I can have a warrant in two hours."

She smiled at that and winced for the effort. "What judge is going to appreciate you waking him up in the middle of the night for something that can wait until tomorrow?"

Touché. "I suppose in your business it pays to know all the loopholes."

Jade shook her head. "I told you, we haven't used the cameras since Mr. Morton took over, and the tapes before he came have been destroyed."

"Why?"

"Use your cop brain and figure it out."

"Were you with Townsend Saturday night after midnight?"

"He left with Genevieve."

Jase smiled and moved in a few inches. "You're a very smart lady, Jade Devereaux."

Jade shrugged. "I'm educated."

"Educated and smart aren't necessarily the same thing."

"I graduated cum laude from Stanford. I speak five languages and can calculate algebra in my sleep."

"Impressive. Now that we have established you understand English, answer my question."

Her eyes narrowed. "I did, and be happy I didn't insist on my attorney sitting next to me."

Jase smiled tolerantly and moved another few inches closer to her. She had fully recovered from the shock of her encounter—gone was the skittish kitten, gone was the fear in her eyes, gone was her uncertainty—now a spitting, hissing she-cat, poised to pounce, faced him. He liked her better this way. He was never comfortable consoling people, especially women.

"I asked you if you were with Townsend after midnight last night, not who he left with."

Jade smiled, the gesture pure saccharine. "I gave you my answer."

She tossed the towel into the sink and turned back to face him. "I'd like you to leave now."

Jase decided he'd rather have her think he was satisfied, then push. Instinctively, he knew she wasn't going anywhere. "I'll go, but I'm advising you not to take any out-of-town trips until we have this case solved."

"Are you saying I'm a suspect, Detective?"

"I'd call you a person of interest."

"As in, you think I killed Andrew Townsend?"

"The evidence will prove who killed him." Jase turned to leave but turned back to her, noting that the swelling on her face had increased despite the ice. "I think you should see a doctor."

Jade shook her head and moved past him. "No thanks.

I'm going upstairs to clean up, when I come back down here I want you gone. And lock the door on your way out."

She swept past him and ran up the staircase.

Detective Sergeant Jase Vaughn disturbed Jade on several levels. He was a cop, he was smart, he had her pegged as Andrew's killer, and she was attracted to him. What unnerved her the most was her attraction to him. Sex was a weakness, a weakness that had cost her more than she cared to admit. Yet her body did things in his presence it had never done before. It felt . . . good. She wanted him. She wanted him on the most basic of levels. The admission stunned as much as it terrified her. Her body shivered in excitement and fear.

Intuitively, she knew Jase wasn't the type of man to abuse a woman. In fact, he seemed to be the type of man who delivered the opposite, but there was a dark undercurrent to him. He didn't trust easily, either, and because of that he was convinced she was a prostitute, and a murderer.

She strode into her bedroom, her sanctuary, the one place she could relax. But not tonight. Otis's presence cast a pall over her home. Andrew's death cast a pall over her life. A hard tremor jerked through her entire body. She felt as if the world were closing in around her.

Jade stood in front of the mirror in her bathroom and stared. Her right eye was nearly swollen shut and her lip was twice its normal size. She blanched at the sight. Great. She wouldn't be able to show her face at the club tomorrow night. Not like this.

She slid the towel off her shoulder and smiled. She had to hand it to Jase, even with her body parts exposed his eyes hadn't lingered. She respected him at least for that.

She slipped out of her dress and held the silky sheath in her hand. It wasn't repairable. She opened her fingers and let it drop to the floor, where it pooled at her feet. She slipped off her thong undies and stepped into the roomy shower. It was what she loved about her town house. It was open and spacious, almost 2,500 square feet. But out of the entire space, only her bedroom gave her comfort. Tina's bedroom had been stripped of her sister's essence. Yes, there was a room for her when she came home for breaks, but Jade wanted her to stay away. She needed to be away from Jade and her life. She didn't want her baby sister to know what she did for a living. Or what she had done in her past.

Sighing heavily, Jade stepped into the shower and, in robotic mode, she washed herself. She refused to think about Townsend, except for wanting to call in a favor and find out how he died.

If she were responsible? It was an open-and-shut case of self-defense. The question was, would she take her chances and admit it? And with the admission take the chance of losing Tina forever. For Jade there was only one answer. If she had to, she'd lay low. She could not prove she defended herself against Townsend's attack. There were no witnesses to her attack, but there were to his threats earlier that evening, and first thing in the morning she'd get rid of the knife.

Showered and feeling a trifle better, Jade pulled on a pair of comfy PJs. She tossed the multicolored pillows from her bed to the floor and pulled back the soft downy comforter. A soft knock on the door startled her; she started and turned around. Jase stood at the doorway, her .357 dangling from his fingers.

"I hope this is registered in your name."

Jade flung her wet hair over her shoulder and strode up to him, holding out her hand, palm up. "Actually, it isn't."

Jase cocked a dark brow. "I could take this with me."

Jade cocked a brow. "But you won't."

He handed it to her butt first. "Get it registered."

"Yes, sir."

Jase looked around. "Nice room. I like it better than downstairs."

"This is me, downstairs is Jade Devereaux."

"Who *are* you?"

"A very tired woman."

She set the gun down on top of her dresser and said, "I'm going downstairs for some drugs and ice. I'll see you out."

Jase didn't argue. He could see she was tired, beat-up, and if he pushed harder she'd push back more. Patience was his friend. Besides, if he was going to follow her tomorrow he'd need some sleep, as well.

Bright and early the next morning, Jase sipped his coffee and watched the garage door of Jade's town house open and the black BMW back out. From what he could see, Jade had on a baseball cap and oversize sunglasses. She headed south on Hurst. He followed. He had the GPS device in hand and would take the first opportunity presented to attach it to her car.

It didn't take long. She pulled up in front of a large non-descript home in south San Jose. He called in the address to Dispatch.

After a moment he had his answer. "Seventeen, that is the Lost Lambs Shelter for Battered Women and Children."

Jase whistled. Was she going as a victim? Despite what

Shannon had divulged about her suspicions that Jade had been raped, Jade didn't strike him as a victim of anything. But Jase knew all too well victims of sexual assault could keep their trauma buried deep for years.

He wondered then, as he watched her knock on the door and after several minutes saw her allowed in, if that was why she was a prostitute. Weren't prostitutes victims of men, of life, of drugs? Did she let her walls down here?

He took the GPS device out of the box and opened a tube of epoxy. Taking advantage of the opportunity, Jase globbed on a bunch and hurried across the street to the BMW. Nonchalantly, he bent down out of sight of the shelter and slid the device under the driver's door, pressing it up and under the chassis, holding it in place for a few minutes. The street was quiet, but if anyone asked, he'd say he dropped his keys and was looking for them.

Letting go of the device, he smiled. Now he could monitor her.

Jade sadly smiled down at Beatrice Mendoza as she carefully brushed damp bangs from the bandage on the girl's forehead. Bea's poor sweet face was unrecognizable beneath the kaleidoscope of colors, the bruising and the swelling.

"Bea, what happened?"

The little girl, no more than eight, shook her head. Tears slid from the slits that were her eyes. *Mi papá.*

Fernando Mendoza. It amazed Jade how he could be such an absentee father yet show up to use his only daughter as a punching bag. Jade understood the cycle of violence more than Bea knew. In a world where men ruled and women had no skills it was almost impossible to escape. Jade sat up straight. But *she'd* escaped. Barely.

By sheer willpower, desperation, and yes, fear, she'd taken her sister and run. She ran as far and as fast as she could from a life that would have chewed them both up.

It took ten-hour days cleaning toilets and going to night school to carve out a little life for her and Tina. She was only fifteen in an unfamiliar world. But she'd risen above her poverty. She grew up, and swore never again would she bend to a man's will.

She patted Bea's hair and rocked her. "Where is your mother, Bea?"

Squinting eyes stared up at her. "She no come home last night. I'm afraid."

Jade shushed her and continued rocking. "I know you are, sweetie, and I promise you it will get better. You're safe here."

Bea broke down and cried more. Jade did what she came there to do, comfort and reassure. But as Bea's tears began to soak her shirt sleeve, anger swelled. It was one thing to victimize an adult, but an innocent child?

Fernando Mendoza needed to go to jail for this. He'd managed to slip through the cracks by intimidating his children to lie. But this time, Sister Josie told Jade, there were witnesses. Now the little girl had to put her faith in the justice system.

After several long minutes, the girl's sobs turned into deep, troubled breaths. She was asleep. Jade closed her eyes and thought back to her years on the run with Tina. The so-called system had not stepped in and helped two homeless girls. No, the system failed them on so many levels she'd stopped counting. Jade learned early there was only one person on this earth she could trust. And so she worked her fingers raw and did what she had to do.

Exhaustion crept over her and, feeling safe here in the shelter, Jade let the fatigue take over her body. She fell into a troubled sleep.

Several hours later, Jade woke with a start. It took her several seconds to get her bearings but Bea's soft snores against her shoulder calmed her. Gently, Jade moved the little body from hers and rearranged her on the bed, covering Bea with a Little Mermaid blanket. The child's innocence was lost forever and without intense counseling she would no doubt repeat in her adulthood the cycle of violence, picking a man who showed he cared with his fists.

Despite the lost hours of sleep, Jade made her rounds visiting the few children who called the shelter home this week. Although the shelter was sponsored by the Catholic church, it was donations that kept it afloat, and Jade donated heavily and regularly. She also made sure she mentioned it when appropriate to the members at Callahan's. Guilt money was a beautiful thing.

Jade wasn't surprised to see the handsome detective leaning against her car when she left the shelter several hours later. Her stomach did a slow roll, but she ignored it. "Following me, Detective?"

He smiled. "As a matter of fact, I am. Why did you call Andrew Townsend at seven p.m. the night of his murder?"

Jade stopped in front of him and crossed her arms over her chest. It was common knowledge at the club that they had a date that night. "I was confirming our dinner date."

"Did you have dinner with him?"

"Yes."

"What else did you do on your date?"

Jade pulled down her sunglasses and winced at the bright sunlight, then slid them back up again. "Do you want to know if I had sex with him?"

"Among other things."

"First of all, let me explain again, Detective. Callahan's is not a brothel. I am not a prostitute. Nor are any of the other ladies employed there. If I had sex with Andrew Townsend, or any other man I might date, that is my business and would be my choice as a consenting adult. Not to turn a trick."

"Do you have sex with your dates?"

"How is my sex life pertinent to finding who killed Mr. Townsend?"

"Did you like him?"

"Andrew? No."

"Why not."

"He was a bully and he had no manners. Men like that deserve a swift kick in the ass." She moved around the car to the driver's door. "I have to go home."

Jase followed around and stood between her and the door. He raised his hand slowly to her face. She didn't flinch, and he smiled. Gently, he pulled the sunglasses away from her face. "The swelling has gone down."

"That happens when you take mass quantities of anti-inflammatories and sleep on a block of ice."

Jase ran a fingertip along the swollen curve of her lip. "Does it still hurt?"

She slapped his hand away. "It hurts enough."

Jase stood back and allowed her to get into her car. He watched her drive away and smiled. He was getting to her.

He sat in his car and booted up the laptop, then keyed in to the monitoring site. After he put in the necessary data the screen lit up with the area street grid, and the flashing dot on the screen that was Jade. Looked like she was going home.

He called Ricco. "Hey, man, anything from the coroner?"

"Yeah, the prelim came back. Cause of death: asphyxiation. The guy choked on his balls!"

Jase grimaced. "I thought as much. Was the stab wound significant?"

"Hmm, says here, puncture to the left lung. Blade size: four inches long by one-sixteenth by half an inch wide. No distinctive marks. One jab."

"I want a warrant for it. Call Judge Culling—she likes me—and get it signed off. I want to search the residence of one Jade Devereaux."

"But it wasn't the murder weapon."

"It could have been the knife used to whack his balls. Besides, she's lying to me about seeing him later in the evening. I want to know why. I don't know, but the woman has some baggage and she's hiding information. Was there any DNA on the victim other than his?"

"Nothing traceable except soap. There was no semen, so if Townsend had sex he showered and changed, or the killer was the one who washed him down. Probably to get rid of any trace evidence. You think Jade screwed him, then cut his balls off and shoved them down his throat?"

Jase laughed. "If she did, he must have been lousy in the sack."

"Yeah, remind me never to piss off a woman like her in bed."

"Keep me posted," he told his partner, then hung up.

Jase watched the beep that was Jade's car on the grid turn toward the club. So, she'd changed her mind.

Moments later, Jase drove by the back lot of Callahan's.

Save for Jade's BMW, the lot was empty. Jase pulled in beside her car and followed up on a few leads.

According to Jade and Mac, Genevieve was the last person to see Townsend alive. Ricco had left her several messages with no return calls. The address Ricco had for her hadn't checked out this morning. Jase smiled. Looked like it was time to encounter Jade Devereaux again.

Jase hopped from his car and strode up to the back door. He wasn't surprised when he tried the door to find it locked. He knocked. A minute later, a small slot in the door opened and Jade's swollen eye peered at him.

"What is it now, Detective?"

"I need your girl Genevieve's address."

"I gave it to you."

"It's bogus."

The metal slat closed and the door jerked open. "What do you mean, it's bogus?"

"Just what I said, my partner went there this a.m. to have a chat with your girl. It was an empty warehouse in Santa Clara."

Jase followed Jade in and she shut the door behind him and bolted it. She moved down a long hall through the kitchen and into a short vestibule that opened to her office. Interesting. It was a fake panel from the inside. Two entries.

Immediately, Jade sat down at her computer and pulled up a file. Irritated, she picked up the phone and dialed a number. "Hi, Genny, it's Jade. When you come in this evening, please bring a utility bill with your name and address on it for my files. Thank you."

She turned to Jase. "I don't like to be lied to."

"Neither do I. Do you have a knife you carry with that gun of yours?"

Her head snapped back. "A knife? As in a steak knife, that kind of knife?"

"Exactly, but something on a smaller scale, say four inches."

Jade stared at him for a long time. She'd forgotten to ditch the damn knife! It was right there in her drawer, attached to her key chain. "I don't recall."

Jase sat down and made himself comfortable. "I thought you were going home. Why are you here?"

"I have work to catch up on, especially since I don't plan on coming in tonight."

"A date?"

"Hardly, Detective. In case you haven't noticed, I look like someone used my face for a punching bag. I can't be seen by anyone here in this condition. The bruises will only get darker as the week goes by; hopefully I'll be able to cover those with cosmetics, but not the swelling. So I get to take a little unplanned vacation."

"Who will run things with you gone?"

"Thomas is quite capable of handling the club for a few days."

"When's the last time you had a vacation?"

"That's a strange question for a detective to ask a person of interest."

"Off the record."

"I took my sis— I took a trip to San Diego a few months ago."

"You have a sister here?"

"No, she's away. College."

"Does she know what you do for a living?"

"Just what *do* I do for a living, Detective?"

"Officially or unofficially?"

"Since you seem to know all, why don't you give me both versions?"

"C'mon, Jade. You can't expect me to believe after what I saw last night and what I overheard last night that you aren't running girls through this place."

"Did it ever occur to you, Detective, that I might use people's perception of me to further my position?"

Jase sat back in the chair and relaxed like he had all day. "Explain."

"Last night I was followed by a man who had two misperceptions of me. One, that I was someone named Ruby; and two, that I was a prostitute. I couldn't get rid of him even though I am not this Ruby person. But to gain leverage in a volatile situation I allowed him to think I was on the clock. He thought I had another client, and because of it he left."

"He left because you pulled a .357 on him."

"I did, but as you can see by my face, that didn't deter him, now did it? I'm sure he assumed you were my next john."

"I'm going to arrest him for assaulting you."

"No, you are not."

"It's not your call."

"Detective, my life is complicated enough as it is. The last thing I need is the likes of Otis Thibodeaux making it worse."

"If he's in jail, he can't."

"If he had money to join Callahan's, he has money to buy his way out of jail with a shark of an attorney, and if I'm a hostile witness? Why waste the taxpayer's money?"

Jase nodded. "The law-enforcement part of me aside, as a man, do you have any idea how difficult it is for me to do nothing to a man who uses a woman as a punching bag?"

Jade smiled. "You cannot be every woman's knight in shining armor, Detective."

"I don't strive to be. Now, explain Hiro."

Jade sighed. "Mr. Hiro and I go way back. Up until last night he had been a perfect gentleman. Maybe the full moon brought out his frisky side. I doubt I'll see him again anytime soon. He ditched me."

"Tell me about Jack Morton."

She shrugged. "Not much to tell. He bought out Sam Callahan two months ago. My gut says he's new money, and he's in trouble. It explains why our membership has taken a slide into the new-flash pool."

"As opposed to old money?"

"There's a difference. It's a rare new-money mogul who doesn't let everyone know he's loaded. Their wives? All flash. No subtlety. They wear it like a sign. 'Look at me, I have money and now I'm better than you.' The men come in here and think all they have to do is snap their fingers and the girls will drop. We don't, they get pissed, and we have a problem."

"Did Townsend expect you to drop for him?"

"Yes."

"And when you refused?"

"He put his hands on me. I told him if he touched me again, I'd cut his balls off and shove them so far down his throat he'd choke to death."

Jase froze. "I beg your pardon."

Jade smiled, the gesture stinging. "Mac stepped in, and even then Townsend pushed. Finally, he left with Genny."

"Then what?"

"Then I went home."

"You're lying."

"Why do you think so?"

"I heard the nine-one-one tape, and you did a lousy job disguising your voice."

"Hire a voice expert, and you'll see it wasn't me."

Jase nodded. "Don't think I won't."

"I would expect nothing less from you, Detective. Now please, go do your job so I can do mine."

Jase slid into the unmarked and called his partner.

"Maza."

"I have some rather interesting info."

"Shoot."

"It seems our Miss Devereaux told Townsend when he wouldn't take no for an answer the other night, that if he persisted, she'd cut his balls off and shove them down his throat."

"No shit. A sideways confession?"

"I don't think so, she was pissed, and she's too smart. Maybe she didn't hack him, but the person who did him must have overheard her threaten Townsend and knew we'd find out."

"You think someone is trying to pin this on her?"

"Maybe. But my gut says she's involved somehow, I'm just not sure how. I'll bet my new house she was the one on the nine-one-one tape."

"I've already sent it out for analysis."

"Good. Did you run down Otis Thibodeaux?"

"Yep, just got it. He likes the good life. Suite nine-twenty at the San Jose Fairmont. You want me to visit him?"

"I'm on my way right now. Do we have any more from the coroner? Or the techs? I need some DNA."

"Lab is backed up. Most of it's going to county, where we take a number."

"You'd think with a San Jose resident as the murder victim they would speed it up."

"Nah, the sheriff has cracked down on cuts. We wait our turn."

"That's bullshit."

"Agreed."

"Run down a William Trent MacDonald, and Katsuo Hiro—"

"Is that the chap Jade left with last night?"

"Yeah."

"You know he's the CEO of SyTech, don't you?"

That was why he was so familiar. Global SyTech, Japan's answer to Microsoft.

"I knew he was connected. Be quiet about it, he got a little overzealous with Miss Devereaux last night at dinner. Not sure what would have happened if I hadn't interrupted."

"She's turning tricks in restaurants?"

"It looked that way, but now I'm not sure."

"Don't fall for the crack, man."

Jase laughed. "That's my line."

"I'm serious. Even for the hit-and-run master you are, sometimes all it takes is one woman to geld you."

Jase laughed again at his friend's misplaced concern. "Look, Ricco, I appreciate your concern, but even if I twisted up the sheets with Jade Devereaux, she'd be the one clinging on. Life is too good. Why mess it up with emotional bullshit? I don't do relationships, on any level."

"Lust ain't a relationship, man. It's a drug. Addictive. It'll kill you. Take it from a guy whose been there and done it and has the damn T-shirt to prove it. And you forget, brother, I've seen her, and you know how damn selective I am, and she gave me a twenty-four-hour boner!"

Jase laughed. How could he fault his partner for what he and every other man in the state would be guilty of in her presence?

"Jase, I Googled her, and the pics that come up with her on the arm of every Fortune 500 CEO in the world tell me she is trouble. Big trouble. She—damn, I can't explain it, she has some serious mojo going on. Steer clear."

"So noted, amigo."

"Yeah, I can hear it in your voice."

Jase laughed and hung up the phone. But when he pulled up in front of the Fairmont, he didn't get right out. Ricco's words echoed in his brain.

He had always been an aesthete in his hygiene, clothes, work ethic, and in keeping his emotions in close check. He made no bones about his distrust of women. He had every right to his feelings. And he had never felt the need to augment them. He was a loner, a guy who liked women but who didn't like any enough to trust them. And he was okay with that.

Jase shrugged off Ricco's warning. He was in complete control of his dick. He got out of his car and tossed his keys to the valet, then strode into the San Jose Fairmont. He liked the San Francisco version better. The new one was new flash, whereas the grand dame in the city had a few age spots.

As he made his way up the elevator, he wondered what Jade was going do with her night off.

CHAPTER

6

When he'd seen her on Fox News two months ago on the arm of some upstart California congressman, he'd recognized her immediately. Her face was forever burned into his brain. It didn't take long for him to track her down.

And while she fooled those around her and even herself, she didn't fool him. Ruby Leigh Gentry might be more of a looker than she was eleven years ago, but she still had that air about her, like she was smarter than everyone else. Otis choked back a scornful laugh and tried the handle on her back door. Locked. But Ruby was careful that way. She probably had an alarm system, too. He stood back on the small back porch of the town house and scanned the roof line. No box, no camera.

He ran his fingers along the top of the doorframe and just as he was about to retreat, his fingertip touched cold metal. "Not so smart are you now, Ruby Leigh?"

Quickly, he let himself in and carefully locked the door

behind him. He'd find the proof he needed, and when he did, he'd make her life so miserable she'd have to give him what he wanted. And if she didn't? Well, he knew all her dirty little secrets and so would everyone else.

He bypassed the tidy kitchen and the meticulous living room. He knew she was too smart to have reminders of who she was and where she came from out in the open, but there was a place somewhere in the house where her secrets lay hidden. He'd find that place and when he found the proof he needed, he would have her.

Hastily, he made his way up the stairs, the plush carpeting silencing his steps. His heart rate accelerated when he pushed open her bedroom door. Her lingering scent enveloped him and for a minute he stopped and let it engulf him. His dick twinged and his hands balled into fists. The colonel had wanted her all for himself, but when Daddy couldn't get it up, he sicced that lowlife stable manager Donavan Le Blanc on her.

Donny, the girls all cooed. *Donny, my ass.*

Otis's breath quickened as his hand slid to the bulge between his thighs. He'd watched Ruby and Donny Boy, watched Donny hump her till she couldn't move. He watched her cry afterward. Anger consumed him. He'd wanted to kill Le Blanc, strangle him slowly and watch his eyes bulge out of his head while he struggled to breathe for what he'd done to his girl. Didn't he know Ruby was his?

But when Otis told Ruby Leigh he could do more for her, she slapped him and told him he was the last person on earth she'd let touch her.

Miss High and Mighty was in love, and he could never fill Donny's shoes. No matter how much money he had or who his daddy was. Didn't he know Donny and her were getting married as soon as she turned eighteen? Then they were taking Crystal and leaving Sykesville for good.

Furious and realizing his precious Ruby Leigh was slipping away for good, he shattered her schoolgirl dreams right then and there. It gave him more pleasure than fucking her ever could have. He'd never forget the day Ruby Leigh Gentry's perfect world blew up in her face. It was the last time he saw her, and his daddy never forgave him.

Otis stepped into the room. The soft inviting colors meant nothing to him. He would find what he needed to rightfully take back what was his, and he didn't care how hard he had to play. He had nothing to lose.

His eyes scanned the room. Everything about Ruby was neat, tidy, and cold, except this room. Here, her personality seeped through the chilly walls of the town house. For a common whore, she had expensive taste. Always did. Made sense if what Daddy said was true about her father being some Yankee blue blood her mama screwed when she went up north for a winter. But she'd never know about him.

Otis carefully scanned the room, and his eyes settled on a tattered brown fabric bear on her pillow. He went to it and touched it. Closing his eyes, he brought it to his nose and inhaled her scent. It was burned into his DNA. Stupid girl, if only she'd loved *him*. His eyes flashed open and he threw the bear hard against the wall. A small crackling sound caught his attention.

When he picked the bear up, a gravelly sound, like broken glass, rumbled from inside the floppy thing. He turned it over and found a zipper. He smiled and unzipped the toy. "You can run, girl, but you can't hide from Otis."

He pulled out a small framed picture surrounded by shattered glass. A miniature version of Ruby sat beside her on the tree stump behind the trailer. Crystal Blue, Ruby's baby sister. The "baby" would be about eighteen now. It was obvious the girl didn't live here, but he knew Ruby better than that. She was a tiger when it came to her sister. Crystal was close but untouchable. Well, he'd just see about finding her and see how Ruby wanted to handle matters when he did.

In the meantime, he slid the picture into his pocket. He had what he'd come for: Proof that the darkly exotic, cold-as-ice bitch who called herself Jade Devereaux was none other than Ruby Leigh Gentry, whore to his daddy and murderer of her own mother.

As Otis began to leave the room he stopped midstep, then slowly turned around. His gaze swept across the room again. The slow rage that had simmered for eleven years boiled over. He stepped back into her lair, her sanctuary, the place she went to get away from her life. She didn't deserve this place, not after what she'd done to him. He closed the door behind him. When he was done she'd have nowhere to hide.

The minute Jade walked into her house from the garage, she knew someone had been there. She could smell salty male sweat. Carefully, she set down the two bags of groceries in her hands and backed into the garage. Always prepared, she went to the planting bench in the corner and opened the drawer. She pulled out a small-caliber pistol.

Silently, she made her way into her house. The large living room was undisturbed, as well as the formal dining room. She hugged the walls and crept into the family room. Nothing looked out of place. The kitchen was intact.

She turned and made her way up the circular stairway,

her steps slowing. The door to her room was wide open, as she had left it. She listened for any sound and was greeted with silence. Letting out a long breath of relief, Jade walked into her bedroom and screamed.

Jase walked out of the Fairmont, unable to locate Thibodeaux, when his cell phone rang. "Vaughn."

"Detective Vaughn, this is Jade Devereaux. My house has been ransacked."

"Don't touch anything, I'll be right there."

Jase hung up, jumped into his car parked at the curb, much to the valet's rancor, and made a quick U-turn, calling Dispatch with her information.

He called Jade back. "Hello?" Her voice sounded scared, like a little girl.

"Where in the house are you?"

"In my bedroom."

"Go into your bathroom and lock the door. The perp might still be in the house."

"I checked, he—"

"Do it now!" Jase didn't mean to yell, but dammit, she could end up dead before he got there.

"I'm in the bathroom and the door is locked."

"Good, now tell me what happened."

"After I left the club I went to the grocery store, then came home. I knew the minute I entered someone had been in the house."

"How?"

"The smell, sweat."

"What's damaged?"

"My bedroom is trashed. It looks like someone went on

a rampage, like they took their hate out on my personal belongings."

"Who has such anger toward you?"

"I—I don't know." But she did.

"Jade, I have a feeling this may be connected to Townsend somehow. You need to think hard—who has it in for you, and him?"

"What are you saying?"

"I'm saying I think you are the connection between these two crimes."

"Are you accusing me—?"

"I'm not accusing you of anything, but there is a connection." He heard the siren through her cell phone. "That's the uniform I had dispatched. Let him in."

"Okay."

"Try not to touch anything. The techs will go over every inch of your house."

Jade didn't argue. Instead, she hung up on the arrogant cop and opened her front door to a cop barely out of high school.

Minutes after she let him in, Jase screeched to a halt in front of her house. Great, the neighbors were gonna never let her hear the end of this.

Jase hurried up to her, his eyes scanning every inch of her body. "I'm fine," she said, exasperated.

He nodded to the uniform. "Stand by." Then he took Jade gently by the elbow and steered her into the house. He let go and hurried up the stairs, she followed. What greeted him was not a big shock, but he had to admit the length the person responsible went to—single-handedly destroying every piece of furniture, clothing, and accessories—was unmatched.

Stuffing from the pillows and comforter littered the floor. It reminded him of a Tahoe blizzard. The bed was broken, the headboard smashed, the mirror on the listing dresser shattered. Her stuffed animals were torn and strewn and her clothes were shredded, the heels ripped off her shoes. Strangely enough, the bathroom was untouched.

Pictures were ripped, their frames broken. Hate fueled this attack. Jade choked back a sob as she darted into her room and grabbed the teddy bear Jase remembered seeing on her pillow last night. Only now it was shredded, the brown fur hanging in slivers from the eyeless head.

"Jade, you can't touch anything, you might destroy evidence."

"My bear! He killed my bear!"

Jase had noticed last night it had seen better days. Now it looked ravaged. Her sobs intensified and then her anger surfaced. "Son of a bitch! Who does this?" She turned angry eyes on Jase. *"Who does this?"*

"Someone who wants to hurt you. Tell me about Otis Thibodeaux."

Vehemently, she shook her head. "I don't know him!"

"Talk to me, Jade. Tell me what the hell is going on."

She shook her head. And clutched the skin of the bear to her chest. "I don't know." In a sudden realization, she cried out: "My picture!"

"What picture?"

Jade closed her eyes shut and held the bear closer. "The one of my baby sister and me."

Jase scanned the room. "It's probably somewhere under all of this mess. Once the techs go through it, it'll turn up."

It occurred to him that he hadn't seen any other pictures of her or her family. "Is that the only one you have?"

She nodded, her eyes far away.

For the second time in twenty-four hours Jase resisted the urge to comfort Jade. The feelings that spurned him to such an uncomfortable gesture confused him on a most basic level. It wasn't because he was an unempathetic asshole and didn't want to comfort another human being. With Jade it was the complete opposite. His powerful urge to go to her went deeper; it was more. He felt her pain, and her fear, and he wanted to be the man to make it all go away.

Jase heard voices downstairs. He moved to the landing and called down to Ricco and the techs, "Up here, but put the bunny slippers on, and bring me two pairs and some gloves."

As Ricco entered the bedroom, he and Jase exchanged a look before Jase gave him the rundown.

"Why don't you get her out of here and I'll take over from here," Ricco offered.

In a mild state of shock, Jade allowed Jase to take her downstairs. He sat her down at the kitchen table and told her not to move. Quickly, he slipped on the booties and gloves and moved around the house, checking every point of entry. Nothing forced, no windows unlocked. He moved through the door to the garage and checked the door to the backyard. Locked. He opened it and walked to the gate. He looked down at the immaculate lawn. The grass was cut so short, footprints were impossible to detect, yet he followed it to the decent-size backyard. He scanned the flower beds.

There at the edge of the deck was a heel imprint in the dirt. Another a foot away, and some of the dirt on the deck. The sprinklers must have just been on when the intruder walked on the lawn, because the dirt had caked into mud.

The partial imprint of what he figured to be a size twelve was clearly visible. Jase followed the natural course of the criminal: he reached up and found the key. He slipped it into an evidence bag, then knocked on the back door.

As Jade opened it, he held the bag out to her. "Do you always make it so easy?"

CHAPTER

7

"I—"

"For a lady with so much gray matter, this isn't too bright. I can't believe you'd leave a key out, especially in your business."

Her anger flared. "My *business*?"

"Yes, dammit, your business. You lead men on, for Christ's sake, you act like their girlfriend. *You're a paid prick tease.*"

Jade stood. "Get out of my house!"

"Sorry, it's a crime scene, and I'm a cop."

"Have your friend upstairs do what needs to be done, I don't care to have any more interaction with you."

"Can't handle the truth about yourself?"

Jade threw her hair over her shoulders and strode into his space. "I have dealt with truths you can only pray you never have to face. And I'm still standing. Go preach your sanctimonious bullshit to someone who gives a damn."

Jase stood his ground. "It's not sanctimonious bullshit.

In your business, you deal with men, horny men who pay a lot of money for your company, and I bet most of them, like Andrew Townsend and Katsuo Hiro, think you owe them more than dinner and conversation. So isn't it remotely conceivable to you that one of them might just try to force himself on you? *In* your home, where there would be no witnesses?"

"You have a colorful imagination, Detective."

"No, I have a realistic imagination. It doesn't take much to imagine what a man who thinks he got ripped off will do to a prime piece of ass."

His words stung. Jade shook her head and stepped away from Jase. "You are no gentleman."

He reached a hand out to her and abruptly retracted it. "That was wrong. I meant—"

Jade smiled, not feeling any joy from their exchange. Her life had been and continued to be all about perception, and right now her survival depended on this cop's current perception of her. But despite all of that, it bothered her much more than it should that he believed what he did about her. Inwardly she shrugged. So be it. It was what it was.

"I know what you meant, Detective. And I hear you loud and clear. You obviously aren't a fan of women, and you certainly think I'm something you scraped off your shoe. I understand it, but please keep your private bigotry to yourself."

Jase made to move closer. She stepped back. He stopped where he stood. "Look, Jade, maybe we need to start over here—"

"I don't start over, I just move forward." She moved past him and said over her shoulder, "How long will your people be here?"

"As long as it takes."

"I need a few things from my bedroom."

"No can do," he said from behind her.

"Fine." She dug in her purse and pulled out a card. She scribbled her cell phone number on the back, then handed it to him. "Please call me when they're done."

Jade turned then and left the house. Anger bit hard at her subconscious. She'd never given much thought to what anyone thought of her. Tina thought she was a manager of a private club, which she was, though she'd never gone into detail about the kind of club. She had no girlfriends, no family, no social life. It was easier to keep her secrets that way.

But it bothered her more than she cared to admit that this Detective Vaughn thought she was nothing more than a high-priced hooker.

Would he offer to pay for her time? That would be the ultimate insult.

For the second time in as many days, Jade felt the stirrings of loneliness. She had run too long and too far for anyone to come into her life and disrupt it. She would fight for her privacy and fight to keep her baby sister safe from the ugliness that was once their lives. The day she took her sister's hand and ran away from the woman who gave them life, she vowed neither one of them would ever have to be subjected to such abominations again. She would make her own way, and no man or woman would have a say in her life.

Jade gunned the BMW. Hot tears stung her eyes. She needed a cry, a real good one. It had been more than a decade since she had shed a tear for anyone, least of all herself. With her refusal to allow anyone in her life, for her own self-preservation, she had denied herself the most basic of human requirements. The touch of a man, a kiss, a caress.

A warm flush skittered across her skin when she thought of Jase's large hand sweeping across her skin, lighting her up, stirring deep latent desire. What would it feel like to be loved by a man like him?

The chirp of her cell phone interrupted her thoughts. "Hello," she softly answered.

"It's Vaughn."

Her back stiffened but butterflies skittered along her skin. "Did you lose a criminal?"

He laughed and said, "No, I just wanted to let you know the techs are going to be here through the night. Do you have somewhere you can stay?"

Jade let out a long breath. It wasn't like she could go back and get her clothes. They were destroyed. Her insurance carrier was going to crap a golden cow when they got the estimated replacement cost. She had tens of thousands of dollars in wardrobe, shoes, and accessories. Luckily, most of her jewelry was in a wall safe in the pantry. It hadn't occurred to her to look when she was there. If the jewelry were gone? It didn't matter, it was just metal, rocks, and minerals. None of it held sentimental value.

"I can stay at the club."

"I thought you were taking the night off?"

"I am, I'll go in after they close up."

"And sleep at your desk?"

"We have sofas."

After a long pause, Jase said, "Let me make you dinner."

Jade let out a long breath. "Too little, too late, Detective."

"Don't read anything into it, Jade, it's simply an offer."

"No thanks again. I look like hell and feel like hell. I just want to curl up in bed and sleep."

There was such a long pause Jade thought the detective had hung up. "Hello?"

"I'm here. I have a friend who's out of town. His place is clean and comfortable, you're welcome to crash there tonight."

"Thanks for the offer. I'll stay in a hotel."

"If you change your mind, you have my cell number."

"I won't. Good-bye." Jade hung up before she did change her mind. The sudden yearning for human contact knocked her off balance. It seemed unnatural to her, but more than that, it seemed like the most natural thing to want. Yet she had never felt the urge before, not like this. Was she finally beginning to feel again? Had the numbness of her abuse worn off? Did she dare step back into the fray of an emotional life? She shook her head no. Being so comfortably numb had its advantages.

She turned up 880 with the intention of hitting Santana Row and restocking, at least on a minimal level, her wardrobe. Shopping always made her feel better.

Three hours later, Jade felt even worse. The sense of emptiness prevailed over the six thousand dollars' worth of haute couture she had amassed.

Forty-five minutes after that, she found herself sitting in front of her house. The unmarked police cars were gone, leaving only the crime-scene van. She felt—gypped. She was hoping Jase would still be there. For what? Waiting for her? Why the hell would he do that? He thought she was a high-priced whore. And maybe she was. Eleven years ago, the price she'd charged for sex was love. The price her mother had charged meant she had to save the family from ruin, her sister from Social Services. She'd succumbed to both.

She'd been played by one man for love and her mother

for financial gain. Sex to her was a dirty word; it only conjured up hurt, pain, and shame. She doubted she would ever have a normal sex life. And up until the day Jase Vaughn walked into her club, she had not had one spark of desire for a man in eleven years.

Maybe this time she could blame her melancholy on hormones. Still, it didn't change the fact that she didn't want to sleep at the club and the thought of an impersonal hotel room, even a five-star hotel, held no appeal. She wanted the cozy comfort of her bedroom. She wanted to put on her PJs and have someone cook her dinner and tell her stories and make her forget her past, her present, and the unknown future.

She pulled her cell phone out of her purse and stared at it for a long time. She hit the last incoming number and held her breath.

"Vaughn."

"I changed my mind."

"Are you hungry?"

"Famished."

"T-bone and cab sound good?"

"Perfect."

He gave her an address and she entered it into her car's navigational system. In twenty minutes, she pulled up in front of a new home in a very nice subdivision. Her gut told her she was making a colossal mistake. The little girl in her ignored it. She didn't want to be alone. Never mind the man behind that door thought she was a prostitute and a murderer.

Jase smiled when he opened the door and she entered, telling herself she was a big girl and could leave anytime she wanted, that no one would force her to stay against her will. That it was her decision for herself, not someone else's for his own needs.

Her terms.

Upon entering, Jade noted the masculine yet comfortable decor of the house. She liked its wide-open space. A fire crackled in the fireplace and the deep browns and burgundies of the studded leather were inviting.

A bottle of wine sat decanting on the black granite countertop. Jase had changed from his designer suit into a pair of worn acid-wash blue jeans and a white T-shirt. His feet were bare. Normally, she didn't like to look at men's feet—she pushed the reasons for it from her mind, the image making her stomach roll—but Jase had strong square feet, the nails square, the toes symmetrical. They looked . . . sexy.

She looked up and smiled at him. He smiled back.

"Do my feet muster up?"

"Long story, but yes."

He poured her a glass of wine, then handed it to her. "Have a seat. Dinner will be ready in about twenty minutes."

"Can I help?"

"Nope, just curl up on the couch. There's a throw somewhere over there. Get comfortable."

Sometime later, Jase gently shook her awake. "Jade, wake up, dinner's ready," he softly said close to her ear. She started and cried out, the unexpected touch alarming her. Confused by her surroundings, instinctively Jade pulled her feet up under her and hugged her knees to her chest and looked wildly around.

Jase squatted down next to her, not touching. "Jade, it's okay, you're safe."

Reason quickly settled in. Suddenly she felt foolish. "I—I'm sorry, I forgot for a minute where I was."

He smiled, his eyes level with hers. "Just my place." He stood and offered his hand to her. Her wild eyes darted from his hand to his face, then back to his hand. She reminded him of a terrified rabbit about to be snatched up by a circling vulture. That urge to protect her surfaced again. This time he allowed it to stay.

"I won't hurt you," he softly said. He kept his hand extended. Her big green eyes blinked back what he could swear were tears. He pretended not to see. The woman had a streak of pride running through her as wide as the state of California.

Just as he was about to withdraw his hand, she reached out and took it. Her fingers were cold and her hand trembled. He wrapped his warm fingers around hers, then backed up a step, guiding her up. He walked her into the kitchen, where the table was set.

He pointed to the chair near the window. "I took a chance and took you for a medium-rare kind of girl."

Jade smiled, and his heart melted a little bit. The gesture on her bruised and battered face was that of a victim trying mightily to overcome trauma. A new respect for the woman began to grow.

Jade's defenses went on high alert as Jase held the chair out for her. The detective was too accommodating.

As she made herself comfortable, Jase poured her a fresh glass of wine. "Try it, it's perfect."

Warily, Jade picked up the glass, swirled the rich burgundy-colored wine around, then took a sip. Rich cherry and floral flavors erupted in her mouth. "Very nice."

Jase grinned and sat down across the small table from her and poured himself a glass. He raised it to her and said, "Here's to good wine and good food."

As she clinked her glass against his, Jade asked, "Isn't this highly unusual behavior, Detective?"

He sipped his wine, then said, "My name is Jase."

"My point exactly."

"If you're referring to me having you as my guest, in my home, I suppose it could be construed as unusual."

Jade set her glass down and picked up her knife and fork. The only thing on her plate was a steak. She almost smiled. Typical guy fare, she supposed. Just protein. "But not if you pump me for more information?"

"That isn't the reason I invited you here."

She cut a piece of meat and looked straight at him. "Why did you?"

Jase shrugged and dug into his meal. "You looked like you could use a friend."

"I don't do friends."

Jase chewed a piece of meat, swallowed, then sipped his wine. His look was thoughtful. "You don't seem to do much in the way of personal interaction, and what you do do is an act." She stiffened, setting her fork down. "Truth hurts."

His candor shouldn't have rattled her, but it did. He had a way of doing that to her. "Without sounding like a crybaby, in my life, Detective— Jase, the people I counted on let me down. I learned early not to expect. With no expectations, there is no room for disappointment."

He raised his glass and clinked it against hers. "Here here."

"Did your family let you down?"

He nodded and took another bite of his steak. "I suppose. In a sense."

"Tell me about yourself." Jade was surprised by her question, but this man intrigued her on several levels. She wanted to know what made him tick.

"Not much to tell. Single white male."

"Have you ever been married?"

Jase coughed. "Never, and it isn't an aspiration of mine."

"Don't you like women?"

He flashed her a smile. Her stomach did a slow roll in response. "I love women. I just don't trust them."

"As a rule?"

Jase nodded. "As a rule."

"Hmm, so why would a hunky cop who loves women not trust one if his life depended on it?"

Jase shrugged and chewed a piece of beef. "I just don't."

"Did your mother abandon you?" she asked. His eyes narrowed and she smiled a slow sad smile. Ah, so the detective's mom wouldn't win any mother-of-the-year awards. Small world. "Mine did, not physically, but emotionally. I had to take care of myself and my sister. My mother wasn't—capable."

Jase nodded, the gesture barely perceptible. "My mother had a constant string of men through our house. My sister, too. No sooner would one walk out the back door than another would be coming in the front door. They took what they could from each of them before they sent them on their way," he said.

"So you think all women want the same thing?"

"I don't know. I've never cared enough to find out."

"What about your father?" she asked.

Again, Jase shrugged. "I never met the man."

Jade smiled. "Me, either."

Jase set down his fork and gave her a long, steady look. "We're a lot more alike than I thought."

Jade nodded. Maybe they were.

"Why don't you like to be touched?"

His question caught her off guard. She laughed, nervous. "I—why do you think that?"

"Why do you always answer a question with a question?"

"Maybe I don't like giving the answers."

"Maybe if you were honest about the answers, you could move on."

It was her turn to shrug. "Maybe I like just where I am."

"Do you really?"

Jade shrugged again, avoiding his gaze, and moved a piece of beef around her plate with her fork. "I'm right where I want to be in life."

"I doubt that. Seriously, if you could be anywhere, doing whatever you wanted, what would you do?"

Jade looked up at him and pondered that question long and hard. No one had ever asked her what she wanted. And surprisingly, she had no answer. "I don't know."

He frowned. "No childhood dreams of falling in love and having a family?"

Jade suddenly felt very cold. More like childhood nightmares. "I don't believe in love. Not that way."

"Which way?"

"The romantic kind. But," she smiled, "I love my sister. I'd do anything for her."

"Even at the expense of your happiness?"

"I am happy!"

"Really?" Jase leaned toward her and pinned her with his blue eyes. "You're happy leading men on for a living? You're happy having to constantly steer clear of a man's roaming hands? You're happy working twenty-four/seven and not doing anything for yourself? Are you happy being numb? Don't you want to *feel*, Jade?"

Jade laid her fork down on the edge of her plate and speared him with a glare. "You seem to think you know an awful lot about me, Detective. You don't know me at all. And for someone who asks a lot of questions about feelings and love, you just told me you have no aspirations of ever committing to a woman. Isn't that the pot calling the kettle black?"

"I never said I didn't like relationships. I like them, a lot, so long as they are short."

"Wham bam, thank you, ma'am?"

Jase grinned like a little boy and shook his head.

"I like to feel, Jade. I like to feel a lot of things. Like the softness of a woman's skin. I like the physical connection of good sex. But I make it clear to my partners I'm not a long hauler. It works for me, *and* for the women in my life."

Intrigued, Jade asked, "What exactly does sex mean to you?"

"A physical connection. A good time."

"No emotion?"

Jase grinned. "Is lust an emotion?"

"I don't know."

"Have you ever been in lust with a man?"

Jade frowned. The question brought back too many memories she had long ago buried. "I thought so once. But I—it wasn't."

"Why do you hate men?"

"I don't hate men. Men pay my bills. How can I look a gift horse in the mouth?"

Jase reached across the table to her hand. She let him touch her. "What happened to you?"

She snatched her hand away. It was time to fold and go.

She pushed away from the table and stood. "I made a mistake coming here."

Jase stood up and came around the table, then reached out to her shoulder. She flinched, moving away. "Not all men are bastards, Jade."

"That may be true, but I don't care enough to find out."

He pressed his fingertips to her skin. "Not all men hurt."

Her body stiffened under his touch. Not because she found it unpleasant. Quite the contrary. She found it soothing. Moist heat stung her eyes. What would it feel like to walk into this man's arms and let him hold her, and feel safe for just a minute?

He moved closer to her. His warm breath brushed her cheek. She dared not look up. He would see her fear, see her lies, and see her vulnerability. He'd see her for the fraud she was.

Her back arched, her legs trembled. When his hands slid around her waist and gently brought her into his embrace, Jade resisted before she relaxed into the warm strength of him. He smelled good. Masculine, spicy, strong. His arms tightened around her and he held her. Not asking anything from her, only offering his strength. And it felt good.

She pressed her cheek against his chest, his heart beat a solid steady rhythm against her.

"Does that hurt, Jade?"

Jade closed her eyes, and not trusting her voice, she shook her head. It was the wine getting to her. She rarely drank and wine always had that warm cozy effect on her. What should have been an impersonal dinner had turned into something she was not prepared to handle.

She stepped back out of Jase's embrace. She wanted to minimize what had just happened. "Thanks for the hug."

Then she proceeded to clear the table. When she turned back a moment later to look at Jase, he stood where she'd left him, a small smile quirking his lips.

"What?" she demanded.

He shook his head and walked toward her, taking the plates from her hands. "Take your wine and go sit by the fire. I'll clean up."

For reasons he could not explain, Jase held back the questions burning to be asked. And it wasn't easy. Jade Devereaux intrigued him as a woman just as much as she intrigued him as a suspect, and he knew if he went any further she'd bolt. And for purely selfish reasons that had nothing to do with the case, he wanted her to stay.

When she curled up on the sofa and wrapped the throw tightly around her shoulders, Jase threw a few more logs on the fire and left her staring into the flames. After he finished up in the kitchen, he checked on her. Her eyes were closed and he noticed that her wineglass was empty. Maybe she'd sleep for a while. He had computer work to do and now was as good a time as any.

When he came downstairs several hours later, she was sound asleep on the long leather couch.

He stood for a long time staring at her, watching the soft even rise and fall of her breasts against the throw. And for the hundredth time, he wondered who the hell had damaged her. He wanted to break the bastard's neck. His protective feelings toward her confused him. As a cop he was sworn to serve and protect, and he did just that for the general populace. It was part of his job. He just did it without any emotional involvement. He'd seen too much shit over the years and had for self-preservation constructed walls around his heart.

But somehow this woman had breached his security system and gotten to him. He wanted to go out and fight her battles for her. He swiped his hand across his chin. "Hell," he muttered. She was no damsel in distress. Jade Devereaux was quite capable of slaying her own dragons. She was a survivor, like him.

Yet there was a vulnerability about her he couldn't deny. Jase looked at the burning embers in the fireplace and debated leaving her on the sofa or attempting to get her into the guest room bed. He opted for the bed.

When Jade woke the next morning, she started just as she had the night before. She sat up in the bed and looked wildly around. Her senses took over. A strong, spicy, masculine scent infiltrated her nostrils and she calmed. Jase. His house. She looked around the nondescript room. A guest room? She didn't remember climbing the stairs. She looked under the covers and blew out a sigh of relief. She was still in the clothes she'd shown up in.

A piece of paper on the nightstand caught her attention. In his dominant-male scrawl, Jase had written: *Coffee on. Breakfast in the oven.*

Jade sank back into the pillows and frowned. What was he up to? He got her drunk last night on that great cab, embraced her, then carried her up to bed and didn't touch her? Not even an attempt? She touched her shirt. Every button was buttoned, nothing out of place. He'd told her not all men were bastards. She figured he was stringing her along. It's what men did.

To add insult to injury, he leaves her with coffee and breakfast? Jade shook her head, wondering why she felt so odd. The last thing she wanted from any man was to be taken advantage of, but this feeling that she was less of a woman because Jase hadn't? What did that mean?

She slipped out of bed and hurried into the adjoining bathroom and found a toothbrush, toothpaste, a towel, and soap on the counter.

Jade brushed her teeth and washed her face. After she pulled her hair back into a ponytail, she inspected her face. Not too bad. The swelling was nearly gone, and the bruising wasn't nearly as bad as it could have been. With a little concealer and heavier foundation, she'd look as good as new.

Jade sipped her coffee and nibbled on the ham-and-egg biscuit that constituted breakfast, wondering about the man who'd made it for her. What did he really want from her?

Jade scribbled a quick thank-you note and headed out. She had to get her house in order, but first she stopped by the club to pick up Genny's address. A note on her desk in Mac's handwriting informed her that Genny had never come in. Jade stood, staring at the note. How odd. Hastily, she called Genny's cell phone number. It went immediately to voicemail.

"Genny, it's Jade. I'm concerned you didn't come in last night. Please call my cell as soon as you get this." As she hung up, Jade began to wonder if Genny was afraid to come in or worse, was she hurt? Had Townsend damaged her before he sprung on Jade? Should she tell Vaughn? She chewed her fingertip, not sure how to proceed.

First on Jase's agenda for the day was to track down Otis Thibodeaux. When he knocked on the suite door this time,

Otis opened it and immediately tried to shut it. Jase stuck his foot between it and the jamb and paid for it in pain. He shoved the door back and entered the room.

"Hey, unless you got a warrant, you can't come in here."

"Call the cops," Jase said.

Otis walked farther into the messy room. Jase followed, slammed the door shut, and locked it. Otis demanded, "What do you want?"

"I'm Detective Vaughn, Montrose PD. How do you know Jade Devereaux?"

Otis's eyes darted to the ceiling, then left, then right. "I just met her the other night."

Jase stepped closer to the lying bastard. "How did you know she was working at Callahan's?"

"I didn't. I saw her for the first time when I went the first time." Otis backed up a step, the bed stopping his backward progress.

Jase moved in so the only escape Otis had was across the bed.

"Who did you think she was and why were you at her house the night before last?"

"I thought she was someone I used to know." Otis swiped at his damp brow with the back of his hand.

"Who?"

"I don't have to tell you that. I don't have to tell you nothing."

"You can tell me here or downtown, your choice, doesn't matter to me which."

"I thought she was a girl named Ruby Leigh. I was wrong."

"Ruby Leigh?"

"Ruby Leigh Gentry."

"From where?"

Otis pursed his lips. "You're a cop, you figure it out."

Jase smiled harshly. "I just need to look you up, Otis. I know you're from Louisiana, and I'll find this Ruby Leigh, or at least her past."

"Then go do your job," Otis said with sudden bravado.

"Maybe you need some time to think, like in jail."

"On what charge?"

"Battery, to start with."

"I heard about you California cops and how you slap bogus charges against people you don't like. Well, I got friends here, Detective, high-up friends. Go on and arrest me. I'll be out by lunchtime."

Jase stepped into Otis's very personal space and softly threatened, "You might get out by lunchtime, but you can be damn sure that lily-white Southern ass of yours will get screwed six ways to sundown before you do."

Otis shut his mouth.

"Yeah, you're yellow to the core just like I thought. Only a coward slaps a woman around." Jase's hands opened and closed. It was all he could do to keep his hands off the bastard.

"I—"

"Shut up, Thibodeaux, before I slap you myself."

Jase wrestled with what he wanted to do and what Jade asked him not to do. He'd made inroads with her last night. If he arrested this son of a bitch for battery, Jade would clam up for good. Against his better judgment, Jase left the sniveling Southern prick and called Ricco. "Go deeper on Otis Thibodeaux. Start with Louisiana. Any hit with his last name, put it in a file. Also, dig around for a Ruby Leigh Gentry, same state."

"Got it. The coroner released Townsend's body today. We can't keep cause of death out of the papers, but we can keep the details out."

"All right, but make sure the ME and her staff keep their mouths shut. I don't want the details leaked."

"I told her, and she gets it, it won't be the first time. So where does that leave that long drink of water?"

"She's involved, and she's lying to me about some things."

"Do you think she knows who killed him?"

Jase scowled. "I'm not sure. But she has information, info she isn't divulging."

"Maybe she's being blackmailed by the killer."

"I think that club is a high-class whore clearinghouse, and I think she knows it and I think she's part of it."

"You think she's turning tricks?"

Jase paused and realized, especially after last night, for someone who had such an adversity to human touch, Jade Devereaux just might not be emotionally able to perform sex for money.

"If she isn't, she's pimping those girls." Jase cringed inwardly. The connotations of that statement bugged him deeply.

"I've worked this town for a lot of years, only done the UC thing for a few years, and we've never had a problem, not even a whisper of impropriety from Callahan's. Hell, the chief stops by once in a while," Ricco said.

"I heard that. But the new owner is strapped for cash. Maybe he's pressuring the girls. Maybe he's making promises to the members and when a guy has a hard-on for a woman and he's told to go home with blue balls, shit happens."

"I've been by Morton's house twice. No luck."

"Jade told me he was out of the country. I don't buy it. I'm going to swing by there right now. Did you get any other addresses on him?" Jase asked.

"Two: one in Woodside and one at the Harbor Marina in San Francisco, where he's got a yacht. I'll hit each one of the addresses. Plus, I have a lead on the Genevieve girl. I don't mind the legwork. You keep close to the crack, man."

Jase smiled. "I appreciate that, man. Also, Jade left Genevieve a message yesterday to give her her correct home address, I'll see if she has it and call you back."

Jase felt his mood lighten at the prospect of talking to Jade. She answered on the third ring. "Hello." His blood warmed the instant that honeyed voice of hers answered.

"Good afternoon."

"Hi, thanks for the coffee."

"Any time. Did your girl Genevieve leave her address?"

"No, and she didn't come in last night, either."

"Is that unusual?"

"Genny is flaky, but while she has only been here for a couple of months, she hasn't *not* shown. No phone call, either."

"Is there anyone who has been to her house who could give us a lead on where to find her?"

"No."

Gauging her tone, Jase had no reason not to believe her.

"I have two references here on her resume."

"Give them to me, and I'll have Dispatch do a reverse."

Jade gave him the numbers and said, "I'm worried about her. I'm calling them now."

"Get back to me ASAP."

"I will."

Two minutes later, Jase's cell phone rang again. "I left messages at both numbers."

"How thoroughly did you check her out when you hired her?"

"Very thoroughly. Down to a physical."

"Do you have the girls screened for STDs?"

With no hesitation, Jade answered, "Yes."

"Why?"

"Because, Detective, I am not so naïve as to believe that there wouldn't be occasions when the girls hit it off with a member and things lead away from the club."

"But isn't it a conflict of interest for a member and employee to hook up?" he pushed.

"We as a business cannot deem who our employees can and cannot socialize with. We can between fellow employees, but not members of society at large."

"Is that why you shot Mac down?" Jase clenched his jaw.

"What?"

"Mac, because it was against company policy?"

Her voice turned frosty. "I'm entrusted with maintaining and upholding company policy. Mac knew better than to proposition me, so of course I turned him down."

Jase scowled. So, Mac *did* have the hots for Jade. She'd shot him down. The guy went up a few rungs on the suspect ladder. For his own personal knowledge, Jase asked, "Would you have said yes if it weren't against policy?"

"That is none of your business."

Well, there he had it. Another dead-end conversation about men with the ever-elusive Jade Devereaux.

Jade hung up the phone, her frustration over Jase's belief she was a prostitute gnawing at her more than it should.

For the first time in years, she cared what a man thought of her.

No sooner had she hung up the phone than her office door opened. Jade looked up, ready to tell the rude person to knock first, but she held her tongue. "Mr. Morton. I thought you were in Milan."

"Jade," he said, walking slowly into her office like a big cat stalking a mouse. "I came home early."

Jade came to the realization immediately that they were alone in the building, and while she had no cause to fear for her safety, she had never felt as comfortable with Jack Morton as she had with Sam Callahan. Her savior. Sam was a benevolent old man, and if he hadn't taken her under his wing all those years ago, she shuddered to think where she might be.

Jack Morton was the polar opposite of Sam. Jack was short and slick, and his black eyes appeared to see all, and worse, see through her. "It seems we may have a bit of a problem."

"Mr. Townsend's death cannot be linked to the club."

"I wasn't speaking of Andy."

She frowned, perplexed.

"What then?"

"I received a rather indignant call from a certain CEO two nights ago."

Jade's spine stiffened.

"Apparently, he was less than satisfied with the service he received."

"Mr. Morton, Mr. Hiro received the regular treatment. Nothing changed on the club's end."

Jack smiled, and the gesture reminded her of a reptile. "Perhaps when I gave you that hefty raise, you didn't understand how it affected your job description."

"It was my understanding, sir, that my raise was part of the sales agreement with Sam."

Casually he looked around her office, and said, "If you haven't noticed, operations are . . . different now."

Jade kept her composure, even knowing where the conversation was going. "I understand the stringent guidelines for membership have been relaxed, and with that the quality of members has dipped. It has created problems."

Jack moved in closer to her. "No, you have created problems by not accommodating the new clients and the expectations of the established membership."

"Are you implying that membership includes physical interaction?"

"Let me spell it out for you, Miss Devereaux. Katsuo Hiro paid a bonus for dessert. He didn't get it. I had to refund him his fee and now he refuses to come back until you go to him at his suite at the Fairmont and make things right."

"Let's speak plain English, Mr. Morton. The bonus was for sex."

"Exactly." He stared at her hard and unwavering. "This was not negotiable."

She stood. "I'm not for sale."

"Everyone is for sale."

Jade shook her head. "Not me."

"That's not what I hear. And quite frankly, it doesn't matter. If you value your position here, make sure our members are satisfied in every sense of the word. If you can't perform, then I'll find someone to replace you. Genevieve has experience in this field as well. Whores, even high-class ones, are a dime a dozen."

Jade slapped him, and as much as she regretted it, she wanted to do it again.

CHAPTER
8

Morton didn't flinch, except to slowly rub his cheek. His dark eyes glittered maliciously. "Under different circumstances, that would have cost you your job. But as it is, *Ruby Leigh,* I think you'll apologize and do what is necessary to see to our members' needs."

Jade froze, her blood slowed in her veins, and she felt the sudden onslaught of defeat. So that's how Otis got in. "There seems to be some misunderstanding, Mr. Morton. You and a new member, Otis Thibodeaux, seem to have me confused with this Ruby Leigh person. I have no idea who she is, and would really appreciate it if you would refrain from calling me that. And if Mr. Thibodeaux continues to harass me, I will go to the police."

Jack smiled, the gesture unnatural. "You're a cool one, Jade. I'll keep your little secret, so long as you keep mine."

He turned then and walked out of the office, not giving her a chance to tell him to go to hell. In his wake she paced the small space of her office. She'd been outed! She felt trapped—suffocated, pushed against a wall. And no matter which course of action she took, she would lose, and lose huge. The sudden urge to run fast and far overcame her.

"Miss Jade?" Rusty asked from the door.

He startled her from her thoughts. She turned to see him calmly regarding her. Her tension eased.

"Rusty, what are you doing here?"

He smiled and blushed. "I left early last night, so I came back to clean up in the stock room." He moved into the room and squinted at her. "What happened to your face?"

Jade inhaled deeply, then exhaled. She smiled at the timid boy. He looked so concerned. "I got a little too close to a wall."

"Oh, sorry."

"I'm okay. I have some paperwork to finish up here. You can stay as long as I'm here, but I'll be leaving in about an hour."

Rusty bobbed his head and backed out of the room. "Okay, holler if you need anything."

She smiled again. "I will."

As Rusty left the room, she let out a long breath. Immediately, guilt grabbed ahold of her. She felt like a rat on a sinking ship. Rusty depended on her for an income, just as the others here did. And while someone like Mac or Thomas or Bernard her doorman could walk into a job anywhere, someone like Rusty couldn't. He was slow. He'd been desperate when she'd hired him six weeks ago, desperate, hungry, and willing to clean toilets for pennies just so long as he had a job. She gave him a chance. Many of the girls who graced the rooms of Callahan's, while beautiful, were in similar situations. They had siblings they looked after or, like Dominique, student loans to repay. Jade knew all too well the hardships of being the one everyone looked to for survival. She didn't want anyone to have to go through what she had gone through. So, here in her small part of the world, she could make a difference. Or had been able to. What Jack Morton wanted to do with the club would change everything. There was no pride in prostitution.

Angrily, Jade got back to the business of the club's books. As she entered each number into the spreadsheet, her anger mounted. How dare Jack Morton! She deleted a file and started over, realizing she had put the bar order in with the linen order.

Rusty popped his head into her office and smiled. "I'm done, Miss Jade!"

Her mood instantly softened. "Thank you, Rusty. I'll see you tonight."

He left with a big grin on his face.

Jade finished up her paperwork and headed out of the office. She needed some air, she needed to get away, and for the second time in her life she needed to run away.

Squeezing the steering wheel so tight her knuckles whitened, Jade maneuvered south, suddenly finding herself driving through the Santa Cruz Mountains. She hadn't planned on going to the club tonight, but Rusty had changed her mind. She needed to micromanage now. Too much depended on the club not being reduced to an all-out brothel. Despite her attack, the bruising was minimal and the swelling gone, and she could, with appropriate cosmetics, hide the evidence.

Her cell phone rang.

"Hello," Jade said.

"Katsuo is waiting at the Fairmont, suite four forty-five,"

Jack Morton said. The drone of the dial tone hummed in her ear. Angrily, she pulled over and then did a quick U-turn, heading back toward San Jose.

Forty-five minutes later, she pulled up in front of the Fairmont, handed her keys over to the valet, and went up to the fourth-floor suite.

As Jase stepped out of the elevator, he watched Jade enter the lobby. He stood back and watched her hit the up button to the set of elevators leading to the suites. Was she going to see Otis? Just as the doors closed behind Jade, Otis stepped out of the elevator that opened to the lobby. Jase stood back. If she were there to see Otis, she'd be back down in a few minutes. If not?

He waited almost an hour before she came back down. Her flushed and disheveled demeanor told the story of what she'd been doing for the last hour. Anger flashed hot and violent through Jase. He was a bigger fool than any of the members at Callahan's.

Jase strode into the vestibule and caught her arm, frustration driving his actions. "Do you always take a room at the Fairmont in the middle of the day? Or are you working?"

Jade cried out and pulled her arm from his grasp. "Are you following me?"

"What if I am?"

"Then you have a problem. Leave me alone."

She started to walk through the lobby.

"Why do you do it?" he challenged.

Jade ignored Jase's question and felt the shocking sting of hot tears. He wouldn't understand. She wasn't sure she did.

She kept walking, but he grabbed her arm again and

spun her around. He grabbed her other arm and pulled her out of the main lobby area and into a plant-shrouded alcove. She didn't struggle; she refused to make a scene. When he roughly pushed her up against the wall and the long length of his body pressed against her, she felt a sudden hot swell of desire. It stunned and terrified her. He felt it, too. The hot flare in his eyes spoke volumes. Jade didn't understand what happened next. Jase's lips slammed hard against hers, taking, not giving, not caring. He invaded her space. He gave her no quarter, and to her utter shock, she allowed him. She didn't recoil. She didn't have the urge to run away, she didn't feel violated.

She felt emancipated.

Just as quickly, the kiss ended. Jase cursed and pushed her away as if she'd burned him. He stepped back, swiped his hand across his mouth, and stalked past her. Breathless, she slumped against the wall and suddenly felt very cold and she began to shake.

He watched her slip from room 445 and his blood pressure spiked. Fury encompassed every cell in his body. She'd lied to him. She'd lied to them all! When the elevator closed behind her, through his angry haze he glanced up and down the hallway, then hurried to the door and knocked.

"Who is it?" Mr. Hiro called.

"Jade sent me," he answered in a low husky whisper.

The door immediately opened. The CEO smiled, his kimono open, his erection twitching, and said, "I'm glad she—"

He shoved the smaller man back into the room. "Shut up and turn around," he ordered.

The door closed heavily behind them. "What is the meaning of this? Where is Jade? Who are you?" Katsuo demanded.

"I'm her avenging angel. Now turn around and put your hands behind your back."

Jase continued cursing. Son of a bitch! He slammed his fists against the steering wheel. She was a fucking whore! And a liar! And for the life of him, he couldn't keep his hands off her. She'd invaded his dreams at night and his every thought during the day. She lied to him, she was breaking the law, and she was withholding evidence. And all he could think about was how fast he could get her out of her clothes.

Shit!

His cell phone rang. Grateful for the interruption to his raging libido, Jase answered. "Vaughn."

"Jack Morton was seen leaving Callahan's earlier today," Ricco said.

Fuck me. "I thought he was out of town."

"Apparently not, and he doesn't want to talk with us. But he talked with your lady."

"She's not my *lady*."

"Back down, just a figure of speech."

Jase fumed. "Where is he now?"

"Not sure, but I've got a car on him, he headed up the one-oh-one. My guess is he's headed to the city."

"I have to take care of a few things here." Jase let out a long, exasperated breath. "Can you go up there and talk to him?"

"Not a problem."

"Do you know anyone who works at the Fairmont?"

"Nope, what do you need?"

"I need to get a look at the current guest list. Miss Devereaux just spent an hour in one of the rooms."

"Maybe she got a massage," Ricco joked.

Jase was not amused. "Maybe she gave one."

"How much do you think a woman like that charges?"

"I have no clue." And Jase didn't want to know.

"Ask her."

"She swears she's not in the business."

"You don't believe it?" Ricco asked.

"No. I don't. Too much points the other way. Not only is she turning tricks, she's hiding something, something other than her involvement with Townsend. It's connected to Otis Thibodeaux."

"I got a hit in Avoyelles Parish, Louisiana. On a Colonel Leland Thibodeaux. Deceased. I'm digging some more."

"Send me what you have. There's a connection there, and I'd bet my next check our Jade Devereaux and this Ruby Leigh are one and the same. I want to know why she's running."

After Ricco hung up, Jase sat in his car for a long time, wondering why the hell he wanted a woman who, like his mother and sister, could not be trusted, and why it bugged the hell out of him she was lying to him.

He closed his eyes and rubbed his chin, then his temples. Jase expelled another long breath. Maybe it was just sex. With the exception of a few weeks ago, it had been months. Coming out of his last UC assignment, he'd taken some much-needed downtime in Cabo. No shirt, no shoes, no problems. And no sex. He didn't want interaction on any level, he just wanted to feed his soul with utter nothing.

It had come to him down there on the white beaches of

Mexico that he would never have what his longtime friend and mentor Ty had: a woman who made him a better man than he'd been without her, a woman who loved him unconditionally, a woman he could trust. A woman who wouldn't trot off the minute a better deal came along.

Jase grinned as he thought of Ty and Phil. He never thought he'd see his buddy settle down, much less get married and turn into a freak over a woman. He supposed anything was possible. He sure as hell never thought he'd find himself thinking about a woman like he did Jade Devereaux. While he did not trust her, he admitted he lusted for her. And that was as good as he gave.

Jase understood the true ways of a woman very well. He'd lived it, what with the parade of men his mother brought through the house: always trading up, and realizing many times too late she had actually traded down.

Mother had taught them well. By the tender age of eight, Jase knew that if the front porch light was on when he got off the school bus, he was to play outside and not come in. His older sister, Dawn, would take him down the street to her boyfriend's house, where he would have to sit in the living room while she went down the hall with Kyle. Jase learned quickly that the sounds coming from his sister's boyfriend's room and the ones coming from his mother's room were one and the same. Like his mother, Dawn grew bored easily. Jase didn't fall far from the tree. He'd lost his virginity at thirteen and went through girls quicker than his mom and sister went through lipstick.

Why then, he wanted to know, did he feel this unnatural attraction to a woman who got paid for her revolving bedroom door? The very things he despised in his mother and sister he despised in Jade. So, why the pull? She was beautiful, exotically so, but that wasn't it. Was there some type of chemical reaction? Would sex tamp it down? Sex with a suspect wasn't a good thing. He'd seen it cloud the judgment of his buddy Reese. Jase smiled. Despite the fact that Reese followed the crack, he'd found a damn good woman in Frankie, she had been suspect *numero uno* in a murder investigation. Jase wiped his hand across his face and clenched his jaw.

He knew if he got Jade out of his system, he could move on. Jase shook his head. Yeah, like she'd feel like relieving him of his hard-on. He turned the key in the ignition. Stranger things had happened. He'd go to the club tonight and watch her. She was guilty of many things, and by applying pressure by his presence alone, she would start to crack.

Frustrated and feeling as if her life was coming unraveled at both ends, Jade headed back to the club. In a valiant effort she tried to push all thoughts of a certain detective from her mind. But each time she tried, her blood quickened. Unable to beat him from her brain, she threw in the towel, pressing her fingertips to her lips and reliving the hard kiss. Jade moaned, the ache in her loins flaring. Dear lord, what was happening to her? How, *why*, did she respond to him as she had? And what the hell was she going to do about it? Nothing! This time, adamantly, Jade forced Jase from her head. She needed to focus. To take her mind off him, she tried Genny again. And finally Genny answered her phone. She didn't sound well. "Genny? Are you all right?"

"Hi, Jade, sorry I didn't call you back, I've been puking my guts up."

"Flu?"

"No, food poisoning, I think. I feel better today, just a little weak."

Jade got to the point. "Genny, Andrew Townsend is dead, and the police want to talk to you."

"Oh my god! What happened?" Genny asked, clearly shocked.

"I'm not sure, but after he left Callahan's Saturday night he was found dead a few blocks from here."

"Oh my god, Jade, this is terrible. Do—do the cops think I did it?"

"I don't think so, they just want to talk to you. You were the last person to see him alive."

"Okay, Jade. Tell me, what do I do?"

"Are you up to coming in tonight?"

"Yeah, I think so. I just ate some soup and crackers, but I need to get to my place and clean up. I'm at my brother's right now."

"About your place, Genny. Why did you give me a bogus address?"

She was answered by silence.

"The truth, Genny."

"I—I didn't have a place lined up at the time, and I had to give you something. So I made an address up. I'm sorry."

Jade's mood and tone softened. "Genny, you can come to me with anything, I hope you know that. Now, after you get home and shower, call my cell and let me know how you feel. I need you here tonight; maybe the detective can talk with you here in my office. And, Genny?"

"Yes, Jade?"

"We must be discreet."

"Always."

"Okay, I'll call the detective and let him know you'll be here."

As she hung up the phone, Jade's belly fluttered. She wondered why Jase unnerved her on so many levels, yet she couldn't wait to hear his deep husky voice when she called to tell him about Genny. But what made her more anxious was the knowledge that he would be here, at the club, where his dark angry energy would encompass her like a warm blanket.

As Jade cleaned up her earlier debacle of paperwork, her mind wandered to her recent encounter with Katsuo.

Like her kiss with Jase—for reasons better left alone—she wanted to push her hourlong session with the CEO as far from her conscience as humanly possible. Jade closed her eyes and hugged herself, her skin cold, gooseflesh scattering across her arms and legs. Slowly she opened her eyes and stared, unseeing, at the white wall. He would not be visiting again. And she would leave it at that.

"Vaughn," Jase said into his cell phone.

"It's me, Jade."

He knew that when he saw the number spring up on his LED. His body immediately reacted and silently he cursed. Jase cleared his throat. "I know."

"I just spoke with Genny. She's been sick with food poisoning."

"Then why hasn't she been at her fake house?"

"She said she's been at her brother's place. She's coming in tonight. I told her you would want to speak with her. Here in my office is fine."

"What time will she be in?"

"By six-thirty. I'd prefer you talk to her before we open for dinner. Once she's out on the floor, I don't want her disturbed."

"Of course."

"Look, think what you want about me, but give Genny a break. She's a good girl working her way through college."

"Is that how you paid for college?"

He couldn't blame her for hanging up on him. Damn if Jade Devereaux didn't push him where no other woman had. He'd insulted her again. It wasn't his style. He was losing his touch. And with it, he was losing control. This day-to-day police bullshit sucked. He much preferred the looser life of undercover. He'd thought he wanted back in a PD. He thought a break from the rigors of undercover work would kick him back into a normal life. A life where, while he didn't have the latitude he had in UC work, he would have the structure of general orders and be free of the burden of pretending he was someone he was not. He was wrong. Dead wrong.

Everything he hoped for had a strangle hold on him. He felt trapped by the constraints of the rules, on edge because he had Big Brother looking over his shoulder, frustrated because he could not just do his job by whatever means necessary, and overriding it all, he was horny as hell. He flipped his cell open and scrolled through a few numbers before he found the one he wanted, then he hit call.

"Hello, stranger," a low sexy voice said.

Jase grinned. "Hello yourself."

"You left without saying good-bye."

"Sorry about that. I promise next time I won't."

"What makes you think there will be a next time?"

"C'mon now, Stacey, you know it's good between us."

"It's better than good; if it wasn't, I would have hung up on you by now."

Jase laughed low. "How about a late dinner, then dessert? Or we skip dinner and go right to dessert?"

"I'm on a diet, so no entrée. I'll be waiting for you."

"About nine?"

"Perfect. And, Jase? Don't disappoint me. I don't give second chances."

His dick swelled, but he realized as he hung up it wasn't Stacey's model-tall golden body that had him rising against his slacks. It was a dark voluptuous beauty who had it throbbing. Jase forced a smile. Well, after a few minutes wrapped up in Stacey's honey-scented embrace, Jade Devereaux would be a memory. He rubbed his hands in anticipation of that becoming a reality.

Jade finished up the niggling paperwork and decided she needed a massage, then a hot soak in her tub. She didn't look forward to going back to her house and returning it to order. While she was a perfectionist, she didn't want the reminder of her past or what her present had turned into. She decided to hole up the next few days at the Blue Orchid, a quirky little boutique hotel not far from the club.

She'd go home and gather her toiletries, call her housekeeper to go clean up, and then maybe by the weekend she would feel up to returning to her house. Jade made the necessary calls and smiled when she spoke to Jolie, the owner of the Orchid. The masseuse had a cancellation and if she could be there in ten minutes she could get her in. As she exited the building, Jade smiled and waved at Mac as he pulled in. Right behind him was Rusty on his bicycle.

Her smile widened. For the second time that day she was grateful she'd hired the kid. At first she wasn't sure if he'd be able to handle the stress of the job, but with Mac's quiet patience schooling him, the kid had surprised her.

Rusty's big grin and Mac's broad smile washed away the tawdriness of what had become her job. All of her employees, down to Ernesto, her handyman, were good, hardworking people. She trusted their discretion, was grateful for their loyalty, and respected their work ethic. She'd had no problems with anyone over the past five years. She knew with certainty, especially after her conversation with Jack, that there were going to be lots of fires to put out in her near future.

And more troubling to Jade was how she would come through it unscathed.

For the first time since the weekend, when Jade entered the club, she felt refreshed and ready to work. She pushed all thoughts of Andrew Townsend, Katsuo Hiro, Otis Thibodeaux, and Jack Morton from her mind. She would not acknowledge what they represented. Instead, she pretended she was meeting Jase as a normal girl with a normal man on a normal date. It would be the only way to get through the night. The alternative was not an option. She decided it didn't matter what he thought of her, there was nothing between them but a strong physical attraction, and as much as it scared her, it also made her feel good. It made her feel alive. It was good to know she wasn't completely dead inside. And damn little these days made her feel good. A girl was entitled to a little fun. And if it made her more of whore in his eyes? It didn't matter; she couldn't change his mind, so she might as well capitalize on the attraction.

She'd chosen her dress with extreme care. She'd picked up a lovely Versace, a gossamer-thin gold number that came to just above her knees, with a low dipping-open back. It gave the impression that she wore no undergarments. It was the perfect tool for seduction. The gold strappy sandals gave her shapely legs more length. She didn't bother with nylons, the smooth natural tone of her skin made it easy not to.

She knew just how good she looked when Thomas stopped and quirked a brow. "My lord, Jade, are you looking to cause a train wreck tonight?"

She smiled. "I'll take that as a compliment, Thomas."

"Be careful, Jade, I don't think all of us combined would be able to save you from a rabid Romeo tonight."

"I only have one Romeo in mind tonight, Thomas, and he can't touch."

Thomas's brows drew together in a frown. "Not that cop?"

"Yes, that cop. He's been messing with my life, now it's time to give him something back."

"Be careful with that one," Thomas warned.

"Always."

Jade hummed as she headed back to her office. For Thomas to notice was not a big deal, but for him to comment was huge. He was gay, and in the five years she'd worked with him, he had never given even the slightest compliment.

When she strutted into the lounge, Mac's eyes bugged out of his head and Rusty, god bless his heart, couldn't look down at his shoes fast enough. She was primed and ready to rock Detective Jase Vaughn's world.

And true to Thomas's words, Jase bumped into the man in front of him as he walked into the lounge and caught sight of her. Paul DiMarco came in right behind him and slammed into Jase's back. The man in front of them, Eduardo D'Anza, looked up and caught Jade's amused stare and stumbled forward. Only Thomas saved him from hitting the floor.

Jade smiled, turned around, and sashayed into her office, where Genny sat. "Detective Vaughn is here. I'll bring him back."

Jade sauntered to the bar where Jase sat conversing with Amber, a lovely redheaded medical student. When his eyes lifted to hers, Jade felt a hot current zap through her entire body. She slowed and watched him watch her, liking the way his lips quirked, and he half smiled, just for her. Halfway to him, she stopped. And with the slightest movement of her head she beckoned him. He excused himself from his conversation, slid from the chair, and seemed to glide to her. She turned and showed him the way to her office, all the while feeling his hot gaze on her back as solidly as if he'd placed a heated branding iron there.

Jade left them and made her way back into the lounge, where she smiled and laughed as easily as if she were a carefree teenager. She didn't dwell on her past, or her tomorrow, she thought only of tonight and enjoying the power she had over the men here, and one in particular.

Touching her lips, she relived the hot excitement of Jase's kiss. Despite what he thought of her, the sexy detective did something to her. He touched her in a place she hadn't known existed. He excited her, and what excited her almost as much was the idea that she had control of the animal in him. As much as he wanted her, he would not step over the line. Not for passion, not for money, not even for himself.

Unless she gave him the signal. And that she had no intention of doing.

Jase could spot a liar a mile away and Genevieve Monroe was a liar. And she tried to use sex to gainsay him. It didn't work.

According to Genny, she had not been the last person to see Townsend alive. She and Townsend had gone down the street to Delicato's for a drink.

"He was too drunk to be decent company," she said, her lips smiling seductively.

"By 'decent company,' do you mean he couldn't fork over the required cash and rise to the occasion?" Jase asked the little blonde.

Genny's eyes widened, and she had the admirable talent to appear insulted.

"Nice try, sweetheart," Jase said. "If you cooperate, I promise when this entire case goes down, the DA will go easy on you."

"Detective," Genny cooed as she uncrossed her legs in a manner that would have given him a twat shot if he were looking, "Maybe we can continue this conversation later? Over a drink?" She leaned forward, showing off what were an admittedly impressive set of tits. "I'm available on whatever level the law requires of me, Detective Vaughn."

Jase explained he had a date, but didn't shut her down completely. He didn't need another woman scorned, out for his blood. She pouted prettily.

"When did you leave Delicato's?"

"Around one-thirty or so."

"Alone?"

"Yes, the bartender called a cab for Andy."

"Did you see him get into a cab?"

Genny smiled again, then sat back in the chair, arching her back just enough so those impressive tits pointed north. "No, I had left by then."

"Where did you go?"

"Home."

"To that home on Mission?"

Genny scowled. "I wasn't feeling well. I went to my brother's."

"And he can vouch for you?"

"Yes, he can."

"What is his name and is he home now?"

Genny looked up at the ceiling. "My brother's name is Richard. And he went out of town this morning. He's visiting a friend."

Jase believed that as much as he believed in Santa Claus. "I want the friend's info and your brother's cell phone number."

"Dickie doesn't have a cell phone, and I don't know who his friend is or where they live."

"You don't seem to know much about anything, do you?"

She leaned forward and smiled, running a fingertip up from his knee to his crotch. "I know how to please a man," she breathed.

Her touch having no effect on him, Jase sat back in his chair and carefully regarded the young woman. The way this girl used her blatant sexuality on a man might have worked on him a few days ago, but, Jase realized, those days were over for him. He liked a classier woman. One who did not have to flaunt her assets in his face to let him know she existed. Jase was the kind of guy who needed no road map to find a woman. He grinned. Hell, if the pickings were slim, all he needed to do was call Ricco and the ladies swarmed.

"Detective Vaughn?" Genny softly said.

Jase eyed her. She smiled. She really was a pretty girl. But he could tell there was something fundamentally wrong with her attitude toward men. Had she, like so many women in this business, been abused? Suddenly, his ire at this woman subdued. "Were you abused as a girl?" Jase softly asked.

Genny's eyes popped open wide and the color drained from her cheeks. "I don't think that is any of your business!"

"Did you have sex with Andrew Townsend after you left here Saturday night?"

"I am not a prostitute!"

"I didn't say you were. I asked if you had sex with the man. And by sex, I mean was there any trading of body fluids?"

Genny quickly recovered. That cat-that-ate-the-canary looked resurfaced. She leaned forward and touched his knee. "Detective Vaughn, a girl does not kiss and tell."

"She does when a murder is involved."

Genny sat back and crossed her arms. "Dominique says we don't have to talk to you if we don't have a lawyer with us."

Jase cocked a brow and smiled. "Does she now?"

Genny swallowed hard and nodded, not certain she should have let that slip.

Jase stood and flipped his notepad closed. "Don't leave town, Miss Monroe."

He opened the door for the lying little blonde and allowed her to pass through. Several moments later, he exited the room, only to come face-to-face with the hottest thing to hit NorCal in his lifetime.

"Was Genevieve helpful?" Jade asked.

Jase stopped and couldn't help an appreciative glance at her. "Helpful enough."

He didn't fool her. Jade read the heat in his eyes, the slight acceleration in his breath, the way his wide chest moved deeper against the tailored black jacket.

"Nice threads," she said.

He nodded. "You don't look too bad yourself."

She batted her eyelashes and said in her native Southern drawl, "Why, this little ol' thing?"

Jase moved a step closer. They were semisecluded in the vestibule outside her office. He moved her back against the wall. It took every ounce of willpower he possessed not to touch her. His body flared with the heat of a furnace. He bent his head a fraction down to hers, his lips hovering just an inch above hers.

He could smell her. If he were blindfolded and thrust among a thousand women, he'd be able to pick her out by her sultry scent alone. It hit him between the eyes and his cock stirred. His gaze did not waver. Nor did hers. When she licked her lips and the tip of her pink tongue touched his bottom lip, Jase was sure the floor moved beneath him. He groaned and put his hands on the wall on either side of her head. He dipped his lips to hers, only the barest breath of air separating them now. When he spoke, his lips brushed hers. "Now, Miss Scarlett, that sounded just a might too natural to me."

He felt Jade's body swell the minute he spoke. Her breasts pressed against his chest and she closed her eyes and moaned. The smooth skin of her neck beckoned him and it was too much to resist. Jase laved her jugular with his teeth. Jade cried out, her hands grabbed his biceps, her fingers digging into him, she moved hotly against him. "I practice," she breathed against his chin.

Jase's teeth bit into her skin and his tongue licked her. His body pressed firmly against hers, the contact electrifying. "Stop messing with me, Miss Devereaux, or you'll have more on your hands than you can handle."

Jase moved back, the cool air of the hallway swirling into the hot swelter they had manufactured. "Besides, I can't afford you."

Jade slapped him. Jase caught her hand and jerked her hard against him. On a second thought, he pulled her toward her office, opened the door, and slammed it shut behind them with his foot. He turned the lock and stalked toward her.

"Let's stop dancing around each other, Miss Devereaux. Tell me what I want to know and I'll leave you alone."

"I've told you everything."

As he moved closer, she stood firm, her arms folded across her chest, her desk to her back.

"Why are you playing the prick tease with me?"

"Because I can."

"Am I such an easy target?"

"All men are."

"And I'm just like any other man?"

"Yes."

He moved closer, only inches from her. He stroked her cheek with his knuckles. "Am I really?"

Jade nodded, the movement jerky.

"Do all men have to pay to touch you, Jade, or do you give some for free?"

His finger had the misfortune of being near her mouth

when he'd insulted her. She nipped the tip and held on to it. He ignored the pain and moved closer. Her teeth bit harder. He invaded her space so that now she could either meet him chest to chest or bend back over her desk away from him. She bent. He pushed. She bit harder. He growled. In one quick motion, he pushed her back onto her desk, his left hand swiping away any impediments.

Jade gasped, letting go of his finger. He put a knee on the desk between her legs and leaned over her, his hands on either side of her head. "You'll discover, Miss Devereaux, that I am like no other man you've met."

He didn't wait for a reply. He dug his fingers into her intricate hairdo, not caring that he would ruin it. His lips swept down over hers and blood shot to his cock. He swelled so suddenly and so quickly it hurt. He groaned against her parted lips. He knew she felt him against her thigh; she'd have to be dead not to.

What he didn't expect was for her body to go rigid beneath his.

Holding his body over hers, he pulled away from her lips. Her expression stymied him. It wasn't angry, nor was it wanting. Was it regret?

He smiled. "I think, Jade, you have a big problem."

"Oh?"

He dug his fingers deeper into her hair and pressed ever so slightly against hers. He lowered his lips to her ear and whispered, "You want me, and you can't find a way to justify it." He laughed low, the sound not gentlemanly.

"You're wrong on both accounts, Detective. If I wanted you, I would have you."

"What if I didn't want you?"

As she swept the palm of her hand down his burgeoning

shaft, he flinched in her hand. He hissed in a hard breath. "That isn't the case."

Jase grinned. He loved playing these kinds of games. Holding her gaze, he pulled his right hand from her hair and slid it down her shoulder to her arm, then over to her hip. He squeezed. Her body tensed. She knew exactly what his intentions were, and yet she didn't stop him. His body thrummed. His hand slid across her hip and slowly down to her thigh. The heat of her skin surprised him. He sniffed the humid air and smelled her essence. In a slow gesture, he slid his fingers beneath the fabric of her dress and made slow circles upward. Her body trembled. He bent his mouth closer to hers, just as his fingertip touched the opening of her core. Her hips jerked and she cried out. Hot moist heat hit him. In a slow slide, he dipped a finger between her drenched lips. He bit her neck and pressed against her, sliding his finger into her hot wet depths. Jade cried out, grabbing his shoulders. Her head pressed against him. "You lied to me again, Jade," he whispered against her throat.

Her thighs clamped around his hand and he looked down at her. Her eyes were screwed shut and she bit her bottom lip. Jase almost came in his pants. He'd never seen anything so sexy in his life.

"You're a naughty girl, Jade Devereaux. Not wearing panties."

His fingers slowly began to withdraw from her, but she moaned, her hips chasing his hand. He had no intention of letting her go, not yet. He'd just begun. But when he finally took her it would not be here, on top of a desk.

No, when he took her it would be on his terms, and his terms included multiple orgasms, for them both.

His finger slid around her hard creamy nub. She shuddered. His lips moved to her lips. His tongue lapped her swallow lips, as his finger did a slow slide back into her. Jade cried out under his lips, her hips rocking, her fingers digging into his arms. A spasm racked her. Then another. And another. Jase nearly came where he stood, barely able to contain himself.

When her body stopped shuddering, her eyes flashed open. Jase didn't move. God he wanted her. He smiled instead and said, "A body doesn't lie."

She smiled slowly. "Are you so blind?"

"About what?"

"Why, Detective, this is what I get paid to do, isn't it? To act? Let my johns know they are the only men on earth who can make me come?"

Jase moved off her and rearranged his erection. "You're lying."

Jade slid off the desk, the movement slow and fluid, like thick syrup over pancakes. Her dress slid down her thighs, covering her swollen pink lips. His hard-on twitched. Lies or not, she was the sexiest thing he'd ever encountered. And he wanted more.

She didn't waste a movement or stop for a gesture. Jade moved right into his space, her eyes never wavering. Stopping in front of him, she threw her head back and moaned, the deep sexy huskiness of it sending shivers down his back. She closed her eyes and bit her bottom lip, her moans intensified, her hand slid down her belly to her mound. Her hips moved ever so slightly. "Oh," she moaned, "that feels so good, don't stop."

As her hand increased its pressure, Jase stood rooted to the floor, the picture in front of him almost more than he could bear. In quick succession, her body shuddered and her hand moved faster across her mound. Her breaths increased in velocity and her low sounds of enjoyment climbed in time. Just when she was about to come, or pretend to, he grabbed her hand and replaced it with his.

He pressed hard against her mound and she cried out. Her eyes were wide open in shock. His hand cupped her and his other hand grabbed her ass, pushing her hard against his hips. "Now fake it again."

Jade tried to twist away, but he held her firm. "C'mon, Jade, *fake* it again."

"Stop it, leave me alone!"

Immediately, he let go of her. Her breasts heaved hard against the fabric of her dress. His eyes bored hard into her. He quirked a smile and slowly brought his right hand to his nose and sniffed. "That doesn't smell fake to me."

"Get out."

"I'm on my way."

Disheveled, her body throbbing, Jade stood, staring at the door. Anger collided with longing. Humiliation engulfed her. When had the tables turned? How had they turned so quickly? One minute she was in charge of Jase, and the next she was having an orgasm. What the hell had happened? And what the hell was she going to do about it? She wanted him, dammit, but on her terms. His powerful personality made it hard. How could she control a man who was uncontrollable?

She moved into the small bathroom off her office and stared in the mirror. Her makeup was a mess, her hair beyond repair, and along her neck small bruises began to erupt. In no hurry to go back into the club, Jade took her time repairing Jase's damage while trying not to think of the man who just ravaged her.

Thirty minutes later, half-expecting and half-hoping he was still in the club, Jade came out of her office, feeling once more in control. Mac gave her a quick "Are you okay?" look. She smiled and glanced around the lounge. No sign of Jase. The excited swirl in her stomach plummeted.

"How are our guests tonight, Mac?"

"Thirsty, but in good spirits."

"Let's keep them happy and their glasses full." Jade went into hostess mode, the act so common she hardly noticed the switch anymore.

Jase pulled up in front of Stacey's house a half hour early. He was horny, angry, and needed to get laid. He didn't care if she was ready, what he had in mind would only take a few minutes. He strode up the sidewalk and rang the doorbell. Immediately, the door opened and Stacey, tall, golden, and wearing only a shimmery negligee, opened the door wide for him. He grabbed her and kicked the door shut with the heel of his shoe, not wasting a minute. He carried her back into her bedroom, where he tossed her on the bed and began to unbuckle his belt.

Stacey's brown eyes glowed in excitement. "Jase, I missed you, too."

"Shut up and strip," he commanded. She did.

He didn't bother taking his clothes off, he just pushed his pants down and pulled her ankles toward him. He looked at the core of her, her pink lips weeping in anticipation. He hesitated. The vision of Jade as she slid off the desk, the skirt part of her dress hiding what he so desperately wanted, flashed before him. Jase straightened. A whiff of Stacey teased him. His nose twitched. It wasn't the scent he wanted. He backed away from the bed, his erection beginning to wane.

"What's wrong, Jase?" Stacey asked, jumping from the bed.

"It—I—shit, Stacey, I don't know, but I can't do this tonight."

"What do you mean, you can't do this tonight? What is *this* anyway, a quick roll in the sheets?"

He hiked up his pants, zipped up, and began to buckle his belt. "Whatever it is, I'm out."

He turned and hurried out of the room, but not before one of her spiked slippers hit him in the back. He supposed he deserved that.

Jase found himself parked back at the club. His knuckles whitened on the steering wheel. One curse chased another. He would not go in. He would not show her he wanted her. He'd been played a fool once by her, he would not be played again. If she wanted him, she'd have to come find him. That way there would be no question about faking it.

Jase put his car in gear and was just about to pull away when he saw a familiar face pull up. Otis what's-his-name. The next instant his cell phone rang.

"Vaughn."

"Hey, Lucy, your girl has some esplainin' to do."

Jase laughed. Ricco. "What do you mean, Ricky?"

"Katsuo Hiro. Hog-tied in his hotel room, like her other boy toy, Townsend. Guess what SJPD found in his mouth?"

"His balls."

"Bingo. Guess what else?"

"Jade was seen leaving his hotel room?"

"Bingo again."

"Shit!"

"What do you mean? Looks like we have enough to bring her in. SJPD is gonna be all over her. I'm surprised they haven't gotten over there yet."

"Do they know where she works?"

"They do now."

"Shit, Ricco, why didn't you tell me first?"

"I'm telling you now, man, what's the problem? She's a fucking black widow. Let's get her off the street."

"Fuck, give me the name of the detective in charge."

"You're too close to the crack, man."

"Just give me the damn name and number!"

CHAPTER

9

"I want a private moment with you, Miss Devereaux." Otis Thibodeaux wasn't going to take no for an answer.

"Why, good evening, Mr. Thibodeaux. Of course. I'm sure we can find a quiet corner in the salon," Jade easily said.

She kept the smile pasted across her face and her heartbeat at a steady rhythm, and squelched the fear that laced around her lungs, squeezing the breath from her. She doubted Otis would assault her here. But if he so much as laid a hand on her, there was a panic button in each alcove.

The salon had several small alcoves built in especially for private conversation, or other private interactions. She showed him into one to the immediate right. Slowly she turned, prepared to be barraged by threats. Instead, she was met with a slow smile. He didn't fool her. She knew exactly what was behind it. Otis Thibodeaux had been a nasty boy and was now a nastier man.

She pulled the discreet heavy curtain. Instead of sliding into the round-table booth, she remained standing. "How can I help you, Mr. Thibodeaux?"

Otis pulled a sheaf of papers from the inside of his jacket pocket. "Sign these papers, Ruby Leigh, sign them and I'll disappear."

"I've explained to you I'm not—"

He raised his hand to slap her. She didn't flinch. "You got ice in those veins."

She stepped into his personal space and poked him in the chest with a finger. "I'm not going to tell you this again, Mr. Thibodeaux. I'm not Ruby Leigh Gentry. My name is Jade Devereaux; I was born and raised here in California. If you continue to harass me, I will be forced to call the authorities. Now please, leave me alone."

She turned to pull back the curtain, but he yanked her away from it. "You gonna tell the cops how you killed your mama, then burned down her trailer to cover it up?"

Her lungs constricted, the noose tightening. Jade yanked her arm away from him, but his fingers dug deep into her skin. "I told you, I don't know what you're talking about. Leave me alone!"

The curtain opened and Jase stepped in, putting his hand on Otis's left shoulder. "The lady said back off."

Otis sneered and looked from the cop to her. "I see you're hedging your bets, Ruby Leigh. You always knew how to make a man think with his dick." He stepped past her, then turned back to her. "I was always on to you. The colonel thought it was something else. But you and me know the truth."

He walked away and Jade felt a sudden chill encase her body.

"What the hell is he talking about?" Jase demanded.

Jade shook her head, wanting to look away. "I have no idea. He's crazy. He has me confused with someone else."

Jase flashed her a sharp stare. It bored deep into her heart. Her lungs constricted more. She felt smothered, her breath labored, the tightening in her chest sharp, hot, and painful. The thought of this man knowing her dirty past disturbed her more deeply than Otis's presence.

"I swear it! He's lying." The one lesson she'd learned from her mama was that desperate people do desperate things. And right now Jade was desperate. As much as she hated the lie her life had become, if she told the truth now it would shatter what life she did have and that of her only living kin, her baby sister.

"Katsuo Hiro is dead."

Jade gasped. Her knees quivered, then shook. She needed to sit down. Jase helped her to a chair.

"Oh my god, how? When?"

"Same way as Townsend. And you were seen leaving his room today."

"I—I didn't kill him!"

"What were you doing in his room?"

Moment of truth. She glared up at him. "What do you think?"

"I'm done guessing with you. You need to tell me what you were doing in that room and whether he was alive when you left him."

"Yes, yes, he was alive!" Jade grabbed his hand. "I didn't kill him, I swear."

"You swear an awful lot of things, Jade. I don't know what to believe." He removed his hand from hers.

"I didn't kill Mr. Hiro. He was alive and well when I left that room."

"You're going to have to tell that to the San Jose PD."

"What do you mean?"

"You're their number one suspect."

Her skin chilled. "Now?"

Jase nodded. "Detective Kowalski is on his way over."

Wildly she looked around. "No, not here."

"I can take you to him. And, Jade?"

Her big green eyes looked up at him and his stomach rolled. She looked like a scared little girl. "Yes?"

"Call your attorney."

"Yes, yes, of course."

She hurried past him and Jase pulled out his cell phone and called Kowalski. "I'm bringing her to you."

Slowly, Jase flipped the phone closed and wondered just what the hell he'd done.

Jade was grateful Branford Pettigrew was waiting for her when Jase escorted her into the Twelfth Precinct. He was the first membership she'd sold when she began at Callahan's five years ago, and for that first year they spent many hours together. He had been quiet and awkward. But slowly he had opened up into the confident man standing before her. Not much older than she, Branford was forever in her debt for getting him over his fear of women.

"I'd like to speak privately with my client," he said as he strode up to her, putting his arm out and bringing her into the protective fold of a half hug. "Are you okay?" he asked, concern lacing his words and face.

"Yes," she lied.

"Just a minute," a voice boomed from behind them. Jade, Branford, Ricco, and Jase turned to the loud voice. A large man in a bad suit with a ruddy complexion, Detective Kowalski, filled the doorway leading to a hallway.

"Miss Jade Devereaux?" he asked.

Jade nodded.

"Who are you?" Branford asked.

"Detective Kowalski," he boasted.

Kowalski looked at Jade, his wary gaze sweeping up, then down, his contempt obvious. "Miss Devereaux, you have the right to remain silent." He smiled when Jade gasped, but Branford squeezed her arm. "Anything you say may be used against you in a court of law. You have the right to an attorney. If you cannot afford one, an attorney will be appointed to you. Do you understand these rights as I have explained them?"

Jade nodded.

"I can't hear you, *Miss* Devereaux."

Jade stiffened. She glanced over to Jase, who stood next to his partner as stoic as an oak. He refused to look at her but she could see the muscles clench and unclench in his jaw. "Yes, Detective, I understand my rights as you have explained them to me."

Before Kowalski could comment, Branford stepped forward. "Is my client under arrest?"

"We'll decide that after we talk to her."

Branford laughed. "There's nothing to discuss. Either arrest her now or we walk." When none of the cops made the necessary moves, Branford took Jade's hand and started for the door.

"Hold on a minute!" Kowalski bellowed.

Everyone in the room stopped and stared at the frustrated detective. "I might not have physical evidence right now, the lab is as usual decades behind, but I got a body and your client was the last known person to see him alive. I got a cop who puts her there, and she admitted it to him. Now, I can charge her and make you both miserable until arraignment tomorrow morning, or your client can talk to me."

Branford nodded. "I'd like to speak to my client for a moment." He pulled Jade away from the detectives.

Her heart thudded against her chest. Was she going to be arrested and put in jail?

"What the hell is going on, Jade?" he softly asked.

"I don't know, Bran. Mr. Hiro is dead."

"Where you with him today?"

Jade swallowed hard and nodded.

"Did you kill him?"

"No!"

Branford smiled and kissed her on the forehead. Taking her hand again, he walked back to the three detectives.

"Unless you produce physical evidence, my old Stanford Law professor and the current DA, Stanton Wilcox, will toss the charges against Miss Devereaux out the window. I'll request him personally to oversee this case, and while the three of you have your doubts about Miss Devereaux's innocence, I do not. I will strongly argue that point to Stanton."

Kowalski looked as if his blood pressure was about to erupt. Jase stood quietly watching her, a snide smirk twisting his lips. His partner, Ricco, was not readable. Jade held her breath. She did not want to be arrested.

"Miss Devereaux," Kowalski said, his beady black eyes fixed on her, "do not leave the area."

Jade looked up at Branford. He smiled down at her and squeezed her hand. "Good day, gentlemen." He tugged her hand and drew Jade from the cold sterile building.

Once they exited the building, Branford stopped at the top step leading to the precinct and turned to face her.

He smoothed a strand of hair from her cheek and smiled. Lightly, he kissed her on the forehead. "Do you want to tell me what the hell is going on?"

Jade shivered and shook her head. "I don't know, Bran. Two of the club members are dead in less than a week, and I saw both of them shortly before they were killed."

"Was the first Andrew Townsend?"

She nodded.

"I read about it." His eyes softened and he smoothed more hair from her face. "I have to ask you, Jade. Did you have anything to do with Townsend's death?"

She swallowed hard. "I don't think so." God, she hoped not.

He squinted his eyes. "You either did or you didn't, Jade."

She took a deep breath. She could not go to jail. Not yet. "I didn't."

He hugged her to him. "Okay. C'mon, angel, let's get you home."

"No, take me back to the club. My house was broken into; I'm not going back until my housekeeper cleans all of that mess."

"Your house got tossed? Why didn't you tell me?"

And once again, she trusted no one with her secret. "A simple breaking and entering, the cops said. The guy got some jewelry and stuff. Random."

Branford stared at her for a long minute, then continued to walk toward his car. "C'mon."

Jase watched the tender moment between Jade and her *attorney*. Disgust mingling with a sharp stab of jealousy wrestled inside his gut like two terriers going at it over a bone. He turned to Kowalski. "What do you have?"

Kowalski grinned and shook his head, his fleshy jowls swishing in the air. "You hot for that piece?"

"Hardly."

Kowalski snorted. "You gotta be dead not to get wood over that."

"Not my type. Now, tell me what you have."

"Asian male, Katsuo Hiro. Hog-tied, his balls cut off and shoved down his throat. My guess is he choked on his nads."

Jase nodded.

"Your boy Maza says you had one like this Sunday?"

"Yes, same MO, and both members of Callahan's."

"I'm aware of Callahan's. Don't tell me that fine piece that just left here was the last one to see your boy alive?"

"No, she wasn't. At least I can't place her as the last. I interviewed a Genevieve Monroe this evening, she was the last to admit to seeing him alive. She had a drink with him at Delicato's a few blocks from Callahan's. She said she called a cab for him, he was too drunk for anything. His BAC supports it. The guy had enough alcohol to float a boat. Cause of death, asphyxiation. He choked to death on his balls."

Kowalski nodded. "Your girl there could have run into him again, maybe when he stumbled out of the bar."

"Ricco will be heading over there shortly to question the employees. We'll know when Townsend left and how."

"Okay, so let's say he stumbled back to the club. Runs into that harpy and she whacks him," Kowalski suggested.

"Motive?" Jase asked.

"You tell me."

Jase shrugged. "So far, other than the fact that the guy was a scumbag, no motive. And while I'm sure Miss Devereaux works out, she doesn't have it in her to hog-tie a guy."

"What if she had help?" Ricco asked.

Jase narrowed his eyes. "Okay, so she had help. Why? Was Hiro missing his wallet?"

"No," Kowalski said. "Over five grand in his wallet and he had enough jewelry to make my wife happy for decades. But the sixty-four-thousand-dollar question is, what was your girlie doing there before Hiro was whacked?"

Jase scowled and his blood pressure jumped. "I have a hunch."

Kowalski waved a hand in front of Jase's face. "Earth to Vaughn, murder investigation in progress."

Jase's scowl deepened. "I think she was turning a trick." As he said the words, he thought he was going to be sick.

"Ah, so man-hater hooker whacks john. Classic."

The truth bit Jase sharply in the ass. "Call me an idiot, but my gut says she's telling the truth."

Ricco shook his head. Kowalski chortled. "Vaughn, you are way off base. She's a black widow, and she has your dick in her mouth right now. If she confessed, you wouldn't believe it."

"No shit," Ricco muttered.

Jase shot his partner a hard glare. "I haven't lost my objectivity."

Both Kowalski and Ricco hooted over that one. Were they right?

"Tell you what, Vaughn," Kowalski said. "Since you seem to be so cozy with her, why don't you turn up the charm and find out for us poor slobs what she's hiding under that thousand-dollar dress of hers."

Jase nodded. He'd worked too many years of undercover

not to know how to work a suspect for information. The thought of getting between Jade's thighs for information made him feel like he needed a shower. His head snapped up and he grinned. Jase slapped Kowalski on the shoulder, pulled a card from his breast pocket, and handed it to him. "Will do. Keep us posted and we'll return the favor."

Kowalski nodded, and Jase left him and his partner staring after him.

As Jase pulled out from the precinct his mind ran rampant. What the hell was going on? He knew Jade was hiding information from him regarding Townsend. She knew something and was not telling him. And Hiro? If she wasn't the last person to see him alive, who was? And why all of a sudden were two of Callahan's club members ritualistically killed? Had they crossed a line? Was their death revenge for some wrong? He gripped the steering wheel so tightly, his hands cramped. The common denominator was Jade Devereaux.

Jase drove back to the club on autopilot, preferring the quiet peace of nothingness as opposed to the static noise a certain proprietress created. He waited on the opposite side of the street from the parking lot. He could have waited for her at her house, but he decided instead to follow her. Who she left with and the state of that person's health could be at stake.

Long after midnight, Jade walked out to her car. The eerie quiet of the moonless night unnerved her. A cold emptiness filled her. Like an arctic wind, it whistled through each cell, chilling her to the bone. She was emotionally spent, physically wiped out, and afraid for everyone.

She had spent a little time with each of her employees, reassuring them that not only was she not in any danger but neither were they, and that they should just go about their regular business. Their jobs were not in jeopardy. She flinched as if an invisible hand had reared back to strike her. It remained to be seen when the members' murders, less than a week apart, would hit the tabloids. It would kill business. Members would not come to the club for fear of being the next victim. And then she would have to lay off employees. And she would be without a job.

Jack Morton's words came back and jabbed her in the gut. She'd made the decision years ago never to allow a man to touch her for money. Not even for Tina would she go back on her promise to herself.

Somehow she'd have to manage the status quo at the club and keep her new pimp owner happy, and pray for no more distractions. Jade let out a long relieved breath. Even if the papers printed the names of the victims, there would be no tie-in with the club. Their membership list was private. She doubted the cops would release that information. She bit her bottom lip. Or would they? Could they?

Impulsively, Jade reached for her cell phone, then just as quickly she put it down. It was too late to call Jase and find out exactly what the cops planned on releasing. And she wasn't going to be the one to give them any ideas.

It wasn't until she was halfway to the Blue Orchid that Jade realized she was being followed. Fear shimmered through her. The tightening of her lungs returned. Along with the feeling of suffocating. Was the killer following her? She grabbed her cell phone again and called the only person who came to mind.

"Vaughn."

"It's me, I'm being followed. I'm scared." The split second her confession left her lips, she cursed herself.

"Are you sure?"

"Yes, since I left the club."

"Where are you?"

"I'm on Saratoga heading toward the one-oh-one."

"What the hell are you doing there?"

"I—I can't go home. My house . . ."

Her eyes darted to her rearview mirror and the car that had been tailing her turned right onto a frontage road before turning right again. Relief followed by embarrassment flooded her.

"He's gone."

Jase nodded. He gave her more time to continue down Saratoga before he picked her up again. Even if he lost sight of her, he had his laptop and her signal was loud and clear.

"Are you sure?"

"Yes, I must have imagined it. I'm feeling a little shaky right now."

"Jade?"

"Yes," she whispered.

"Do you want some company?"

Every fiber of her screamed yes. Just for an hour, just until she forgot why he was there, just until she fell asleep. "No, but thank you."

"Where are you staying?"

"At the Blue Orchid on Hacienda."

"Who else knows you're staying there?"

"No one."

"Lock your door."

"I will."

Jase drove by the hotel a few minutes later. The front porch light was on, the curvy silhouette of a woman canvassed the upstairs window. His blood quickened, warming his limbs, heating his groin. His breathing accelerated. It occurred to Jase then that he was in deep shit.

Jade spent the next day holed up at the Blue Orchid. She had another massage, a facial, and allowed herself to be pampered. She called her sister and left her a message, she napped, she tried to read, and ultimately found herself bored and restless. It occurred to Jade as she paced the plush carpet of her room, that she was avoiding the world. The world that included her turbulent past, her tenuous present, a life that held little promise of a smooth future. A world that included a man she had allowed on several levels to get under her skin.

Jase Vaughn was never far from any of her thoughts. When she awoke hot and sweaty in the middle of the night, craving his touch, she knew she had a problem. A problem she didn't want, a problem she didn't need, and a problem she had no idea how to handle. She was once again under the control of a man. And this man wanted something from her she had never given to anyone, not even Tina. He wanted the truth.

The truth was something she could barely face herself. With it came pain and the loss of her freedom. Her freedom was crucial to Tina's survival. She'd vowed the day her mother died Tina would never have to want, never have to subject herself to the whims of a man to survive. She would support her sister emotionally and financially, pay for her college, and set her up for a life where she could choose to do whatever she wanted or do nothing at all.

Without her freedom, Jade could not work and no work meant no income. If not for Tina, Jade would walk into the nearest precinct, turn herself in, and take her medicine. She had been dead inside for too long to remember what it meant to feel.

Until Jase.

And while she couldn't put a finger on the emotional aspects of the man, and she didn't want to go there anyway, her body had a mind of its own. She reacted to him on a most basic level. A level that, if she tapped into it, could control her.

Jade sighed and started to get ready for work. She went through the mundane motions of creating the woman men dreamed about. Wet dreams, that is. She trembled as she applied her mascara. It was ironic. Her mother turned her out at fourteen and she had had no clue what a man wanted from a gangly girl. She found out soon enough. For a pervert, the colonel hadn't forced himself on her, but what he did do to her was humiliating and she swore, as she stood there naked in front of him while he jerked off to her baby talk, that she would never allow a man to take advantage of her again. It would be on her terms and her terms alone. It was how she went to work every night, how she dated for money. It was her choice. She picked the men, the time, the place.

She slid the jade-colored sheath down her curvy form. The shimmery fabric matched the color of her eyes spot-on. She'd spent a few minutes in the tanning bed this morning and her skin glowed a healthy bronze. She shivered as she looked at herself in the mirror and visualized Jase standing behind her, his lips tracing a path along her neck to her shoulder. Her nipples stiffened and she felt a warm flush between her legs.

She could almost feel his body heat, the pressure of his large hand, the warmth of his lips on her skin. She'd only allowed one man to touch her so intimately, and his betrayal was almost harder to endure than the betrayal of her mother.

Jade closed her eyes against the sudden sting of tears. "He's not worth it!" she shouted at the mirror. Abruptly, she turned and zipped up her dress, slid on the matching snake-skin stilettos, grabbed her purse, and left the room.

It wasn't until she was halfway to the club that it occurred to her that she was being followed again. She glanced at her purse where her cell phone was but refused to make a call to a man. For as much as men had screwed up her life, she'd managed without one, and she wasn't about to start playing the helpless female role.

Jade pulled over to the bike lane without signaling and waited for the car behind her to pass. Her heart rate elevated when the dark-colored vehicle pulled over, as well, but nearly fifty yards behind her. Anger swelled and she did a too-stupid-to-live move. Jerking the car door open, she stepped out and strode angrily toward the car.

When the engine revved, it occurred to her the driver might run her down. Instead he or she backed up with the squeal of rubber and did one of those TV cop moves, where the car spun around. Oncoming traffic swerved and horns blew as the car crossed over the median strip and headed the other way. As far as she could see, it was a dark green or black four-door sedan, maybe a Taurus or Corolla. Hell, she didn't know. But she would recognize it again.

Jade hurried back to her car and drove off, keeping a sharp eye on her rearview mirror.

Jase sat at his desk, feeling oddly discontent. A large Styrofoam cup materialized in front of him. Jase looked up to see his partner's dark penetrating gaze. "You look like a lost puppy, Vaughn."

Jase reached for the cup and opened the lid. The rich scent of fresh-brewed coffee teased his nose. "Thanks." He took a sip and set the cup down. "Did you hear what the techs found in Miss Devereaux's garbage can?"

Ricco nodded. "Townsend's cell phone."

Jase nodded and took another sip. "Puts her in a whole different light."

"Prime suspect light."

Jase shook his head and took another sip of coffee. "It could have been a plant, no prints."

Ricco laughed. "Wow, amigo, which head are you thinking with? She had motive, opportunity, and, with some help, means."

Jase's head snapped back and he challenged his partner. "Motive? What motive?"

"A man-hater. Chicks like that hate men, hate the way they control them, use them for sex. Vengeance, revenge, or just because she feels like getting back for the cause."

Jase shook his head. "I don't get that from her. I'll give you this much, though, she's not on the up-and-up and she has no great love for the opposite sex, but she doesn't strike me as violent or vindictive. In fact, she strikes me as the quiet loner type. She's in no hurry to bring the spotlight on herself. So why now?"

"A trigger. Maybe repressed feelings have surfaced. Maybe this Otis Thibodeaux has something on her. Maybe she's setting up the kills to take him out, because he's the original target."

Jase took another sip of his coffee and nodded. "Maybe."

"Despite what her high-priced lawyer said, I think we have enough to charge her. At least for Hiro."

Jase shook his head. "Doesn't matter. If Pettigrew is tight with Wilcox like he says, the DA is going to want indisputable proof. The labs will give us the physical proof we need. She'll either be ruled out." Jase cringed, not wanting to imagine Jade behind bars. "Or we'll peg her."

Ricco nodded. "I wish the lab worked as fast as *CSI: Miami*."

Jase smiled. "No shit. And if the techs carried guns and interviewed the suspects, who would need us?"

Ricco got serious and faced his partner square on. "Look, man, I know you got it bad for that woman, but you need to back down. You could get kicked off this case or out of the department. You have too many years in to throw it all away for a chick who is probably guilty of killing two men."

Jase nodded and sipped his coffee. He looked Ricco dead in the eye. "I'm having déjà vu here. I told Reese the same thing not too long ago."

Ricco shook his head and sat back in his chair. He steepled his fingers and tsk-tsked at his partner. "Just don't shoot me when I say I told you so."

CHAPTER

10

When Jade entered the club later that afternoon, she did it with the confidence of a woman who hadn't a care in the world. In the world she'd created for herself in California, she had no cares. Relief had flooded over her when Branford called to tell her Townsend died of asphyxiation. She had no hand in Townsend's or, she knew for a fact, Hiro's death, and she had Branford to prove she didn't if it came to that.

"Miss Jade," Rusty quietly said from behind her. Jade started and immediately laughed it off. Gracing the kid with a smile, she tousled his chestnut-colored hair.

"You startled me, Rusty."

His freckles darkened and he looked down at his feet and shuffled them. "I'm sorry, ma'am."

"It's okay, we're all a little jumpy these days."

"What's happening here?" he asked.

"I told everyone last night, Rusty, not to worry. Our jobs

are safe. *We're* safe. The club is fine. Just answer any questions the police have and do your job." She set a comforting hand on his shoulder and with her other put her finger under his chin, raising it so his eyes met her gaze. "Don't worry, your job is not in jeopardy."

"Promise?"

Jade smiled and crossed her heart. "Cross my heart, hope to die, stick a needle in my eye."

"I sure hope you don't die next, Miss Jade."

The hair on the nape of her neck sprung straight and the room grew suddenly cold. She swallowed hard and looked into the young man's eyes. "I hope so, too, Rusty. I hope so, too."

As the kid shuffled off, Jade made a mental note to speak with Mac, Thomas, and Bernard. She would strongly stress they were not to discuss the murders with any member or other employees or the press. As the girls started to arrive, Jade had private conversations with each of them. She also took the other staff aside and gave them the same lecture.

As Jade walked back to her office, she watched Rusty make goo-goo eyes at Genny. The girl smiled at him and Rusty blushed ten shades of red. Poor kid. For all of the male employees, with the exception of Thomas, it must be hard working so closely with such exquisite women on a daily basis, knowing even if both parties were consenting there could be no fraternizing.

It was a stringent rule, and one that had Sam Callahan, the original owner not insisted upon, nor Jack Morton supported, Jade would have created herself.

She had been on the fence about firing Mac when he let her know early on that he was interested in her. Her cool rebuff had been taken in stride. But it took years for her to finally feel like Mac had gotten over it. Jealousy was nasty and insidious, and in this climate it bode well for no one.

Despite her earlier feeling of elation, knowing she had not killed Andrew Townsend, the rest of the evening moved by like a slow-motion car crash. By ten o'clock, Jade's head was pounding. She asked Genny to come back to her office and take care of some menial paperwork that needed to be done. Genny had shown interest in the business side of the club and for the first time since she'd taken over as manager, Jade allowed someone into the sanctity of the financial part of the club.

"You don't look very good, Jade. Are you feeling all right?" Genny asked, closing the office door behind her. Jade looked up from the spreadsheet on her computer screen. "Just a headache, nothing a couple of aspirin can't cure."

"Let me get them for you." Genny hurried out of the office. No sooner had the door closed behind her than the fax machine next to Jade's desk began to ring.

Jade ignored it, not wanting to deal with another order or reading one of Jack Morton's nightly memos. Why he didn't use e-mail like everyone else was a mystery to her, but she'd gotten used to his run on faxes. Always the same message: *Customer satisfaction is job one*. Except now he'd expounded on the "customer service" part. Jade turned away from it and rubbed her throbbing temples.

Genny came in with a glass of ice water and handed her two white pills. "Thank you," Jade murmured, then took the pills, chasing them with a long drink of the cool water.

"Who's Crystal?" Genny asked.

Jade's eyes flew open, her temples screamed, the pain radiating to her eyes.

It took a superhuman effort to keep focused and turn to face Genny. Her neck seized, her stress level skyrocketing. Her head felt like it weighed two hundred pounds.

"What?" Jade asked, her voice barely a whisper.

Genny handed her the picture that had just come through the fax. Jade's stomach felt like a runaway elevator. The muscles in her chest tightened, rendering her breaths incompetent. A picture of Crystal's aka Tina's smiling face as she crossed in front of her dorm building happily chatting with a classmate. The words "I found you, do you want me to find Crystal?" were scrawled across the bottom.

Jade snatched the picture from Genny, crumpled it up, and threw it in the trash can. "It's a bad joke, Genny."

"Do you know that girl?"

"No, I don't. Please, can you leave me alone?"

"Okay, but, Jade, if you need help—"

"I'm fine, it's just this headache. Give me a minute."

When Genny finally left the room, Jade grabbed the picture out of the trash can and stared at it. Anger snaked from her pores, a poisonous gas infiltrating the bone-chilling fear that held her captive. She tore the picture in half and threw it into the trash, grabbed her keys, and strode out of her office, nearly colliding with Genny. "I'm leaving for the night, help Mac with whatever he needs."

"I have a date at midnight!"

"Cancel it."

She proceeded to the bar, where Mac chewed the fat with the CEO of a Fortune 500 company. Catching his gaze, she inclined her head toward the other side of the bar.

"What's up?" Mac asked.

"I have something I need to take care of. Can you close?"

Mac's eyes held only concern in their dark depths.

"Of course."

"Thank you."

Jade hurried out to her car and headed to the San Jose Fairmont. When she knocked on Otis's door, he opened it, a grin as wide as the state of Louisiana plastered across his face.

"Hey, suga, you're early." His smile morphed into a frown. A slow knowing smirk followed. "A picture is worth a thousand words, ain't it, Ruby Leigh?"

Jade shoved Otis backward with both hands. When he stumbled, she kicked him in the groin. She steamrolled forward. She kicked him again, this time bringing him to his knees. "If I see or hear from you again, Otis Thibodeaux, I'll fillet you so nice you won't be good for nothin' but catfish bait."

She towered over him and, coward that he was, he cringed away from her. She guessed she must be a sight. Her hair fell wild around her and her hands were fisted by her sides.

She kicked his thigh. "You get that fat ass of yours back to Louisiana where it belongs."

She saw the flash of humiliation flare into anger in his eyes. She didn't care. "You go on and do your worst to me, but if you touch my baby sister, I'll kill you."

Otis managed to stand up. "We ain't playin' by your rules here, Ruby Leigh. You sign those papers, then I'll leave you alone. Not a second before."

"I'm not Ruby Leigh!"

"Yeah, you are. We both know it." He grinned and rubbed his belly. "An' you know what else, Ruby girl? You're gonna do for me what the colonel couldn't do for you. And when

I've had enough of you all alone, when that girlie of yours comes over here, later on tonight, you're both gonna make Otis a very happy man."

Jade slapped him. He backhanded her. Jade screamed and shoved him. Otis's arms windmilled, and he suddenly lost all balance and fell backward. His head crashed against the end of the desk with a sickening thud. Déjà vu hit her so hard in the chest, she couldn't breathe.

Jade scrambled to her feet and over to Otis's still body. She shook him. Relief flooded her when he started to cough. She stood up smoothing her hair and dress, and gave him a final warning. "Don't contact me again."

She turned then and left him lying on the floor, groaning and cursing her to a life in hell. What he didn't know was that she had been living in hell since the day her mother handed her over to the colonel.

For two hours Jade aimlessly drove the streets of San Jose. Emotion built and as it gathered steam, it culminated into a wild unleashing of hot angry tears. When she pulled over, unable to see through the blur of moisture in her eyes, it took long minutes before the racking sobs subsided. It took even longer for her to compose herself, and when she found herself parked in front of a familiar house, tears erupted again. Not for her past or for her present, not for her sister, and not for her lost innocence, but for the realization that she had nowhere to go but to a cop's house, a cop who would arrest her in the blink of an eye if he had enough evidence.

Jase sat staring at the fire, a short glass of Gentleman Jack in his hand. It was his sixth in two hours. He glanced over at the half-empty fifth on the counter.

For the first time in his professional career, Jase was torn. Torn between what his gut told him, what his brain told him, and what his dick told him. Jade Devereaux was lying. Jade Devereaux was quite possibly guilty of murder. Twice. And Jade Devereaux was the sexiest woman he'd ever crossed paths with. And she was off-limits.

The mere thought of her unique scent, its soft musky flavor, the way it circled his senses, teasing, promising, making him want to own it, sent blood coursing to his groin, filling his cells to hurting.

He threw back the rest of his drink and swallowed. The smooth burn of whiskey did little to alleviate the pain below his belt. He slowly shook his head. Amazing, just fucking amazing. Remembering the smell of her had him as hard as a lead pipe.

He poured himself another drink. Jade Devereaux was a lot of things, but the only thing he wanted her to be was naked and underneath him.

"Fuck!"

The sudden incessant ringing of his doorbell momentarily shoved him out of his thoughts. Who the hell was banging on his door at one o'clock in the morning?

When he opened the door he stood transfixed, unable to move. Afraid to even blink. The sight before him moved something deep inside him, something primal, something he wasn't aware he possessed. "Jade," he softly said. Her dark hair was wild, her big green eyes open and unblinking like a startled owl. Dark streaks of mascara blotched her red swollen face. Her right cheek swelled below her watery eyes. The haunted look in her eyes nearly undid him. He reached out to her, and amazingly, she stepped into his arms.

Protectively, his arms tightened around her. He closed

the door with his bare foot and drew her into the warm family room.

Jade fit into him as intimately as a well-known lover, and the thought of her attaining that status renewed the waning heat in his blood. Effortlessly, he walked with her down the short hall. When her body went limp, he scooped her up, and the soft pressure of her warm body against his hard muscles reminded him she was all woman. Not that he needed that reminder. Regretfully, Jase laid her down on the wide sofa. She shivered and moaned something inaudible. He slipped her heels from her feet, his fingertips lingering on the arch of her foot. Her red-painted toenails looked out of place against the rustic suede of the couch. She shivered again. He stood and threw another log on the fire.

He returned to her, sitting on the edge of the sofa. Her arms snaked up around his neck, her long body going taut against him, her lips, soft and hot, reached up to his, like a starved bird.

Jase responded, his body going rigid, his arms tightening around her waist, molding her softness more securely against his hardness. His lips swept down to hers, barely brushing against them. Jade choked back a sob, pressing harder into him. He tasted the warm saltiness of her tears. Emotion overcame Jase, the desire to posses, to protect, and to mate.

He bent down and scooped her up into his arms, meeting her cry with his lips. Shock waves rippled through his nervous system. He lost himself in the smoldering heat of her, the way her skin felt hot and smooth against his skin, the way she melted into him, liquid.

He would have taken her upstairs to his bed, but he couldn't wait that long to mark her. The smell of her skin, her heat, her sex, the feel of her fingers digging into his hair, the fullness of her tits against his chest, the way she moaned and arched against him. Like a sleeping tigress awakening.

For the first time since she was a naïve teenager, Jade didn't question the consequences of her action. She wanted to feel again. It didn't matter that it was with a man who would lock her up. What she wanted to do was forget who she was, what she was. She wanted to indulge herself in this man because it would make her feel good, because it was her choice, because she could. She'd deal with the fallout tomorrow.

"Make love to me," she whispered against the hard heat of his lips. His answer was a deep primal sound like a tiger letting the jungle know he was master.

He stood with her still in his arms, then bent down and snatched the thick alpaca throw off the sofa and flung it to the floor. The fire in the hearth flared as hot as her blood.

He slowly released the pressure of his embrace and she slid down against the long hardness of his body. He was hard beneath his jeans. Fear sprung from where it had been lurking just below the surface. She balked. He sensed her fear. "I won't hurt you, Jade," Jase said softly against her ear, his lips brushing her skin, the result a deep quake that ran straight to her core.

A violent tremor crashed through her. She dared not look up into his eyes, afraid of what she might see there. Jase didn't give her that choice. With his finger, he nudged her chin up to look into the deep dark ocean-blue depths. Only inches separated their warm breaths. His eyes told her so many things. He wanted her, he would make her forget, and she would regret it. Because the only promise his eyes held was one of pure primal pleasure.

And while she had come to him with one intention, the minute he opened the door and his gaze pierced her, she'd had a different intent. She raised up on her toes and pressed her lips toward his. They hovered there, and she licked them. His breath hitched and she felt his body shift. The power his reaction ignited gave her courage. She realized that while she always knew she had power through sex over a man, Jase's reaction to her was different. More complex. More was at stake. She had an emotional investment, and that made it different on so many levels.

"I'm not afraid of you," she answered. Snaking her arm around his neck, she dug her fingers into his thick hair and brought his lips crashing against hers.

Jase picked her up, the force of his embrace causing her breath to hike. Instead of laying her down against the soft fur of the spread, he walked with her to the kitchen table. In one swipe he cleared the surface, the crashing sound of glass excited her. He pushed her down onto the flat surface. Bending over her, his face only an inch away from her, his eyes traveled across her lips, his long lashes hiding the look in his eyes. His hand rested on her hip and his other hand braced his weight next to her head. He dipped his lips to hers, nipping them. Her body arched in response. He growled low and nipped at her neck. Jade squirmed beneath him, wanting him to strip her and take her before she begged him to.

He stood back and pulled her toward him, his hands sliding across the high mounds of her chest. Jolts of pleasure stiffened her nipples, the feeling causing her to catch her breath. She had forgotten . . . she squeezed her eyes shut. She didn't want to remember, she wanted only to live in the present with the man who was making her feel things she'd never felt before.

"How does it feel, Jade, to want?"

"Terrifying."

Jase moved over her, his lips hovering. "That's the first honest answer you've given me." He kissed her, taking her very breath away. His right hand slid down the length of her waist to the cradle of her hip, resting there before inching up her dress with his fingers. "I can smell your desire, Jade. Musky and hot, just like you."

As his hand slid beneath the fabric, her skin trembled, the imprint of his palm burning into her flesh. She bit her lip, gasping in a deep breath. "Touch me," she moaned.

"I'm going to do more than touch you, sweet Jade. I'm going to make you forget everything except me."

He slid a fingertip across the damp satin of her thong. "You are very impatient, Jade."

She answered his taunt with her body, arching and spreading her thighs ever so slightly, giving him more access. He pressed the heel of his hand against her aching mound. Gasping, Jade jerked against the pressure, biting her bottom lip to keep from crying out for more.

She would not beg . . .

He moved his body away from her and she nearly grabbed him back, preventing his withdrawal, but she knew he wanted this as much as she, and she would be patient . . . for the moment.

He trailed his nose down her neck, inhaling her scent, then across her chest. Her breasts heaved beneath the heaviness of his breath. He nipped a nipple through the fabric of her dress and she could barely contain a scream. Her entire body was on fire, the throb between her legs so full she felt its waves pulsate to every nerve flash. And all he had done was kiss her and touch her panties. Could she survive the rest of his assault? She couldn't wait to find out. His head traveled lower, stopping at her waist, where he nipped her again, his lips the only part of his body that touched her. She wanted so much more of him.

He pressed his hand to the hem of her dress and slowly pushed it upward, exposing hot skin to the cooler air. When his nose brushed against her swollen mound, only fabric separating his lips from her core, she rose against him. "Please," she begged, "touch me."

"I am," he breathed, the heat of his breath infiltrating the fabric to the swollen lips beneath.

"Oh god," she moaned. Her soft writhes would change into demanding gyrations if he didn't do something more.

His breath on her bare skin was unbearable. She moaned, arching her hips toward his mouth. When he sucked her clit through the thong, she folded like a deck of cards. He increased the pressure and she exploded in his mouth. His hands steadied her hips and his mouth continued to drive her over one edge, then another. Her fingers clawed at the oak tabletop, her body spasming, her head rolling from side to side as she tried to hold on to something, anything, as her body ran out of control. Finally, she dug her fingers into his hair, her nails biting into his scalp. He answered the violence of her action by tearing his mouth from her. He reared his head back, his eyes glittering like blue lightning on a stormy night.

Jade gasped, the sudden disconnection tilting her spin out of control. Jase smiled, the gesture pure devil. He ran his hands beneath her skirt and pulled at her panties. The satin thong didn't stand a chance against his strength. He ripped it in two and threw it to the floor. His fingers bit into the sensitive flesh of her thighs. His right hand moved so close to her core she could feel her body heat reverberate from him back to her.

He bent over her, his gaze holding her captive. She felt the quick flare of her nostrils as his scent mingled with hers. The cloying air around them held still, then it crackled with energy when he slid a finger deep into her hot wet sheath. Jade cried out, following the sound with a deep moan. "Is that what you want, Jade?"

Her thighs flexed taut, her body went rigid, her breasts speared the air. All she could do was breathe. Barely.

He moved his finger deeper into her and flexed the tip, hitting a spot she had only read about. She felt like she was going to turn to liquid and pour right off the table. She closed her eyes, setting her jaw, wanting the sublime pain of him to never go away.

She felt his large body move over her, his warm breath against her cheek. She could smell herself on his lips. She didn't dare open her eyes. She didn't want him to know she was addicted.

He slowly rotated his finger in a circular motion inside of her and she screamed. The tension in her body wound up so tightly, then unwound in such a juggernaut of pressure she couldn't breathe. His fingers dug into her thigh and he took a nipple into his mouth while the finger inside her was joined by another. Wildly, she bucked against his hand. She could feel her pores open and the perspiration erupt, trying in a vain attempt to cool her heated body.

As the last moans racked through her, she found the courage to open her eyes. She stopped breathing. Seeing the planes of his face hardened in sexual tension, the look in his eyes so intense, fear shivered through Jade. She realized at that moment that this man making her body experience pleasure so intensely was also a very dangerous man. He had the power to ruin her.

In a sudden movement, Jase took himself away from her. The heat of the air was suddenly cold. Jade lay sprawled on his kitchen table, her lips pouty, her thighs parted, and her pussy swollen and weeping for him. He pulled her up by the arm. He kept her from falling by slipping an arm around her waist. He pushed her ahead of him, but kept a steady hand at her back. He dropped to his knees on the furry blanket, dragging her down with him.

"You have two seconds to get that dress off or I'll take it off for you."

Excitement flushed through her, and she quickly unzipped the clothing. Before she had the zipper halfway down, Jase yanked it all the way down, then pulled the garment over her head. She wasn't wearing a bra.

Jase stared at her, then reverently reached out a fingertip to a pouty nipple. The touch sent shivers racing across her skin. Hiking in a breath, she sat on her knees facing him. "Perfectly beautiful," he exclaimed.

He drew her toward him with his other hand around her waist. Bending his head to her nipple, he whispered, "I'll never get enough of you." Then he took her into his mouth. Not a gentle searching touch, but a possessive suck. Like a hungry man too long without sustenance.

Jade closed her eyes, the feel of his wet mouth sucking and tugging at her breast causing more havoc in her body. She was on the verge of sensory overload. If he didn't show her some mercy soon, she would surely explode.

Grabbing his forearm to steady herself, Jade opened her eyes. His dark head at her breast sent an emotional thrill through her. She realized she had not touched him, not really.

She slid her free hand down the hard muscles of his back to his waist. Tentatively, she slid her hand beneath his shirt. The warmth of his skin surprised her. The smoothness of it surprised her more. Jase nipped harder at her and she arched. She couldn't take much more of this, she wanted him naked and inside of her. So did Jase. He disengaged from her, and stood up. She remained sitting on her knees.

Without flinching, without breaking his gaze from hers, Jase unzipped his jeans. He shoved the pants down his legs to his thighs, then to his ankles. Then he kicked them off. Jade sat in stunned silence. He tugged the T-shirt off. He stood only in a pair of black boxer briefs. The complex compilation of muscle, bone, and skin awed her. He was a beautiful specimen. Not overly muscled, but thickly defined and lean at the same time. She didn't look at the high rise in his shorts. Instinctively, she knew there would be no disappointment there. Eager to find out, she rose up and pressed the palm of her hand against the muscle of his thigh, her fingers nearly brushing his scrotum. Jase hissed a breath and his body tightened beneath her hand. She slid it up beneath the fabric, his skin gaining heat with each incremental inch she moved toward him. The heat of his balls surprised her, the thick hardness of his shaft excited her.

With her free hand she pulled down his boxers. His cock sprung from beneath the meager confines of the fabric. His ride was obvious. How could it not be? The thick length of him was admirable, the promise of delivery a no-brainer. She reached up and touched the glistening velvety head. Jase groaned and his body stiffened.

His sex smelled spicy, exciting. She wrapped her fingers around him and gently squeezed. He stood up on his toes, his hands clenched at his sides. "I've never touched a man like this," she whispered against the straining head. "Or tasted a man like this." Her tongue darted out and in a quick lick she tasted him. Jase moaned.

Her admission did him in. He bent down and pushed her back into the soft fur of the blanket. "I've never made love to a woman in this house."

Jade smiled. "I feel honored."

Jase rummaged for his wallet in the back pocket of his jeans. Quickly, he found what he was looking for. His eyes met Jade's surprised look. "I'm always prepared."

Expertly, he opened the condom and as he moved to put it on, Jade stopped him. She took the condom from him. "Let me."

Like a pro, she slid it down the length of him. She just barely had it in place when he pushed her back into the fur. "You have me so worked up, Jade, I don't know how long I can last."

Slowly, she parted her thighs and pulled him down to her. "Let's find out."

When he entered her, Jade lost all breath. She hadn't been prepared for the thick weight of him, or the way her swollen lips would welcome him as a lover long lost. The hardness of him made her feel like the epitome of femininity, and when he slowly began to rock against her, all thoughts fled her brain. He was hers, here and now, he was what fed her soul, her body, her lust. He was a drug, one she had no idea she needed to survive.

Like a heroin addict, Jase wanted more of her the minute he'd touched her. He slid his fingers deep into the thick softness of her hair and brought her lips to his. He wanted to barrel into her, to mark every inch of her, to let the world know this woman was his, that she was off-limits to any man.

Lust rose and crashed like so many waves on a beach, one after another, until the pounding became part of the definition of the sand.

Their bodies slickened, their breaths hot and panting. Their hips moved in perfect synergy, her soft moans of pleasure music to his jaded ears. For the first time in his life, Jase had met a woman with passion for him equal to his passion for her. They were destined to be and he realized with crashing realization destined to never be. He pulled her closer, sinking his body deeper into her.

Jade wanted to cry, the sensations Jase's body wrought from her overwhelming. Her perceived love she'd professed like a fool to Donny Le Blanc in the colonel's barn, and what followed—her deflowering—didn't come close to what she felt with Jase. Jase's deep murmurs—telling her how beautiful she was, how good she felt, and how much more he wanted to do to her—excited her beyond reason.

Jase's thrusts increased in momentum. Jade let her body go, wrapping her arms around Jase's neck. She pressed her body full against him, her legs locked around his thighs. The pressure deep within her mounted, her nerve endings frayed and raw. He hit her sweet spot every time he thrust up into her. "Faster, Jase," Jade called, her voice hitching on her breath. His thrusts pounded into her.

"C'mon, Jade," he urged. "Come for me, sweetheart."

Jade's body tightened and she felt the wave build. Their sweat-slicked bodies slid and stuck, the friction between their skin nearly combusting. "Jase!" The wave hit her broadside, every nerve in her body lit up, then exploded, the starbursts lighting her brain.

Her body had barely peaked when he called out her name, his hoarse voice echoing through the room.

It was several long minutes before they moved from each other. Jase lay on top of Jade, his arm holding the majority of his weight off her. Jade didn't mind, she liked the protective feeling his body gave her. He was big and strong and capable. She felt safe near him.

Jase rolled over onto his back, bringing Jade with him in the crook of his arm. She hesitated, and he caught her gaze. He cocked a dark brow. "After that, you want space?"

Heat flushed her cheeks. "I've never—"

Jase looked hard at her, his dark brows drawn. "What is it, Jade?"

She wanted to tell him she'd never had an afterglow with a man. She had tried with Donny, but he was too busy zipping up his pants. Later she understood why. She squeezed her eyes shut, then opened them. "I'm not the woman you think I am, Jase."

His arm tightened around her shoulder. "You're much, much more."

Those words meant more to Jade at that moment than she could have imagined. She smiled then and lay down next to him, resting her cheek against his chest. The steady beat of his heart so close was reassuring. She had no regrets for having had sex with him. Quite the contrary. She wanted more, soon. Then more after that.

"Why did you come here, Jade?"

"I—I was lonely."

"You work with a room full of men. Why me?"

She turned slightly to look up at him. "I don't like them."

"But you like me?"

She chuckled softly. "I like what you do to me."

He rolled over onto her, rubbing his nose across hers in an Eskimo kiss. "Do you want more?"

"Yes."

His gaze swept her face. He touched the swelling on her cheek. She flinched, his question wrestling her back to her reality. "What happened?"

If she told him about Otis, then she would have to tell him other things. Other things that were better left unsaid. "I bent down to pick up a piece of paper that fell on the floor in my office and hit my cheek on the corner of the table."

"Liar."

She shivered and moved to pull away, but Jase pulled her back into the warmth of his body.

She looked intently at him. "I didn't kill Andrew Townsend or Mr. Hiro."

"Who did?"

Jade moved up onto her elbows and searched Jase's face. "I don't know."

"Did you see Townsend after he left with Genny?"

Jade couldn't lie to him, not while this close, not while this intimate. "Yes, out in the parking lot."

"Were you the one who called nine-one-one?"

"Yes."

"Why?"

Jade closed her eyes, took a deep breath, than looked directly at him. "He was waiting for me, and he wanted to extend our date. I didn't. I'd made it clear earlier. When he forced himself on me, I stabbed him."

"Why didn't you tell me?"

"I was afraid I killed him. It was self-defense, but who would believe me? Bran told me earlier Andrew died of asphyxiation."

"What did you do in Hiro's room?"

Jade stiffened and tried to pull away from Jase, but his

fingers tightened around her arm, holding her close. "Tell me," he said through clenched teeth.

"We talked."

"About what?"

Heat flushed her cheeks.

"What did he want to talk about, Jade, that he couldn't discuss at the club?" Her eyes darted to the ceiling, then to the wall behind him, settling on the low flames of the fire. "Did he want a live version of a nine hundred call?"

She tried to pull away again, and this time Jase rolled over onto her. His gaze held hers. "Is that what he wanted, dirty talk?"

"Yes!"

"Is that what you call what I saw at the restaurant?"

She tried to twist out of his arms. He held tight. "Let go of me!"

"I want the truth, Jade! Were you fucking Hiro for money?"

If she could have slapped him, she would have. "I'm not a prostitute!" Hot tears stung her eyes. He looked so angry, and . . . disappointed. "Coming here was a mistake. Let me go."

"Not until you tell me what the hell it is you do, what Callahan's does. Make me understand, Jade."

She could lie, she could tell the truth, or she could tell him nothing at all. No matter what she told him, he wasn't going to like it. And she decided the lies had to stop sometime and now was as good a time as any. "Everything I told you about the club is true, on the up-and-up. If the girls want to take their dates home, that's between them. *I'm not a pimp.*"

"What about Jack Morton?"

"What about him?"

"What's his take?"

Jade let out a long breath. "I've heard he has cash-flow problems."

"And how does he plan to remedy that?" he asked.

"He's lowered the membership bar—"

"And what else?"

"He . . . he's given some of our new members the wrong impression. Like Townsend, and apparently Mr. Hiro. I was shocked to walk back into our private dining room at La Hacienda Rosa and find him spread-eagle and naked. He has always been the epitome of a gentleman. When I denied him, Mr. Morton had a few words with me, and explained that Katsuo had paid a lot of money for some extra handling."

"And that included dirty talk?"

"Look, I have a sister in college, and her tuition sets me back. My job pays well. Jack told me if I didn't go over to see Katsuo I could pick up the want ads on my way out the door."

"So you went."

"I did. But I did it with the intention of pleading to Katsuo's gentleman side. When he wouldn't bite, we met in the middle. I didn't touch him, and he didn't touch me."

"So he jerked off while you told him how much you wanted to suck him and fuck him." It wasn't a question, it was a statement. And an accurate one at that. "Did you go back feeling humiliated, and whack off his balls?"

Jade gasped, her eyes widening. "He was gelded?"

Jase smiled and silently cursed himself. He'd let that very important fact slip. Had he done it on purpose? Did he want Jade innocent, so he could have her to himself?

"Among other things."

"Oh my god, what a horrible way to die."

"It's not what killed him."

A sudden thought occurred to Jade. "Did—did Katsuo die the same way Townsend did?"

Jase nodded.

"The same killer?"

"Maybe."

"I didn't kill either of them, Jase. When I left Townsend, he had a stab wound to his lung, and Katsuo was naked and happy, drinking sake when I left his room."

"It's a bit coincidental that two club members, both your dates, die the same way, and both times you were the last person to see them alive. Can you explain why Townsend's cell phone was found in your trash can?"

Jade looked surprised and leaned up on her elbows. "What are you talking about?"

"The day you were burglarized, one of the techs found it in your trash can."

"Why didn't you tell me?"

"Why didn't *you* tell *me*?"

She pushed away and he let her. "First of all, I didn't put it there, and if I knew it was there—" She looked hard and long at Jase. "Honestly, if I knew it was there, I would have wiped it clean and mailed it to you."

"You talk like a guilty person, Jade."

"I'm guilty of many things, but killing Andrew Townsend and Katsuo Hiro isn't one of them." She pulled the throw tight around her shoulders.

"How did you get the fresh bruise on your cheek?" And before she could answer he added, "The truth, Jade."

She couldn't tell him the truth and she was tired of lying. "I plead the Fifth."

He nodded and stood up, his great warrior body glowing like burnished bronze in the low flicker of the fire. She couldn't help passing her gaze down his hard abs to the hairline that started below his navel and shot straight to his cock. He was all man, and what made him that way was on the rise. Her eyes moved up to his hard gaze. He stepped closer to her and yanked her hard against him, the velocity of his move knocking the breath from her chest. Despite the offensive move, her blood quickened.

"We can play it your way, Jade, but be warned—your day of reckoning will be your bitter pill to swallow, not mine."

She nodded, unable to form words in answer. She knew more than he, what her end would entail. Until that time came, she planned on living to the hilt. No more worries. She was resigned to her fate, and until it came to claim her, she would not look back or have regrets.

Jade moved into Jase's space. Running her hands up his chest, she dug her nails into his back. "Then let's play while we can."

Jase pulled her head back by her hair, his blue eyes glittered like ice in the firelight. "Play with fire, Jade, and you get burned. Be careful."

She dug her nails deeper into his flesh. His body flinched and she smiled. "Can't handle the heat, Detective?" His cock flexed against her belly in answer.

"I can take it as hot as you can turn it up." He nipped at her bottom lip. She moaned and arched against him. Jase picked her up and spun her around, spreading her on the kitchen table. He pulled her legs toward his waiting cock.

Jade cried out as he speared her. "Oh my god, Jase, you feel so good."

"So do you."

He brought her closer into him. She wrapped her legs around his hips and he moved deeper into her. With his arm around her waist, he steadied her with the other, and their connection was complete.

Jade kissed him, her lips sucking and licking his. His hips moved back and forth in a steady motion, the tension growing with each thrust, their bodies slickening. Her orgasm came quickly, the velocity of it nearly unseating her. Jase's arms tightened, his fingers digging into the tender flesh of her bottom. She cried out just as he released deep inside of her. The force of his ejaculation nearly pushed her away from him, but he hung on to her. Before she could collect herself and regulate her breath, he carried her upstairs and into the bathroom.

He turned the shower on and pushed her in. He lathered her up, then rinsed her, then did the same to himself. He patted her dry and carried her into his bedroom, where he proceeded to toss her onto the soft down comforter. "Get some sleep."

He moved into what she assumed was a walk-in closet and emerged in a pair of flannel pajama bottoms. "I'll be back in a few minutes."

Jase cursed under his breath all the way down to the family room. He wasn't pissed he'd fucked her. Not for the first time or the second time, he was pissed because he wanted a third and fourth time. He picked up the glass bowl, which had once held oranges, from the floor and fished the fruit out from under the sofa and recliner. He pulled the fur throw up off the floor and couldn't help bringing it to his nose. Her sultry scent marked it, mingling with his own.

He tossed it onto the sofa. Why the hell was she lying to him? What was so difficult about telling the damn truth? If she were as innocent as she claimed, what was the big fucking deal? He sighed. She wasn't innocent, that was the big fucking deal.

Jase resisted the urge to run upstairs and shake her until she told him what she was so afraid of, why she couldn't, *wouldn't,* tell him the truth. At the very least, if she were innocent, she was the key to the murders, her or the club, and if she opened up he just might be able to put Townsend's murder to bed, because whoever did him had done Hiro, too.

He set the coffeepot down and mumbled another curse. His cupboards were empty. One of the worst chores on earth to him was grocery shopping. He hadn't been in weeks. At least there was enough coffee for a pot. He'd go out in the morning and get breakfast food. He scratched his belly, he was famished, but it wasn't for ham and eggs, it was for the hot dish up in his bed. Turning off the lights, he jogged up the stairs, looking forward, for the first time since he could remember, to sleeping with a warm body next to him.

He was fucking losing it.

Jase rolled over, expecting to find Jade's warm naked body beside him. Instead, the sheet still warm from her body heat was empty. He jolted upright in bed and squinted at the clock: 3:32 a.m. The bathroom light was on. He lay back against the pillows. He drifted back into the heavy fog of slumber. He woke with a start several hours later. The sheet beside him was cold. It was 6:30 a.m. "Jade?" he called. Silence answered. The bathroom light was off.

He ran downstairs. The coffee was just starting to brew. Next to the pot was a note.

Went to get breakfast, hope you're hungry. PS I took your truck, will explain why when I return, hope you don't mind.

Jase frowned. Why the hell would she take his truck and not her car? He went back upstairs and brushed his teeth and washed the sleep from his face. Just as he poured himself a cup of coffee, the front door opened. Jade came in, a shy smile on her face. She was dressed casually in a sexy sporty pink-and-black workout set. The fabric hugged her curves. Her face was fresh, her hair damp and pulled back in a ponytail.

"Good morning, sunshine," she said in deference to his scowl.

"Where have you been?"

She set the two bags of groceries on the counter. "One night, and now you're in charge of me?"

He set his cup down on the counter next to the groceries. "I don't usually wake up and find my lover *and* my truck gone."

Jade was not to be deterred, and Jase was unsure why he was so angry. It wasn't because she'd taken his truck, it was because he thought she had left him, just as he had done to every woman before Jade.

"I left a note." She picked it out of the trash can and waved it under his nose. "See?"

"I saw it."

"I took your truck—first, because I was almost out of gas, and second, and more importantly, I—I've been followed, and well, I just didn't want to be looking over my shoulder this morning. I went back to the Blue Orchid and took a quickie shower and changed. Then did a little shopping."

He stood looking at her, a mutinous frown on his face. Jade handed him his keys. "I'm a big girl, Jase. If you don't do breakfast after sex it's okay."

"Do you?"

"Do I what?"

"Do breakfast after sex?"

"Since you're the first guy I've ever slept with, I'll let you know. But right now I'd say the chances are slim, seeing as how the guy *I* slept with is a bear in the morning."

"Yeah, well, he's grumpy when he's hungry."

Jade smiled brightly. "I can take care of that."

He moved in and slipped an arm around her waist and pulled her toward him. He kissed her long, languid, and lovingly. "I bet you can," he whispered against her lips.

Jade slipped her arms around his neck, molding her body against his. His warm skin smelled clean and fresh, the muscles supple and fluid. She liked the hard definition of his body, and she liked his cool guarded nature. They were a matched pair in that regard. She knew what effort it took him to admit even on the slightest of scales that he was unhappy she left him, and it would have been equally as hard for her.

She rubbed her nose against his chest, his chest hair tickling her. "I didn't realize big bad Detective Vaughn was a big baby at heart."

His arms tightened around her. "Be careful. This big baby can turn into a big bad wolf."

She looked up at him, her eyes smiling. "And just how bad can you be?"

He ran his hands down her waist to her hips, then pressed his growing erection against her belly. "You're about to find out."

He maneuvered her against the wall and pulled down the top she wore. With one swift movement, her breasts popped out from her bra and he ravaged them. Jade moaned and arched against him, her ardor ferocious. He palmed her mounds and suckled her nipples. His fingers reached up and dug into her hair, disturbing the neat ponytail. Jade threw her head back and ran her hands down his back to his ass, his muscles clenching beneath her palms. She slid her hands between the fabric and his ass. He was so hard, so toned, so much a man, which made her feel the epitome of woman. Jase shoved down her jogging pants and dipped a finger into her waiting heat. Jade moaned and rose on her tiptoes. "Jase, that feels so good," she moaned.

He pushed her pants all the way down to her ankles and followed, resting on his knees before her. Her warm sultry scent swirled around his face, beckoning him to her. "My breakfast," he murmured against the hot flesh of her thigh. He parted her nether lips with his thumbs. Her soft weeping pussy called to him and he answered with his lips.

Jade jerked against him, the sensation of his mouth on her causing spasms to rack through her being. Her knees shook and her legs felt like butter. His tongue teased her clit and his lips sucked at her, but when he slid a finger into her, the motion in perfect synchronicity with his voracious mouth, she came.

At the same time, Jase's cell phone rang. He ignored it.

It beeped a minute later with a voicemail, then his house phone rang. His body stiffened. He had the hottest woman on the planet coming in his mouth and his damn phone was ringing off the hook. It was nearly seven in the morning, who the hell was it? His answering machine clicked on. "Buddy, we got another stiff at the Fairmont. Same MO as the other two." Ricco's voice sounded solemn and impatient. Jade gasped and Jase pushed away from her and grabbed the phone. The answering machine clicked off.

"Say again?" He kept his left hand on Jade, not wanting to lose the connection with her. Until he heard who the victim was. "Otis Thibodeaux. Castrated and hog-tied, within the last five hours. Captain wants us down there with Kowalski," Ricco said.

Jase's fingers tightened around Jade's waist. "I'll call you back in a few minutes, Ricco."

Slowly, Jase hung up. He turned to face Jade, who had lost most of her color. She'd pulled her pants up and adjusted her shirt. She looked guilty as hell. She pushed back against the wall, shaking her head.

"Where did you really go this morning?"

She opened her mouth, then a storm cloud of emotions crossed her face. Her color lightened. "Who's dead?"

"Your buddy Otis."

Jade gasped again, putting her hand to her mouth. It shook. "I—I don't know what is happening, Jase, I swear to you, I didn't kill him!"

"He died the same way as the other two."

She tried to move away from him but he stopped her and realization dawned. Jase grabbed her by the upper arms. "You played me! And I walked right into your trap!" He pushed away from her, disgust twisting his face in anger.

"You came over here last night, pretending to want me, and you fucking used me as an alibi!"

"No! That isn't true." She stepped toward him, he moved back. She read his face as plainly as if he'd written the message in plain English. She disgusted him and he believed she was a murderer.

"I came here last night because you were the only person I felt I could trust! And I don't trust anyone! Then you throw this crap in my face? You think I used you? What about your postcoital info pump? Does Miranda only stand for the moment? You knew I had an attorney, and yet you pumped me for information!"

"Go fuck your attorney, Jade, and make it a good long hard fuck, because you'll need it to convince him you're innocent." She slapped him. He caught her hand when she pulled back for another one. "You're going to be arrested this time, Jade, for the murder of Otis Thibodeaux. And I'll be damned if I'll be your alibi." He shoved her away from him. "Call Lover Boy and tell him to meet you downtown."

Jase moved past her and walked upstairs to his bedroom and slammed the door behind him. He called Ricco and told him to meet him at the station. When he hung up, he heard his front door slam shut. Good riddance. The last thing he needed in his life was another lying scheming woman. He'd become celibate before he allowed another black widow near him. He jumped in the shower and emotionally shut down.

Less than an hour later, Jase walked into the Twelfth and found Ricco ready with fresh coffee. Kowalski paced the tile floor, scowling at Jase. Twenty minutes later, Jade came in with her attorney, Branford Pettigrew, who did not look happy in the least.

"Now what, Detectives?" he asked none of them in particular.

"We're charging your client for the murder of Otis Thibodeaux," Kowalski said, then added, "and as soon as we get the lab work back, Andrew Townsend and Katsuo Hiro."

Branford looked bored and asked Kowalski, "Do you have a time of death for Thibodeaux?"

"Between three a.m. and six-thirty a.m."

"Where was the body discovered?"

"The Fairmont in San Jose," Jase said.

"Fascinating," Branford said. "My client has an airtight alibi from one a.m. this morning to seven a.m. this morning."

Branford looked from one detective to the other, settling on Jase. "Would you know anything about that, Detective Vaughn?"

Jase scowled and looked to Jade, then to his partner, and finally to Kowalski. Both detectives lost considerable color in their faces.

"What the fuck is going on here?" Kowalski demanded.

Branford smiled like he had won the world in a simple sleight-of-hand competition. His eyes focused solely on Jase, and he knew he was screwed. "My client claims she was in your presence at your home from one a.m. until five-thirty this morning. Shortly thereafter she was seen by the proprietor of the Blue Orchid and the checkout clerk at the Whole Foods on Bascom. There was no way she had the time to get to the Fairmont in downtown San Jose to kill Otis Thibodeaux and make it back in time for breakfast."

Ricco speared Jase with a shocked glare. "She was with you, man?"

Jase worked his jaw. "I fell asleep around three, she could have left then."

"But I didn't."

Jase turned to Jade, her dark hair and big green eyes telling him she didn't give a shit what he thought. She had retreated emotionally, as well. Then he remembered waking up and feeling the bed empty beside him. The bathroom light was on, and the clock read 3:32. Fuck! He couldn't say for absolute certainty that she had or had not been in his damn house!

"Was Miss Devereaux at your house all night, Detective Vaughn?"

"She was, up until three-thirty."

"How do you know that?"

Jase's eyes narrowed. "The sheets were still warm and the bathroom light was on when I woke up. The clock read three thirty-two." He turned his hard gaze on Jade. "I didn't give you enough credit. You knew I'd placed a GPS device on your car. It's why you took my truck."

Jade only stared back at him, no emotion flickering across her features. Jase's fury mushroomed. He'd been played by a pro.

Branford smiled, his look that of the cat who'd swallowed the canary. "When you have physical evidence and not all of this bullshit circumstantial crap, let me know and maybe I'll talk to you."

Kowalski stepped forward. "We want to question your client."

Branford slid an arm around Jade's waist and pulled her toward him, his look of possession pure male. "I've informed my client she doesn't have to answer squat. This song and dance of yours is getting tiresome. Either charge my client or we walk."

Pettigrew pulled Jade along with him. All three men stood rooted to the tile floor.

"Hold on, Pettigrew!" Kowalski shouted. Like a big charging bear, he strode up to them. "I'm arresting her for this one."

Jade gasped. Pettigrew smiled tolerantly at the detective. "Arrest her and I'll go to the *Mercury News* and let them know where my client spent the night, and how your detective seduced information from her while she was still under the protection of Miranda. I'm sure the DA will love having his PD's *indelicatos* aired all over the wire."

Jase fumed. Kowalski turned a murderous glare on him.

Pettigrew was good. Real good.

"Now," the snot-nosed kid started, "if you continue to harass my client, I'll slap all three of you with civil and criminal suits." Then they disappeared through the doors.

"What the fuck, Vaughn!" Kowalski screamed.

Ricco whistled and shook his head. He turned to his partner. "Man, what the *fuck* were you thinking?"

Jase shook his head and sat down at his desk. He gave the coffee a scornful look. What he needed was a few shots.

"How the fuck do I know? I'm drinking myself into oblivion last night, she shows up at my door, all weepy and looking too damn good for her own good, and the next thing I know we're going at it like two teenagers on the floor."

"Holy shit, Jase, you need to take yourself off the case. Your ass is gonna be in the wringer over this."

Jase shook his head. "No shit."

And it was. Shortly thereafter, he was removed from the case and given a box of thirty-year-old cold cases.

Jase managed to give himself a decent workout at the gym before he called it a day. When he entered his empty dark house, he realized the absence of Jade's energy was palpable. For the short time she'd been there, she'd lit up the place. He couldn't stop thinking about her. His body yearned for her and his gut was twisted up like a pretzel. He refused to acknowledge the ache in his heart. He was, quite simply, miserable. Lovesick, as it were. He wanted Jade and couldn't have her. He didn't trust her and she despised him. His blood quickened as he remembered her calling out his name as she came in his mouth that morning. He'd wanted her at the station, he'd wanted her as he lifted fifty-pound dumbbells at the gym, and he wanted her now. And nothing short of having her would make the ache go away.

He changed into his usual jogging gear and hit the street. Maybe he could run out the heat in his blood and run out all thoughts of her.

Two hours later, sweaty, hot, and wired to the hilt, Jase jogged up his driveway. He took a hot shower, then an ice-cold shower. Still, his body burned with a deep bone-crushing ache. He wanted more than her body, he realized. He wanted her to take him where she'd never taken anyone before him. He wanted her to open up to him to tell him what scared her, why she was holding back. Who was Otis to her, and why did she want to keep him secret? What did Otis know that scared her, and had she killed him to keep him quiet?

Shit! He turned off the cold water and toweled himself

dry. The ringing of the doorbell had him hustling downstairs with only a towel wrapped around his waist.

He looked through the peephole and went still.

The doorbell rang again.

"I can hear you breathing, Jase, open the door."

Jase stood on the other side, his hand reaching for the knob, afraid if he opened it his entire world would go on full tilt and he would be unable to right it again. Afraid if he didn't, he would not survive another day.

He touched the brass knob, then slowly turned it. When he opened the door, Jade smiled up at him, the smile of a woman in full control. For the first time in his life, he was afraid of what a woman could do to him.

He stepped back. She stepped in. He closed the door behind her. She faced him.

"You may not trust me—and that's okay, I don't trust you, either—but . . ." She stepped up to him and yanked the towel away from him. It hit the floor and his cock sprung up full and ready to ride. "You can't stop thinking of me." She wrapped her fingers around his shaft and squeezed. "And you still want me."

She stood up on her toes and nipped at his bottom lip. When he failed to respond, she bit harder. The copper taste of his blood mingled with her saliva. "You can stand there like a statue, Jase, but your cock doesn't lie. If you don't want me, it does." She slowly pumped him. He hissed in a breath. "See? You want me, and if I let you, you'll take me, right here on the hardwood, like two crazy kids who can't get enough of each other." She looked up into the hard gaze of his eyes. "Admit it, Jase. You'd go to hell and back to fuck me again."

His hard stare unnerved her. But she pressed on with her assault. The look in his eyes that morning, the look of utter contempt, was too hard a blow to take. She needed to know he still wanted her. If he wanted her, he didn't hate her.

"Who hates you enough to set you up?"

She could only think of one person, and he— She closed her eyes and shook her head. He was dead.

"I have no enemies here, and even if I did, why would they kill my dates?"

"To mess with you, taunt you, watch you squirm, a form of torture."

CHAPTER

11

"I didn't come here to talk, Jase." She pushed him down the hall. He resisted. She walked past him and halted at the bottom of the staircase and turned to face him full-on. He'd wrapped the towel back around his hips.

"Right here, Jase. Right now."

Jase stood stock-still. Then he took a step toward her, and another. He stopped several feet from her, unable to go farther. He couldn't.

Jade reached out and tugged at the towel. His hand tightened around the knot. She tugged harder. It loosened. She tugged again, this time freeing the fabric. The only sound was the soft thud of the heavy fabric as it hit the hardwood floor. Punctuating the room was their panting breaths. He had yet to touch her, but his chest moved with his rapid breath. A smooth sheen of perspiration slicked his skin.

When his cock sprung free, he nearly came there on the spot when Jade wrapped her warm fingers around his shaft.

She smiled up at him and let go. Jase jerked toward her and her smile widened. Stepping up to the fifth step, she leaned back against it. With her knees spread, her miniskirt slid back against her thighs, she touched herself. Sliding her fingertip up and down the damp fabric of her panties, she held Jase's intense gaze. "I want you to do that to me, Jase. Your finger, then your mouth, then your cock."

She slipped out of her shirt. Her full breasts rose high, the nipples taut, teasing, beckoning. He dared not touch. Jase held his breath as Jade slipped the thong panties down her thighs to her calves and then to her ankles. Her pink pussy glistened with want, and he wanted to give it what it craved. Jade lay back against the carpeted steps. Her long hair hung around her shoulders, her full lips pouted, and her tits rode way up high, but his gaze lingered at the sweet spot between her thighs. His cock ached and even if he didn't touch her, he'd come right there in the hallway. Jade ran her hand down her belly, softly moaning, teasing him. When her fingertip dipped into her hot wetness, he groaned. Her hips rocked, the air swirling around them growing heavy with tension.

"Jase, that feels so good. Do you want to touch me?" Her gaze caught his and held. Yeah, he wanted to touch her, and a whole lot more. Her hips rotated, beckoning. Her moans infiltrated him, the primal call almost more than he could bear. The ache in his body grew unmanageable.

"Jase!" she screamed as she climaxed. He stepped closer. And when she rolled over and wagged her sweet ass under his nose, he broke. He stepped into her, kneeling on the third step, and speared her with his cock. He closed his eyes, the sublime sensation of being inside of her as one consumed every cell in his body.

Her muscles clamped around him, milking him, pulling him deeper inside. Jade cried out, the pleasure in her voice urging him on. He grabbed her hips, his hands fitting perfectly in their cradle, and pumped into her.

Jade cried out again and again, the feel of him driving deep into her from behind too poignant for words. She keened out a long cry as her muscles constricted and her orgasm exploded deep within her, sending currents of blistering electricity to every nerve ending she possessed. Jase's hard body encompassed her, and his hoarse call as he came sent her senses reeling.

She collapsed against the carpet with Jase on top of her, but he kept the bulk of his weight from her. She rolled over until they were face-to-face and couldn't help a slow, sated smile. She reached for her discarded panties. Taking them, she wiped him from between her thighs. She pushed away from him, slipped her shirt on, and stood, adjusting her clothing to more modest proportions. She started for the door.

"Where are you going?" Jase called, his voice raw.

Jade turned, the balled-up panties in her hand. She tossed them at him and he caught them. "Home." Then she proceeded to do just that.

Jase stood naked in his hallway, his dick still wanting her. His gut felt torn up and empty. He yanked up the towel from the floor, cursing. He'd never had such a chemical reaction to a woman in his life. And while having had her should have put the craving to rest, it only intensified the effect. That and more. Much, much more.

For the first time in his life, he knew what it must feel like to be an addict with the hunger for another fix driving you to the brink of insanity. Jase ran up the stairs and turned the shower on, and several minutes later his teeth chattered under the icy shards of water. He looked down at his raging hard-on. He took matters into his own hands. Only when he'd depleted himself did the edge of tension ebb. An hour later, it was back. Like he'd been drugged, the heat between his legs unbearable.

A hand job wasn't enough. He wanted to possess and to be possessed. There was only one way he could get longer relief, and the only way that was going to happen was to track the object of his obsession down and have his way with her. And god help him, the way he was feeling right now, there wasn't anything on this earth he wouldn't do for one more moment with her.

With superhuman will, Jase dressed and went back to the PD. He had more cold case files than he could go through in a decade. He opened the first folder. DOA Jane Doe, the date nearly twenty years ago. He tossed the yellowed folder onto his desk. Frustrated, he put his hands behind his head and locked his fingers together, then leaned back in his chair and set his feet up on the desk, crossing them at the ankles. Every time his thoughts drifted to the black-haired, green-eyed beauty, he squeezed his eyes shut, gritting his teeth. His dick twitched and he squirmed in his chair. He glanced at the clock: 10:00 p.m. Was she at the club? Was she laughing with another man, rubbing those fantastic tits of hers on his arm, batting her lashes, making sweet promises? Was she allowing the man to touch her? To kiss her, to dig his fingers into the hot wetness of her? Jase jerked up, the impact of his movement knocking him off balance. He caught himself against the desk. "Son of a bitch!" He couldn't concentrate, he couldn't eat, and he couldn't sleep.

All because of a woman.

His mother and sister would have the last laugh. He'd

sworn years ago never to be led by the nose by a woman. He didn't need them, and they didn't need him, and yet here he was, unable to do his job, unable to function normally, unable to do anything but think of his dick in her.

Despite three murders in a week, and despite the fact that she was nearly charged with the murder of one man, with two others hanging over her head, and despite the dark mood of the club, Jade worked the members with a confidence she had never felt. Her coup over Jase earlier infused her with such a feeling of power, of indestructible immortality, that she felt she was unstoppable.

After a particularly engaging verbal sparring match with RomAire CEO Ken Rhodes, Jade strode back to her office, the smile on her face ear to ear. She opened the door and stopped in her tracks.

Sprawled out in her chair with his trousers around his knees was Simon Mueller, and locked onto his considerable cock were Genny's lips. The girl jumped up, wiping her mouth, but Simon only smiled and relaxed back into her chair. "Genny promised me a bonus if I paid top dollar, but I never expected it to be you, Jade."

Fury infiltrated her cells. Jack Morton had reduced the club to nothing more than a brothel.

Instead of answering Mueller, Jade looked at Genny, who had the decency to look chagrined. Barely. "Genevieve, I'm going to get a glass of wine. When I come back to my office, the only person I want in here is you." Jade smiled at Mueller. "Mr. Mueller." Then she backed out of the office and closed the door soundly behind her.

Several thoughts ran through her head. First and foremost, how long had Genny been turning tricks in the club? It was one thing for her to take her business elsewhere, but on premise? No. Never! Under no circumstances. Genny was not going to like what Jade had in store for her.

When five minutes passed and Simon Mueller hadn't emerged, Jade became angrier. Obviously, her word meant nothing. Now she'd have to make a scene.

Just as she started for her office, Mueller came out, tucking his shirttails into his trousers. He had the audacity to grin at her. When he walked past Jade, he grabbed her ass.

When she entered her office, Genny smiled and looked up from her compact as she expertly applied fresh lipstick.

"You're fired, Genny."

"I doubt it," the little blonde absently said.

Jade raised a brow and stepped closer. "I don't think you understand. I am the manager here and I say you're fired. If you would like to take it up with Mr. Morton, be my guest, but rest assured if he doesn't back me on this, I'll let the press know exactly what's going on here."

Finally, Genny looked afraid. "Jade, you can't fire me! I need this job. I have my brother to take care of!"

"You should have thought of that before you gave Mueller a blow job."

"How can you do this to me? I'm the biggest earner here!" Genny demanded.

Jade held her ground. "I can't trust you now, Genny. If I can't trust you, I can't have you here."

The blonde's angelic features morphed into those of a hard-edged harpy. "Hah, you'd be surprised what everyone here is doing behind your back! You think you're so damn perfect! Well, you aren't!"

"Genny, you need to leave now."

Vehemently, she shook her head. "Andy told me all about you. How you were a frigid bitch, and so did your friend Otis. Even Mac says it!"

Her hurt feelings and Genny's firing forgotten for the moment, Jade pressed for other answers. "When did you see Otis outside of the club?"

Genny lost some of the flush in her cheeks.

"Genny, tell me."

"I—I saw him a few times."

"Did he pay you for sex?"

Genny straightened. "I have a disabled brother to take care of. We don't have insurance. I *have* to date outside of the club!" Tears streamed down Genny's face and Jade felt a wave of compassion run through her. She could well relate to the girl's plight. Jade let out a long slow breath.

"I'm sorry, Genny. That doesn't change anything."

"No! You can't do this!" Genny's hysterical shrieks were enough to raise the roof. Jade slapped her. Not out of anger, although she would have loved to put her hands on her and shake her, but more to get her attention, to shut her up.

"I want you to leave this minute. I'll escort you to your locker. If you so much as look like you're going to create a scene, I'll have Mac carry you out. You decide how it will play out, Genny."

Genny choked back a sob as she rubbed her right cheek. She stared up at Jade. "I can't believe you hit me! Who the hell do you think you are?"

Jade moved in closer now, nose-to-nose with her ex-employee and not feeling the love anymore. "If you continue to raise your voice, I'll not only slap you again, but I'll slap you so hard your teeth will rattle. Now, let's go get your belongings and get you out of here."

"You'll regret this, Jade. I know all about you!"

Jade stiffened. Ignoring the barb, she would not let Genny know there was anything to know.

She opened the door and held it open. Giving Genny a sharper glare, she softly said, "Act like the lady I know is hiding in there."

Genny walked haughtily by, stopping at the end of the short hallway to meet Mac's eyes. Her bar manager looked from Genny to Jade, then back to Genny again before he gave Rusty, who had just come in with a case of wine, a nod for the boy to set the case down. Jade watched how the kid slipped in then out from behind the bar. He was good that way. Nearly invisible. It was how the club worked. Food and wine service mysteriously appeared and disappeared. Except for the girls, the employees were not to be seen or heard. The boy caught her eyes and she softened her face. He gave her a fleeting smile before looking at Genny beside her. Then his eyes got all dopey-looking. The kid had it bad for her. Genny acted like he didn't exist. Poor kid.

Genny gave her no more fight except for her parting shot. "You have no idea how much you're going to regret this."

Jade nodded as she watched Genny walk toward her little Mustang parked next to her own BMW. "I already regret you are not the person I had hoped you were."

Shaking her head, Jade retreated back into the back of the club as Genny peeled out in her car, the screeching sound of rubber hard on her ears.

Just as she was about to step into the main lounge, Rusty stopped her, an empty box in his hands. "Miss Jade, is Genny okay?"

"She'll be okay, Rusty."

"Why did she leave?"

Jade sadly shook her head, wishing with all her heart Genny hadn't brought her trade into the club. "She did something wrong, Rusty. I sent her home."

"When will she be coming back?"

"I'm afraid she won't be coming back."

The boy looked stricken. "Why not?"

"She doesn't work here anymore."

"What did she do wrong?"

"I can't really answer that question, I'm sorry. It just didn't work out."

The kid stepped back and there was a flash of anger that rose and fell quickly in his eyes. Jade wasn't sure she'd really witnessed it. "Rusty, don't be angry with her. These things happen."

He shook his head. "I know, it's just that, well, I really liked her."

"So did I."

Suddenly, Jade felt exhausted. She was tired of carrying the weight of the world around on her shoulders. She wanted to unload, to let it all out, puke it up and be done with it. But that was impossible. She also realized that her time at Callahan's was running out. Genny was sure to tell Morton she had been fired, and Morton would turn around and fire her. There was no way she was going to become a madam. He could buy her out of her contract, or she would go public and he could kiss his income good-bye. She let out a long breath and as she sat at the bar and looked up, she found Mac's friendly brown eyes staring at her. "Do you think I'm a bitch, Mac?"

He smiled slowly. "I think you're firm."

Jade nodded her head and looked past him to the bottle of Grey Goose. "I'd like a martini, Mac, you know how I like it." Mac nodded and looked past her. She could tell he was focused on someone by the hard look in his gaze. It changed when he realized she was watching him. "Your cop friend."

Heat rushed to her core and she turned around to see Jase coming toward her. Despite his custom suit, he looked disheveled. Off balance. Hungry. And he was coming straight for her. He touched her elbow and moved right into her space. His lips were so close, she thought he was going to kiss her. "Can we speak in private?"

She nodded, her drink forgotten. "My office?"

He started toward it and she followed. As the door closed behind them, Jase reached over and locked it. He turned to face her, his eyes dark and fiery. He looked all of the predator he was, and excitement over being the hunted nearly knocked the breath from her lungs. She felt her chest rise and fall as excitement filtered through her every pore. "What do you want, Jase?"

He moved closer, stopping a foot away. "I want this to stop."

"What to stop?"

"I want you to stop lying to me. I want bodies to stop appearing after they've been with you. I want you to fucking level with me!"

She blanched at his angry outburst.

"I want you to leave."

His lip curled back. "You're a coldhearted bitch. I don't do fuck and run. Either you fess up, or stay the hell away from me."

A smile tugged at Jade's lips. "What? Can't the big bad police officer stand the heat?"

He grabbed her arm and yanked her hard against his

chest. "I can stand the heat, sweetheart, I just can't stand the lies. There is nothing I detest more than a lying woman."

She nipped at his chin, but he jerked away. She felt the hard rise of him against her belly. She pushed against him, digging her hip into his erection. He hissed a breath and glared down at her. "Bitch."

"I never promised you a rose garden, Detective."

He pushed her away, the instant lack of contact nearly making him howl. God, he wanted her. His hands opened and closed at his sides and he cursed. Just once more to feel her hot wet depths surround him—one more kiss, then he could forget she ever existed.

As Jade moved toward him, he moved back. If she touched him, there would be no retreat. He was weak when it came to her. She was his kryptonite, his Achilles' heel, his silver bullet.

She walked him into the door. Running her fingers up his jacket, she pressed her body full against his. Soft curves molded intimately against him. "Do there have to be messy words? Why can't there just be you and me and what happens?"

His dick strained against the fabric of his pants, the blood pounded, demanding release.

He gritted his teeth, his jaw clenching, his hands flexing open and closed at his sides. "There is you and me, but your lies get between us."

Jade laughed, the sound soft, beguiling, and he fell for it. His body pressed back against hers. She snaked her arms around his neck, her fingers twisting in his hair. She reached up on her toes and pressed her lips to his mouth. "No lies, Jase, just us."

He pulled her hair back by a hank, his gaze bore into hers. "Tell me who ruined you."

Jade gasped and attempted to step back. He held her close, forcing her to stay face-to-face. "Who made you hate men? Who made you think so little of yourself you cock tease for a living?"

"How dare you?" she hissed. She tried twisting out of his grip, but he was relentless. She cried out. Instead of loosening his grip, he reduced the small space between them. "Tell me, Jade, why do you hate men so much?"

"You don't know what you're talking about!"

"Should I call you Ruby Leigh?"

Jade stood, openmouthed. "Don't ever call me that again!" she snarled.

Jase moved closer, while she backed away. He did not release his grip. "Who, Ruby? Who ruined you?"

Her body started to shake and she shook her head. The hot sting of tears burned her eyes. "Leave me alone. You have no right to interfere in my life."

"Tell me who hurt you."

"Let go of me."

Reluctantly he did, but Jase stood his ground. He would have his answers and he would have them now.

And for the first time ever, she wanted to give some. Jade's body loosened for the briefest of moments before she crossed her arms over her chest and straightened up. "My mother turned me out when I was fourteen." She threw him a glare, daring him to put her down for it.

Jase stepped toward her. Unwrapping her arms, she stepped back, putting a hand up to stop him. "Don't touch me!" She stepped around to her chair, putting more distance between them, and sat down. Pulling a tissue from the top desk drawer, she dabbed at her eyes. Her makeup was ruined. She blew her nose and looked up to see Jase standing patiently, waiting for more answers. She expected a sneer. Not tolerance. "What else do you want, Jase? A play-by-play?"

"I want to know why a mother would do that to her daughter."

Collecting herself, Jade shrugged. "We lived in a small town. There were mouths to feed and no work to be had. You either starved or found a commodity. I was the commodity and there was a man in town willing to pay."

"So, you went to this man so your family could eat?"

"That's about the long and short of it."

"Bullshit, Jade! Why the hell didn't your mother go instead?"

Jade laughed, the sound acidic. "My mother was a dried-up drunk. She didn't have her two front teeth. Some john knocked them out after my sister was born. My mother couldn't have snagged a sex-starved rapist. I was the prize, and she sold me to the highest bidder. End of story."

"Where is she now?"

"Dead, and so is that fourteen-year-old girl."

Jase's voice softened as he moved toward her. "Not all men are pigs, Jade."

She looked up and smiled. "Who are you trying to convince, Jase? Me or you? Just take a look at the men out there," she said, pointing toward the lounge. "I caught Genny giving a member a blow job an hour ago, here in my office. Do you think Genny did it out of the goodness of her heart, or do you think that bastard offered her money? I had to fire her! Townsend was a pig, and so was Hiro. They came here hoping for some side action. It's all about the sex, Jase. And up until last week, it wasn't an issue for me, because I was dead inside."

"What happened to change it?"

She looked up at him, her eyes dry now. The barrier went up and she could admit to herself he had touched her where no man or woman alive had. *Had,* past tense.

"Nothing. Just please leave."

"Stand up, Jade." The tone in his voice left no room for argument. And quite frankly, she was tired of arguing, she was tired of running, she was tired of pretending her past didn't exist, and more than anything she was tired of living her life. But—as long as Tina needed her, she had to keep up the pretense. In four years, Tina would be out of school and Jade could finally do something for herself. Start her own business, something, anything other than what she was doing now.

Reluctantly, Jade stood.

Jase moved toward her and she flinched, anticipating his touch. He ran his knuckle gently down the left side of her face. "I'm not like other men, Jade."

She closed her eyes, wanting to believe him, but knowing he wanted from her what every other man in her life wanted from her, and he was as willing as they were to say anything to get it. "I gave you what you wanted, what more do you want?"

"All of you."

Her heart twisted. If only it were true. "No, you don't. You see me as a challenge. I'm not worth it, Jase. Believe me when I tell you there is no future on any level for us. I'm tainted goods and that will never change. Go find yourself a nice girl."

"I'm not looking for a future. I want you, me, us. Here and now. Nice or not."

Jade smiled, the hard pull of the gesture reminding her

she was not smiling in joy, but bittersweet realization. "I have to hand it to you for your brutal honestly, Jase. Most men promise me the stars for sex, but you—" She touched his cheek with her fingertip, the contact combustive. "You speak plain English. You want sex with no ties. Sex for as long as it's good for you. Sex on command. Sex regardless of what I might want."

He stiffened at her last words. "It's not—"

She shushed him with her fingertips over his lips. "It's okay, you have elevated yourself from scumbag to Lothario."

He nipped her fingertip, holding it between his lips. He licked it before releasing it. "Does it change things if I tell you I've never wanted a woman like I want you?"

She shrugged and leaned into him. "No. And even if it did, it wouldn't matter." She regarded him from beneath long thick lashes. "You don't understand, Detective Vaughn. While I may not be guilty of crimes here in California, I am guilty somewhere else."

"Of what?"

"Murder."

CHAPTER
12

The impact of her confession nearly knocked him off his feet.

He didn't believe it.

He wanted so desperately for her to be innocent. Jase pushed her away to watch her face when he spoke, but he still kept his hands on her arms. Cocking his head, he narrowed his eyes. "Murder? How? Where? Who?"

Jade made it easy for him. She pulled her arms from his grip and meandered over to the fax machine, then turned around and looked him hard in the eye. "It doesn't matter. It's done."

"It does matter!"

"Why? So you can arrest me this time?"

"No."

"Then what, Jase? I'm confessing! What kind of cop are you if you wouldn't arrest me for murder?"

"I don't believe you."

His words stunned them both.

"What are you saying? You believe me now?"

"I believe you aren't a coldhearted killer."

"But you believe I am capable of murder?"

"I believe every person has a flash point."

Jade smiled and sauntered toward him. His dark spicy scent filled the small room. His dark hair, blue eyes, and dark scowl intrigued her. She knew full well the hard feel of his muscles and skin. She wanted him again, and it didn't matter that he only wanted her body. She'd come to terms with the fact that her time here was at an end. Otherwise, she never would have admitted what she just had to Jase.

The papers Otis wanted her to sign would have given him custody over the colossal trust account the colonel left her. At this point, it didn't matter that the money was tainted. Tina would be taken care of. And she . . . well, Jade could buy another identity and fly off to Costa Rica.

And for the first time in her life, live for the day and not tomorrow.

As that thought settled over her, a calmness swept through her. She had an out. She didn't have to do this anymore. Her mother had sold her to the colonel for booze money, but the colonel had given her the keys to freedom through his perverted money. And she was not too proud to take it. Indeed, she'd earned it. It would be her sister's salvation.

"What's going on in that head of yours, Jade?"

Lost in her thoughts for the moment, Jade started at Jase's deep voice. "I was just thinking how much I'd like to fuck you."

Jase moved forward and slipped his arms around her waist, bringing her close. "Such unladylike words, coming from such a beautiful mouth." He brushed his lips across hers.

Jade raised a brow and cocked her head back, exposing the smooth skin of her neck. "I'm no lady, Detective Vaughn. I thought you'd have figured that out by now."

Jase nipped at her neck and dragged his teeth down the column of her jugular. "You don't give yourself enough credit." His hand slid down her waist to her butt. "I want you to tell me where you come from, and why you ran away," he said against her ear.

Jade stiffened in his arms. "There is nothing to tell. That girl died eleven years ago."

"Tell me, Jade, tell me who you think you murdered, tell me why you're working here, and tell me what Otis Thibodeaux wanted from you."

If she told Jase the truth, who Otis was, it would only take him a matter of a few days to deduce her hand in her mother's death. He'd have indisputable proof then. She'd have the money in her offshore account by noon the next day and she'd be on a plane to Costa Rica the day after that. She would drive down to San Diego and say good-bye to her sister and then be off. "His father left me some money. Otis wanted it."

"Did you give it to him?"

"No."

"Why did his father give you money?"

"I guess the old bastard had a conscience after all."

"I'm off the Townsend case, you know."

Her eyes widened. "I didn't realize that. Why?"

Jase smiled. "You."

"Me? I didn't call and rat you out."

"You didn't have to."

"So, that's what happens when a cop screws the suspect? He gets taken off the case? Not fired?"

"Sometimes. But with me, there was some latitude."

"Why?"

"I've spent the last eight years of my career undercover. Sometimes deep cover. You forget sometimes you're a cop."

"So, you forgot you weren't supposed to screw the suspect?" She cocked a brow. "Or was it your way to pump me for info? Like when you're undercover?"

Jase gave her a sheepish look, like a little boy who got caught with his hand in the cookie jar. "Maybe both."

She smoothed back his hair. "I appreciate your honesty. Now, I do have a job for the time being, and I need to get back on the floor."

She moved to break the circle of his arms, but he stayed her with a firm hand on her shoulder. "Jade, you can't run for the rest of your life."

"I don't intend to."

She held the door open for the handsome detective and felt a sharp stab of regret. "Good-bye, Detective Vaughn."

Jase stood for a long time, staring down at her. He reached out a hand to touch her face. She flinched and pulled away from him. "Please go."

Jase nodded and walked past her, then out of the door and out of her life. Her knees shook. If she had been gut kicked, it would have felt less painful than what she experienced at that moment, knowing she would never see Jase again. She crossed her arms over her chest and leaned against the wall, a sense of shock permeating her. She knew there would never be another man like Jase in her life, and somehow knowing that made life not seem worth living.

Every sense, every emotion, every feeling she possessed emptied out of her heart. She was empty. There was no wishing that if things were different she would pursue him.

Because things weren't different. She'd killed her mother. Her sister needed her, and she would sacrifice her own happiness to see her taken care of. End of story.

She walked back into the club and painted a smile on her face for the last time. And strangely, it felt good. There would be no sad sloppy good-byes, she had no loyalty to Jack Morton, and Mac and the others would move forward in their lives as she faded to black. The only regret she had was not being able to see her sister at will. But Tina could visit her, and, truth be told, the girl would be better off without the likes of Jade around. Tina was a good, sweet girl. If Jade's past caught up with her, it would only bode poorly for Tina.

She doubted the girl remembered much of that fateful night. It had become a haze even to Jade. She'd pushed it so long and so hard from her mind, the night was a blur. Thank god, Tina had been in the other room, and even at seven years old she could not have possibly understood what happened, and Jade would never tell her. There was no point served if she did. Her actions were her own cross to bear, regardless of the fact that she had saved her sister from the same fate she had suffered at their mother's hands.

No, she would not take back that night if it meant that Tina would not have to endure. No child deserved what she had been through, and she'd been fourteen at the time. How her mother could even have contemplated shipping Tina off to some old coot in New Orleans was beyond her. Jade smiled. She'd made sure that didn't happen.

The rest of the evening for Jade passed by in a slow abstract swirl. While her heart already missed her sister, it was Jase who played the heaviest on her emotions. She missed him before he left the building, the minute she'd made her decision. She missed the passion they shared. Most of all, she missed what could have been.

She didn't bother cleaning out her desk. There was nothing worth keeping. It was all a lie anyway.

Jase drove home and hit the computer. The woman who called herself Jade Devereaux was not a cold-blooded killer. His gut screamed it, and dammit, he was going to prove it.

All he had to go on was Otis's last name and Ruby Leigh Gentry. It took some searching, but he found the obit for Colonel Leland Thibodeaux. The old man died at seventy-six of a heart attack. The coroner was quoted as saying that the old goat never had a sick day in his life, and they were all shocked by his sudden death. Jase scanned back eleven years. He put in "Ruby Leigh Gentry" and came up with zero. Several hours later, Jase hit the mother lode.

An article in the *Sykesville Holler* dated more than eleven years ago read:

MOBILE HOME FIRE KILLS ONE

What is assumed to be the body of Bobbie Jean Gentry was found burned beyond recognition Saturday night. Her two daughters, Ruby Leigh and Crystal Blue, were not home at the time of the blaze. Witnesses say the girls fled shortly after what neighbors reported was a family dispute. The police had no comment, but said the blaze appeared suspicious.

He scanned for more articles. He found an article on Bobbie Jean's funeral. No one attended, but a statement from the cops said that Ruby Leigh had not surfaced, and she was wanted for questioning in her mother's suspicious death. While they didn't go so far as to say the old woman was murdered, Jase knew how cops thought. Ruby Leigh was suspect number one and if they hadn't charged her in absentia, the minute they knew she was in California they'd extradite her.

Jase pulled up articles on the philanthropic colonel. He followed one link to another, but there wasn't much to go on. While the superhighway of technology was fast and furious in California and everywhere else, it seemed like the rural town of Sykesville had a lot of catching up to do.

Although he couldn't locate a picture of Jade, he was sure she was Ruby Leigh. While she hadn't admitted it, she did admit to knowing Otis. Where was the sister? It was who Jade was protecting.

He called Ricco.

"Hey, man, anything come up on the Thibodeaux case?"

Ricco responded with a long silence, then said, "I shouldn't be telling you this, man, but they found a picture in his hand."

"Of what?"

"Not of what, of who. A teenage girl who looks suspiciously close to your woman. The words 'I found you, do you want me to find Crystal?' written across it."

"Shit!"

"It gets better, man. The fax number it came from is the hotel number, and guess who it was faxed to?"

"Callahan's?"

"Bingo."

"Shit!"

"Yeah, Kowalski wants to bring her in and book her. The DA wants physical evidence, since her alibi is airtight. He's pretty pissed, Jase. It's an election year and the last thing he wants to air is the fact that his lead investigator on another case that's tied to this one was sleeping with the prime suspect. You'd better hope your girlfriend doesn't take off."

"She's not going anywhere."

"Look, I pulled up some info on Otis Thibodeaux. The guy was a player in his home state of Louisiana. He liked the whores and the ponies. His old man died last year, and from what I gather, there was a sizeable estate. The guy ran straight through it. I haven't figured out how he's connected to Jade."

"His old man left her some cash. The son came to claim it."

"What made him so cocksure she'd sign over a fortune?"

"I guess he had something on her. Or thought he did."

"Don't tell me."

"Her mother died mysteriously. I've been digging online for days and I'm not coming up with much. I want to get to the bottom of this. I'm taking a few days and flying out there tomorrow. I need to know what the fuck is going on."

"I think it's pretty clear, dude."

"Yeah? Why don't you tell me?"

"You're being played. She's a man-eater. She knows you're tracking her! Fuck it, Jase. She's a damn black widow. Watch your damn back."

"I'm going to Avoyelles Parish and getting to the bottom of this. Whatever the hell is going on started there over a decade ago."

"Jase?"

"Yeah?"

"Listen, there was another piece of evidence in Thibodeaux's room."

Jase rubbed his hand over his eyes, dreading the information. "What?"

"A video."

"Of what?"

"I think you should come down here and see for yourself."

Jase sat rigid in his chair and watched as a very young Jade was seduced by a man easily ten years her senior. She couldn't be more than fourteen. The man looked like a stable hand. He was slick, and it was obvious he knew there was a camera in the room, which looked like a barn office. He worked her good, cajoling her, telling her how much he loved her, how they would run away and leave Sykesville and find work. He promised her she'd never have to see the colonel again, or his snotty-nosed son, Otis.

"Otis wants you, darlin'. He told me if his daddy didn't take you, he would. I clocked him good. I told him you and me were in love." He reached out and touched her on the shoulder, shoving the thin strap of her sundress down her shoulder. Jase could see the gooseflesh rise on her arms. The way her big green eyes looked up into the prick's face, so trusting, so in love, it made him want to puke.

"I told Otis I loved you and you loved me. I told him I'd kill him if he so much as looked at you wrong."

"Donny! You could have gotten fired!"

"Darlin'. I don't care about this job. I care about you." He pressed a kiss to her naked shoulder and maneuvered her around so her back faced the camera. He looked directly into the lens and smiled, then turned her back around so the hand squeezing her breast was in full view.

"Oh, Donny," she sighed, her sweet little-girl voice breaking his heart. Jase watched in disgust as Donny maneuvered her clothes off her body and in her sexual inexperience she fumbled with him. He saw it in her eyes. She wasn't sure. She was afraid. The bastard was less than gentle with her. She cried when he entered her, his loud panting making Jase sick to his stomach. But what made his blood boil was how Donny Boy smirked into the camera lens as he thrust into her, her eyes closed, the tears glistening on her cheeks.

Jase stood, the fury of his action so violent his chair skittered halfway across the room. "I've seen enough!"

Ricco looked at him, his eyes curious. "There's more. It gets worse."

"I said enough!"

Ricco hit the stop button. The screen went blank. "How is it we have this and San Jose doesn't?"

"I asked Kowalski for a dupe for our case files since all three murders are connected."

The bile rose in Jase's stomach. "I bet Kowalski and the guys at the Twelve are having a boys' night out with this tape."

"Look, Jase. This Donny piece of shit knew he was being filmed. I don't know who commissioned it. Hell, maybe it was Otis, and that's why Jade killed him."

"She didn't kill the prick, although knowing he probably was getting his rocks off to a girl being taken advantage of, he deserved it."

"The rest of the tape is like what you said, but she is more willing. Looks like she thinks she's in love. All the time, she's being taken advantage of."

"Do we have a last name on Donny?"

"No."

"I'm going to find out." Jase strode for the door.

"Don't do anything rash, man!" Ricco called.

Jase turned and looked at his partner. "Never." Then walked out the door.

Strangely, as Jade said her final good-byes to the employees at Callahan's, she felt no sadness. She felt no excitement, either; mostly she felt trepidation. She was giving up so much. But if she stayed, Jase would find out she'd killed her mother, and he'd find out how the colonel used her, and how Donny had disgraced her. She couldn't bear the shame of it.

It didn't take Jade long to pack. She only had the clothes she'd recently purchased, and the cosmetics in her bathroom. She looked around the town house. She'd go to the title company tomorrow and put it into her sister's name. She'd pay the taxes on it for the next four years, as well as the insurance and mortgage. Tina could do what she wanted with it. She'd prepay Tina's tuition and deposit a lump sum into her sister's account to cover living expenses. Jade sighed. In the morning, she would call Jack Morton and tell him she was no longer his employee. She took a long hot bath and moved into her sister's room, since she had yet to redo hers.

Despite the imminent changes in her life, Jade fell asleep almost as soon as her head hit the pillow. Her last thoughts were of a young girl's dreams of love with the perfect man . . . and Jase.

The soft touch of warm skin woke her. Two strong hands running up her waist beneath her baby doll PJs. His scent told her who he was. She arched, her breasts begging for his hands. He did not disappoint. Hot lips pressed to hers and she moaned, reveling in the manliness of him. Her thighs spread of their own accord, only natural with him. He made her feel every bit a woman. How could he not when he was the epitome of all things male?

He slid her panties down her legs. The smooth hardness of his body pressed against hers, and reading her thoughts, he filled her so sublimely she cried out. This was how it was supposed to be. Two bodies, two hearts, two souls united for eternity. The slow rhythmic thrust of his hips against hers, meeting his, in time, in passion, and in a bright newness, love.

"Jase," she breathed against his cheek.

He smoothed her hair from her face, his fingers tangling in her hair. His lips hovered above hers. She didn't open her eyes, she just wanted to feel him, imagine his bright blue eyes looking deep into her longingly, lovingly. She bit her bottom lip. Foolish dreams of a foolish girl. She'd been had once, and she swore never again. Not with Jase, not with any man.

"Open your eyes," he murmured.

She shook her head, her hips slowing. "Don't be afraid, Jade, I won't hurt you."

A hot tear slid down her cheek. He kissed it. Another followed, then another. He kissed them all away, encouraging her with his body to open up to him. Open her heart, her soul. She couldn't.

"Open your eyes, sweetheart. Look at me."

A sudden rush of adrenaline infused her, giving her courage. Slowly, her eyelids flickered open and she gasped. Jase's eyes had morphed to black in the dim light of the room, yet their intensity, their passion, their love? They burned brighter than any torch. He smiled and kissed her nose. "See? No bogeyman."

She wrapped her arms tightly around his neck, drawing him closer. "Jase, don't leave me tonight."

"I'll stay," he whispered against her ear. And he did.

Jade stretched the next morning, feeling like an overindulged cat. She sprung up in bed when she realized the sheets next to her were cold. Had she dreamt Jase's tender lovemaking? The slight ache between her thighs told her otherwise, that and the fact that she was bare-ass naked.

She slipped her robe on and hurried downstairs and found Jase at her laptop. He smiled, but there was something behind it. Anger?

"Who is Donny?"

At the sound of the name, Jade felt the room tilt, then right itself.

"I—don't—"

Jase stood, anger flicking in his eyes. "Stop the bullshit, Jade. Who is the motherfucker?" His shout yanked her back into the here and now.

"How do you know about him?"

"Stop answering my questions with a question and answer me, dammit."

She pulled the robe tighter around her body as if to shield what had happened to her from Jase. "He—he was a boy I knew."

"Boy or man?"

"A man."

"Was Otis Thibodeaux blackmailing you?"

Jade was startled. Did he know the details of her mother's death? Before she could answer, Jase did for her. "The cops found a video and a picture of your sister in his hotel room. Tell me what the hell is going on so I can help you."

"You can't help me."

Jase stood and strode toward her, but Jade moved backward, putting her hand out to stop him. "Please, Jase, don't do this. You'll only make a bad situation worse for me."

"What did Donny do to you?"

She sucked in a deep breath and held it, wishing she could just evaporate. The last thing she wanted was to relive what had been one of the most shameful moments of her life. Everything that happened in Louisiana was connected, and it was all ugly. Jade let out a long breath. Maybe if she told Jase, he would finally see her for what she really was, and if she couldn't force him away, the image of what she was might. "If I tell you, will you stop asking me questions about my past?"

He nodded, but only after taking his time.

"I mean it, Jase. No more questions."

"Tell me."

She moved over to the coffeepot and poured herself a cup. She took a sip, allowing the hot liquid to soothe her insides. "On my fourteenth birthday, Mama dressed me up in a homemade dress. She told me the colonel—that would be Otis's daddy—had a big surprise for me. Mama had a drinking problem, but when she was sober she could sew like a fashion designer. She'd been working on my party dress for weeks, wouldn't let me see it until that night. It was beautiful. Ruby red velvet. She even had a matching pair of shoes to go with it.

"I don't know how she got them, probably stole them. Like I said, we didn't have two pennies to rub together. My sister, Crystal, and I could count on one meal a day, two every other day if we were lucky. Mama would go out at night and come back with a bottle and a few dollars, and maybe a burger for us. I stopped asking where she went when I was ten. She just told me to shush and be happy I had food that night. I figured out after that what she was doing.

"I saw the way the respectable ladies in town sneered at my mama, and then at me after I started going up the hill to the colonel's. So Mama tells me the colonel has a big surprise for me at his house that night. That surprised me because—well, I'd only been up there once, and that was the year before to take his wife, Miss Audrey, who was ailing, some embroidered hankies Mama had made. Mama couldn't go because she was sleeping off another bender. I remember the colonel looking at me kind of funny, like he was shocked or something. It was after that that Mama started paying closer attention to me, making sure I wasn't seeing any boys, and god help one if he came around. She scared them off with the shotgun. Didn't matter it wasn't loaded, the boys didn't know that. Pretty soon, Mama had me taking all of the sewing up to the big house. Miss Audrey died that winter, but the colonel wanted his stuff mended by Mama. She even sewed a few of those smoking jackets for him that he liked. She probably got the fabric for my dress from the colonel. Afterwards, she told me it was a gift from him."

Jade took a breath and a sip of her coffee. She stared at the floor, unable to make eye contact with Jase.

"Before I left for the big house that night, Mama told me to be real nice to the colonel. He was a good man and lonely since Miss Audrey passed away. I was to do whatever he told me, because if I wasn't nice, then he wouldn't give Mama business, and with things the way they were in Sykesville, we'd starve for sure. As it was, she told me, he paid the rent on the trailer out of the goodness of his heart. And when Crystal had gotten so sick with her asthma the month before, it was the colonel who'd sent his doctor. Without the colonel's help, we would starve. Crystal gave me a big wet kiss and hug before I left. She said she loved me and thanked me for being nice to the colonel so he could help us."

Jade laughed. "Little Crystal was only seven, but she knew who was paying the bills. I walked to the big house and the colonel himself opened the door. He had that look in his eyes again. I was beginning to understand it. It was the same look the boys at school gave me. It was the same look Donny Le Blanc, the town heartthrob, gave me when I went into town."

Jade's hand shook as she took another sip of her coffee. Jase remained quiet.

"The colonel told me how much he had loved his wife, and how he regretted never having a daughter. He asked if I would like to be his daughter. Seeing as how I didn't have a daddy, it seemed like a good idea. He told me as long as I was a good girl, he would make sure Crystal had her medicine and Mama didn't have to go into town looking for other work. I knew what he meant by 'other' work. As the colonel was coming closer to me, Otis came walking in, and asked, 'So, Daddy, when you gonna let me have a piece of that?' The colonel slapped him and told him never to speak such gutter talk in front of me again. Otis gave me a look that scared me to death. The colonel patted my hand and brought me over to sit on his lap."

Jade took a deep breath. "When he put his hand in my lap and pressed against me, I cried out. For an old man he was strong. He pulled me back into his lap and said real close to my ear, 'Ruby Leigh, you do what I tell you, girl, and no one gets hurt. You go screamin' off, your mama and sister will starve to death and I'll call in Sheriff Taylor and tell him you stole my wife's jewelry.' I sat back down. My knees were shaking and I started to cry. He tried to soothe me, telling me he would be a good daddy. He made me take off the dress that I hated now, and touch him."

Jade sniffed back a laugh. "The old fool couldn't get it up. Then he figured out that if I stood in front of him and touched myself and talked dirty to him he could jerk off. He never did touch me after that. But he liked his dirty talk. I dreaded going up that hill every weekend. But Mama was happy, Crystal was healthy, and I figured so long as he didn't touch me I was still a good girl.

"Then Donny came to work for the colonel." She looked at Jase. "What can I say? I was young, looking for someone to love me for me, and he seemed to fit the bill."

"But he didn't turn out to be your knight in shining armor, did he?"

She closed her eyes and slowly shook her head. She opened her eyes. "Not even close. He intentionally seduced me. Promised me we would run away and get married, that we could take Crystal with us, that he had saved money working at the general store. He knew what was going on with the colonel, and he didn't think less of me."

She laughed again, this time the sound sharp. "He told me how much he respected me for looking out for my family. Then in the barn office, he convinced me to have sex with him."

"How did you find out about the tape?"

Jade set her cup on the counter and walked to the window and looked out. "I—I . . . even though I was convinced

Donny loved me and I loved him, I felt bad about what we did in the stable. I knew what I'd done was wrong."

She sucked in a huge breath and slowly exhaled. "When I went up to the big house the next weekend, Otis cornered me. He was furious. Somehow he'd found out about me and Donny. He begged me to kick Donny to the curb and take up with him." Jade squeezed her eyes shut. Hot tears ran down her cheeks. "Otis was a nasty boy. He—he did things that were perverse. I always steered clear of him. But he was so angry." She opened her eyes, ignoring the sting of her tears. "I told him to leave me be. I told him Donny and I loved each other and we were running away when I turned sixteen."

She turned and faced Jase. "He showed me a tape. It was of me and Donny in the stable office. I knew then that Donny had used me, just like the colonel." Jase stepped toward her. Jade stiffened, his pity too much for her to bear. "Don't touch me, Jase."

He stopped in his tracks and dropped his hands to his sides. "I'm so sorry, Jade, I had no idea."

She shrugged it off. "When I left that day I swore I would do whatever I had to do to get my sister and me out of there. I was too angry at the time to go home. I hated my mother for turning me out. I hated the colonel for being a dirty old man, and I hated Donny for betraying me. But, Jase . . ." When she looked up at him, her eyes were brimming with tears. "When I came home the next night, Mama acted like nothing had happened. It wasn't until Crystal came out of her room all smiles and giggles to show me her ruby red velvet dress and to tell me she was going to meet the colonel that I—" Jade coughed back tears. "She told me he wanted to be her daddy like he was my daddy."

Jade shook, her heart wrenching as she relived the night. "Mama was drunk and forbade me to cross her. She said the colonel had a friend down in New Orleans to look out for Crystal. I knew what that meant."

Jase had moved to within a foot of her. "Then what happened?"

She raised her teary eyes to the only man with whom she truly felt a connection. And thought about how now it was based on something more than lust, more than passion, something deeper, more profound than the act of making love. But she couldn't tell him what had happened. He'd hate her, and that she could not stand.

"I took Crystal and ran away to California. I went to work for the original owner of Callahan's, as a house cleaner while I went to school at night. He and his wife took us in. He helped me legally change my name."

"What happened to your mother, Jade?"

"She died that night. The trailer caught on fire. I didn't stop to look back. I just ran."

CHAPTER
13

"Was your mother alive when you left, Jade?"

Lying wouldn't change her plans. He couldn't arrest her just because she admitted to a murder in another state. Could he? "Do you really want the truth, Jase?"

"Yes."

Their gazes clashed and held. "Can you handle the truth?"

"Yes."

She tied the sash tighter around her waist. "When I told Mama that Crystal would leave over my dead body, she slapped me and told me nobody told her what to do. I shoved my mother. She hit her head on the corner of the Formica table. There was blood everywhere. I grabbed Crystal and ran. I never looked back!"

"Jesus Christ, Jade!"

She laughed, the sound hollow, hysterical. "I knew it. You can't handle the truth. Detective Vaughn thinks he can fix all the problems of the world. Well, try and fix this one."

He shook his head. "I can't."

"I know." She sucked in a huge breath and slowly exhaled.

"Jade?"

As if her eyelids were weighted down with lead, she raised them slowly. The salt from her tears burned. "I know. When you have the proof you need, you'll take me back there and have me arrested."

"I'm leaving this afternoon."

She smiled. "I didn't give you enough credit, Detective. You figured it out."

"I saw the video, Jade."

Heat flashed her skin, humiliation choking her. She pointed toward the door. "Get out."

"Jade, I—"

"Get out!" she screamed. "Don't come back here unless you have a warrant for my arrest!"

She ran from the kitchen and when she heard the front door close, she ran down and locked it. Tears blinded her. She felt like a rat caught in a steel trap. She was anchored by her sister and her conscience, yet if she didn't chew her foot off she'd go to jail and lose everything, including her freedom.

What does it matter? she thought. She had nothing but Crystal. But could she face her sister behind bars? Could she watch Jase sit in the courtroom, on the witness stand, telling the court she admitted to killing her mama?

Could she bear his pity, then his anger, then his disgust? What if they tried to pin Otis's murder on her? Would they show the tape? The tape of a fourteen-year-old girl being preyed upon by a twenty-five-year-old gigolo? She'd never confronted Donny. How much did the colonel pay him to seduce her so he could watch and get off?

She picked up the phone and dialed Crystal's number.

"Hello?" a sleepy voice answered.

"Hey, sleepyhead," Jade managed in her brightest voice. "Don't you have class this morning?"

"Not till eleven. Are you okay, sis?"

Jade smiled, her sister's sweet voice cleansing all the bitterness from her life. "I'm doing great. I wanted to tell you, I quit my job, and since you're in college I'm going to take some time to travel."

"Oh my god, Jade! You're finally doing something for yourself? There is a god!"

Jade forced a natural-sounding laugh. "I'm finally taking your advice. I want you to know, just in case anything happens to me, I'm putting everything in your name. Branford is handling it all."

"What do you *mean*, if something happens to you? Where are you going?"

"Where aren't I going is the better question. I'm going to come down tomorrow to see you before I take off. I'm flying out of LAX tomorrow night to Costa Rica. I have a friend who has invited me to stay a few weeks with him." She knew that would seal the deal for Crystal.

"Oh, now I understand. You have a boyfriend!"

"Yes, and stop being such a smarty about it. I found a great guy, and I'm going to give this relationship thing a chance." Jade cringed, hating to lie to her sister, the only family she had left in the world, but she needed to sound convincing.

"What time will you be down?"

"I have a four o'clock flight. I should be to you by six at the latest."

"I can't wait to see you!"

"Me, too," Jade softly said, then said good-bye.

Jade hurried to the shower. She had a busy day ahead of her.

After she left Branford's office, assured that all of the paperwork would be handled, Jade headed back to her house. She felt bad lying to Bran when he asked her if she were planning on leaving the country. She assured him she was not. She was in fact preparing for her possible incarceration. He assured her that would not come to pass. "If you're innocent, Jade, you will not spend a day in jail."

She'd swallowed hard and smiled. She was guilty as hell.

She tried not to think about the life she would live as a fugitive. She tried not to think of the life she would lead void of a man like Jase.

Her feelings for him confused her. It couldn't be love. She had no idea what that meant anymore. Except in the case of Crystal. She had imagined herself in love with Donny, but realized that was a schoolgirl crush, a fatherless girl looking for an older man to take care of her. In all the years since she'd fled Louisiana, she had never met a man she was remotely interested in, until Jase. What did that mean? They had great sex, and he certainly was her match in every way.

Emotionally, they were both mental cases. Physically, they could go at it all night, like rabbits. Intellectually? He was her equal. And if his house, threads, and vehicles were any indicator, he had serious bank.

Could it be possible he wanted more from her as a person than sex? She shook her head, her heart crushing inside her chest. It didn't matter, since, she would never find out.

Turning onto Highway 101, Jade glanced in her rearview mirror to merge and screamed. A black car drove straight up her rear end. She hit the gas but the car hit her hard, the inertia driving her into the far left lane. She bounced off the guardrail and into the car in front of her, causing it to swerve across traffic. She straightened out her car, only to be hit again, this time harder, at a velocity that sent her through the guardrail and into the oncoming traffic on the other side of the highway. It was the last thing she remembered.

Jase was just picking up his carry-on bag to get onto the plane when his cell phone rang. He considered ignoring it. But as he handed the flight attendant his boarding pass, he answered, "Vaughn."

"Jase, it's Ricco. Jade Devereaux has been in an accident."

Jase's blood flashed to freezing. The hair on his arms stood straight up and he felt like a heavyweight boxing match was going on in his gut.

"Is she alive?"

"I think so. They took her over to Valley Memorial."

Jase had already turned around, and now he ran to his car and sped to Valley Memorial, the only trauma ER in the South Bay. He didn't think of the reason that she was there. He just prayed she would be alive when he got to her.

He didn't ponder why his heart felt like it was squeezing dry. He didn't imagine never seeing her again or never touching her. He didn't question his rampant out-of-control, almost hysterical dread at the thought of losing her.

Somewhere in the back of his mind, he knew there would

be a way for them to work things out. He didn't understand why he wanted to. He didn't ask if it was love. He was clueless to what that emotion entailed. He'd never experienced it before, not even for a pet dog. He had always just gone through life servicing his physical needs—and to a point, his emotions—as they came up. He'd never looked past tomorrow, not even with his job. It was why undercover work suited him. No roots, no emotional entanglements, at least not real ones. Easy come, easy go. But when he thought of Jade, he saw them as a couple in the future. It was vague and hazy, but it was the future. As much of a future as he could muster.

He pulled up into an ambo stall and jumped out of his car, then sprinted into the ER. He didn't wait to be asked if he could be helped, but went straight into the trauma unit. The admitting tech yelled at him, but he flashed his badge and she went back to her seat. He grabbed the first white coat he saw. "Jade Devereaux, where is she?"

"And you are?" the doc asked.

When Jase flashed his badge, the doctor inclined his head to the left. "Room four A."

Jase burst into the room and stopped cold in his tracks. Jade lay motionless, her face as pale as the white sheet covering her. An egg-size knot swelled at her temple. He moved cautiously toward her, her name escaping his lips. Her eyelids fluttered open, and she managed a weak smile. She raised a hand, an IV taped to its back. "Shhh," he whispered. "Rest."

She nodded weakly and closed her eyes. The door opened behind him and he turned, expecting to see her doctor. Instead, Kowalski strode in. Jase's hackles instantly rose. "What are you doing here, Kowalski?"

The fat detective smirked and gave Jade a once-over before he dragged his eyes back to Jase. Jase knew exactly what the bastard was thinking.

"I guess I could ask you the same question. But after seeing her in that video, I can guess why."

Jase cocked his arm and punched the pig in the mouth. Kowalski slammed against the glass wall, rattling the room. Jase stepped in for another one. Kowalski put his hands up. "All right! I asked for that!"

"Get out of here, Kowalski, before I make you a permanent part of this place."

Kowalski swiped at his lip, smearing the blood. He looked at his fist and cursed. He grabbed a tissue from the box next to him on the counter. He dabbed at his mouth, eyeing Jase. "I need to know who the hell ran her off the road. I've got three witnesses who said a black sedan rammed her twice, the second time sending her through the median barrier."

"Anyone get a license number?"

Kowalski shook his head. "She was damn lucky she didn't get hit head-on. She ended up sideways in the canal alongside the highway. A bunch of low bushes kept her from slamming into it head-on."

Jase looked back as Jade's eyes fluttered as if she were fighting consciousness. It might be his only chance to find out if she knew who did this. Was it the same guy who'd broken into her house? The one who she had said followed her? The same guy who'd killed the men?

He moved toward her and smoothed back the hair from her face, careful not to touch her erupting bruises. He leaned toward her face and whispered, "Jade, can you hear me?"

Her eyes fluttered open. Her body stiffened and she cried out. "It's okay, baby, you're safe. I won't leave you."

"Jase?"

Jase looked up at Kowalski and scowled. The detective had the good judgment to look a little chagrined. "Yes, it's me. Jade, I need you to tell me who did this."

"Same car that followed—me. Told you."

Guilt creamed his heart. He'd written off her tales of being followed as a simple red herring tact.

Her eyes fluttered open. She smiled weakly. "I pulled over and got out, I scared him away."

Jase felt like a colossal lump of shit for doubting her. "He came back, Jade. Did you recognize the driver?"

She closed her eyes and shook her head slowly. "No, he was in dark clothes and a baseball cap. Could have been a woman. Not that big."

"Are you sure it was the same car as before?"

She nodded.

"Do you know what model? Old, new? Distinguishing marks?"

"All black. Black windows and no hubcaps. No license plate. It was ugly."

Jase looked up at Kowalski, who was writing it all down. At that moment, a white coat walked in. He gave both men a scowl. "Gentlemen, are either one of you family?" In tandem, Jase and Kowalski flashed their badges. "You can leave then. My patient needs her rest."

"No," Jade whispered. "Jase, stay."

Jase raised a brow at the doc and then smirked at Kowalski, who obviously wanted to be included. "Whichever one of you is Jase can stay." The doc looked pointedly at Kowalski. "The other needs to scram."

Kowalski put his notepad into his breast pocket. "I'll be waiting outside, Detective Vaughn."

"By all means, Detective Kowalski, wait as long as you'd like."

The doctor flipped open the chart he'd pulled off the door, made some marks, and turned to look at Jade. Gently, he touched her arm. Jase broke the tense silence. "What's the damage, Doc?"

"Miss Devereaux?"

"It's okay, tell him," Jade said, her voice barely audible.

"You have a contusion on your right temple, a concussion, and four broken ribs. You also have seat belt burn, and you can thank it for saving your life. Without it, you would have been a bullet through the windshield. You're lucky to be alive."

"What does she need to do?" Jase asked.

"She needs to manage her pain, rest, and not do anything strenuous for six to eight weeks, until her ribs heal."

"When can she leave?"

"Tomorrow morning. She'll need a ride home and someone to watch over her for a few days until her pain is manageable."

The doc looked at Jade and asked, "How is your pain level now?"

"I'm feeling no pain," she slowly said.

"Good. I'm going to give you a sedative shortly. It should get you through the night. Is there anyone you'd like me to call?"

Jade closed her eyes and shook her head, then barely perceptibly, she said, "There is no one to call."

The doc looked up at Jase and he nodded. "I'll take her home and stay with her until she can be alone."

Jase didn't have to think twice about what to do. He'd call in and take a few personal days, put off his travel plans for the time being, and take Jade home to his house and tend her.

By day two, Jade was howling mad because Jase wouldn't allow her to do anything but sit in bed and eat off a tray. By day three, she refused to take any pain meds and demanded he allow her to go home. He relented only when she begged for a real bath instead of the sponge baths he had insisted on.

His attention and lack of sexual interest surprised her. When he drew her bath and he helped her into the hot soapy water, she cooed like a baby. Her ribs were tender but she was healthy and getting stronger by the hour. The luxurious bubbles surrounded her and she happily luxuriated in the oversize tub. Several moments later, the thick movement of water indicated company.

She opened her eyes and watched Jase sink naked into the frothy bubbles. Her heart fluttered in her belly. He was such a man. And, for the moment, her man.

"I was wondering when that libido of yours would kick in."

Jase grinned like the bad boy he was. "My libido has been just fine, thank you, and you can beg all you want. But no sex for you until your ribs are healed."

"Ha! I'll bet you won't get out of the tub with that erection of yours intact."

Jase grinned and slid close to her. "If I don't, it will be by my own hand." He scooped up two handfuls of lathery bubbles. "I think, though, you need some help bathing. I'm here to help."

Jade smiled and carefully turned around in the tub, presenting her back to him. "Be gentle."

Jase extended his legs and gently brought Jade against his chest, where she semireclined. His erection speared her in the back. She smiled when Jase rubbed against her and groaned.

He lathered up the soap in his big hands and slowly he spread them across her skin. He was careful around her ribs, but when his hands, slick with lather, crossed over her breasts, Jade gasped. The hitch in her breath hurt, but the feel of his fingers playing with her nipples was worth it. She wanted his mouth on her. She wanted to turn around and slide down on him.

It took every ounce of restraint she possessed not to arch her back when his mouth laved down the side of her neck, or when his hands submerged beneath the water and caressed her thighs. She opened her legs in a wanton display. "Please, Jase, touch me there."

His fingers swept softly across her mound. Jade closed her eyes, forgetting her pain. Jase steadied her from behind, his left hand pressed against her belly while his right hand played with her slick folds. She wanted to open wider and arch, giving him greater access to her body, but the pain was too intense. She settled for his light petting, his wanton mouth, and his erection rocking against her back.

"Jase, let me turn around."

The tension in his body lessened. Carefully, she got up on her knees and turned around, his blue eyes boring into her and his glorious erection standing up straight and proud. As much as she wanted to slide onto him, she knew the minute she did her body would tense in sublime pleasure and her ribs would protest in sharp pain.

She settled on the other side of the big round tub facing him and smiled. "Touch yourself, Jase."

He didn't need to be told twice. He wrapped a big hand around his erection. "I wish that was your hand." Slowly, he pumped. "Or those sweet lips of yours."

His body jerked and he moved his hand faster, his strokes long and sure.

Heat generated at her core and just as swiftly as Jase's hand moved up and down his shaft, it infiltrated her nerve endings. Her hips responded in silent rhythm.

"Jase, that turns me on, watching you like that."

"Touch yourself, Jade."

She hesitated only a brief moment before she touched her fingertip to a nipple. It hardened. Jase groaned, the sound of his enjoyment dissolving her modesty. Her hands cupped both her breasts and rubbed them as Jase's hand moved faster up and down his burgeoning shaft. His eyes speared her, the planes of his face hardened in sexual tension.

She wanted to touch him, to be the one to make him come. Jade slid up on her knees and moved toward Jase. His eyes widened and he slowly shook his head. "Don't tell me no, I'll stop if it hurts."

Carefully, she positioned herself over him. When she lowered herself to him and he impaled her, she sucked in a breath and yipped as a stab of pain zinged her.

"Stop, sweetheart, I don't want to hurt you."

She opened her eyes and smiled. Taking his face into her hands, she brought his lips to hers and kissed him, and she slowly moved down the long length of him. The sensation of him filling her up was almost more than she could humanly bear. If she died right now, she could not feel more content.

"You feel so good, Jase."

His wet arms slid around her waist, steadying her. He nuzzled her breasts. The urge to flex, to arch, to give more of herself to him had her at her breaking point. But he steadied her, and slowly he moved beneath her, doing all the work.

The undulation of their bodies sloshed the water up and over the tub. Jade wrapped her arms tightly around Jase's neck, digging her fingers into his damp hair, wanting to be as close to him as humanly possible, ignoring the pain in her ribs. She wanted him more than it hurt not to.

Their lips met, their tongues clashed, and their bodies slammed against each other. "Jade," Jase breathed as he thrust deep into her, "I promise you, we'll work everything out."

He kissed her then and she felt the overwhelming urge to weep. He meant it, and she truly believed that if any man could come to her rescue it would be Jase. But she didn't fool herself. This time together would be their last time together.

Her orgasm hit her hard. Her body stiffened and she cried out in sublime pain. Jase came right after, pushing up into her, his fingers digging into her ass, steadying her while one spasm racked through his body after another.

The next morning, Jade woke to find her head resting in the crook of Jase's arm. He was on his back, snoring softly. She smiled and would have reached up to kiss his lips but the movement would have caused her too much discomfort. It occurred to her that for the first time in her life someone was taking care of her and asking for nothing in return. Well, except that she lie in bed and get better.

She almost believed what he said last night, that it would work out. That there would be a "them" when she recovered. But she remembered her plans. And he would be on the next plane to Louisiana in less than twenty-four hours. If she had any intention of staying, she'd have a big problem with that. As it was, she was not.

She'd agreed that she would stay at his place while he was gone, but when he returned she would be in Costa Rica. Jade hated lying to Jase. She let him think he'd find vindicating evidence in Sykesville. That way he'd go on his journey of closed doors, thinking she awaited his return with her 'get out of jail free' card.

She'd called Tina the day Jase brought her to his home and explained she had been in a very minor fender bender and that was what had kept her. And while her sister had insisted on flying up and tending her, Jade assured her there was no need to. When Jade called Tina later in the day, she would tell her she'd be down the following day. Jade didn't know how she would manage to sit in an airplane for the hour or so it would take to fly down, or even manage her luggage. *Forget the luggage,* she thought. She forgot she had enough money to buy ten wardrobes.

And so that was the plan. Jase was leaving later in the morning. She'd argued with him, asking what the point was to go, but he insisted that he needed to know all of the facts.

It didn't matter. She would be long gone when he returned and he would not be able to arrest her.

When Jase kissed her good-bye, he did it slowly. When he ended it, he took her face into his hands and whispered, "I don't know how, Jade, but somehow this will all work out. I promise."

Tears welled; they came easy these days. She smiled and

knew that while he believed he was her knight in shining armor, he could not cast a spell and erase her past.

The hot Louisiana air hit Jase like a sheet of plywood when he exited the terminal. He rented a car and headed north on the interstate toward Sykesville. He'd made contact with Sheriff Taylor. The old boy remembered quite clearly the death of Ruby Leigh's mother and said he'd be happy to chat about it. And by the way, Sheriff Taylor asked, did the detective know where Ruby Leigh was these days? There was a warrant out for her arrest for the murder of her mama . . .

Two hours later, Jase sat in the office of the good ol' boy who had been sheriff for more than two decades.

"Now, tell me again who you are?" he asked Jase.

For the second time, Jase showed the rotund man his ID. "I'm working on a homicide that may involve your Ruby Leigh Gentry. I'm here to find out if the suspect we have using an assumed name is one and the same. Do you have pictures of Miss Gentry?"

"As a matter of fact, I do. You gonna tell me Ruby Leigh's new name?"

Jase grinned and nodded, but his smile faded as Taylor slid him pictures of Ruby Leigh in middle school. There was no denying the similarities. It was Jade, unless she had a twin. Next, Taylor slid pictures of Bobbie Jean Gentry and the sister across the desk. Luckily for Jade, she didn't resemble her mother. Except for the eyes. Those big green eyes were prominent in all three of the Gentry women.

"How'd she die, Sheriff?"

"Not sure if she died from the blunt trauma to her head or if the fire did it. Either way, she didn't die of natural causes.

Witnesses say they heard Ruby screamin' at her mama." He opened a file folder, shuffled some papers, and read, "'I won't let you do it to Crystal. I'll kill you first.'"

"And what do you suppose Ruby meant by that?"

The sheriff shrugged his wide shoulders. His cheeks flushed red. He suddenly found the floor more interesting than looking Jase in the eye. "We live in a depressed area, Detective Vaughn, ain't much that keeps us going except for the few oil fields still wet. The colonel had two on his property, an' he owned the mineral rights to 'em. He kept the locals employed."

"So, because of that, you all turned the other cheek while he exploited underage girls?"

"Now, listen here, son—"

Jase stood up and swiped his hand over his face. "Let me get this straight. You stand by and let Bobbie Jean Gentry turn her fourteen-year-old daughter over to a dirty old man, and then when her mother wants to turn the seven-year-old sister over to him, too, and her big sister has a problem with it, you all have a problem with *that*?"

"Well, sonny boy, if Ruby had stuck around for us to question her, maybe she would have shed some light on the topic." He scratched his big belly. "Coz 'round here, even us Southern folk know two plus two equals four. And since we're that smart, we figured that added up to Ruby Leigh killin' her mama to protect her sister. So don't think I don't have a problem with the threats, Detective, I just have a problem with the fact that the girl carried them out."

"How do you know the old bat didn't fall and hit her head?"

"Maybe she did, but she didn't set that fire. There were accelerants used. It was deliberate."

"How long after the fight did the place go up in smoke?"

"Well, I don't rightly know."

"How can you *not* rightly know? If what Jade—er, Ruby says is true, after the fight, she took her sister and ran and never looked over her shoulder. That would mean someone else set the fire. What was the official cause of death?"

The old sheriff sat back in his old wooden chair, the slats groaning under his considerable weight. "The coroner's report was inconclusive, the body was so badly burned. But the skull showed definite signs of blunt trauma. Entire back of the head bashed in. Witnesses said after the screaming, there was the fire."

"I'll bet you my pension Bobbie Jean Gentry was alive when that fire was started, and it wasn't Ruby who started it."

"Well, now, son, why don't you bring that girl back here and we'll figure it all out?"

"I plan to, Sheriff Taylor, but before I do I want all of the facts. How well did you know Otis Thibodeaux?"

"Well enough. He took over the running of the oil fields when his daddy the colonel died suddenly. He wasn't the good soul like his pa, though."

"You call a man who buys girls from their hard-luck parents 'a good soul'? C'mon, now, Sheriff. Even in California we aren't that deviant."

The sheriff pushed his ponderous bulk up from the groaning chair. "I don't need to take your insults, son. See your way out."

"I apologize for that. Had you heard old Otis kicked the bucket in sunny California?"

Taylor squinted and blew a low breath out. "Let me guess, your two plus two equals Ruby Leigh Gentry."

"Maybe."

Jase left the station and jumped into his rental car. The heat was oppressive and the AC in the small car didn't work. Afterward, he took his map and headed down to the old trailer park where Ruby Leigh Gentry had grown up. As he pulled up to the third-rate motor park, he cringed. From the derelict looks of the place, it wasn't fit to house animals. He drove past it to the paved road that he knew lead to Bleak Hill, the colonel's palatial plantation house.

Jase whistled as he pulled up into the big circular drive. The large white house rose from the verdant greenery around it, the doric columns holding up a large wraparound veranda. It looked just like he envisioned the colonel: old, overfed, and lazy. Despite that, the house held more than a hint of grandeur. It must have been very intimidating to a fourteen-year-old girl. The pervert that owned it would have been, too.

He gave the rental some gas and headed back down the paved road to the Last Chance Mobile Home Park. No shit. It sure lived up to its name.

He drove down to spot number 31. Another trailer, a puny single-wide, sat on the cinder-block foundation. He got out of the car and walked up to the trailer on the spot next to it and knocked on the rickety door that hung from one hinge. An ancient snaggletoothed woman answered the door. She was so hunched over, her upper torso was horizontal with the ground. "Wha' chu want, Fancy Shoes?"

Jase bent over to make eye contact and flashed his badge. "I'm Detective Jason Vaughn, from California."

"Lordy, lordy, what does a fancy detective want with the likes of us here in Sykesville?"

"I want to ask you about Ruby Leigh Gentry and her sister, Crystal."

"A ha! Ruby done settled in California? She always was too smart for the likes of us."

"Do you remember the last night she was here?"

"I remember. Do you want me to tell you out here in this heat, or do you want to come in where it's cooler?"

Jase smiled. As she ushered him in, the screaming swamp cooler did little to cool the stuffy confines of the trailer. It smelled like fried catfish and pickles.

"You want some mint tea? I just brewed a fresh pot."

Jase smiled. "I'd love a glass."

She got busy in the tiny kitchen right next to one of the two chairs in the tiny space. He looked down at what may have been a hallway and saw a futon-type bed at the end. Despite the shabbiness of the abode, everything was neat and clean and in its place. "My name's Millie, Millie Saunders."

"Nice to meet you, Miss Millie."

She chuckled and bustled into the room, handing him a glass of iced tea. "Nice to see a young man with manners." She hoisted her glass and took a long drink before she sat in the overstuffed chair next to his. "Now, why you come 'round here asking about Ruby Leigh?"

"I want to know what happened to her mother."

"She done died, fried right next door, some eleven years ago."

"Can you tell me what you remember?"

"'Course. I might be gettin' up in years, but the old noggin still works." She grinned and tapped her head.

Jase waited patiently.

"All right, so it's suppertime. I hear ol' Bobbie Jean yelling at Ruby Leigh to hurry up and get in the trailer, she done got a surprise for her. Ruby's a good girl. I never paid no never mind to her goin' up the hill to the colonel's. Ruby knew if it weren't for what she done, her baby sister would have up and died of that cough of hers. Ruby never complained. And Bobbie rode her hard every chance she got. That poor girl deserved more than she got. And her mama got just what she deserved. Why, drinkin' an' whorin' all those years sucked her dry. She—"

"Miss Millie? What happened that night?"

"Oh, yes, 'course. Well, after Ruby done gone into the trailer, I heard her yelling at her mama. Telling her no, she wasn't gonna let no friend of the colonel's take care of Crystal. Said her mama would have to kill her afore she let that happen. Well, one thing you didn't do was back talk Bobbie Jean, 'specially when she'd been drinking, which was pretty much any time of the day. I heard a hard slap, and then the baby cryin'. There was quiet for a while after that. I thought Ruby done took her sister and skeedaddled. But I looked out front there and saw Ruby pacing the dirt yard. When she went in a few minutes later I heard yellin' an' screamin', then she run out with Crystal and took off for the woods with only the clothes on their backs. Haven't seen hide nor hair of either of them since."

"Millie, I want you to think real hard about my next question. Did anyone else come into the trailer after Ruby left? Did you hear anyone or anything before or after the fire?"

Millie scrunched her face up and scratched her chin. "I reckon I did hear some screamin'. Most likely Eda Mae and Herbert. Those two were always slapping each other, then making up. I don't know what was worse, the screamin' or the caterwauling!" Her old eyes narrowed. "You think someone came in and finished Bobbie Jean off?"

"Why didn't you tell Sheriff Taylor about the screams right before the fire?"

"Well, he never asked me, and—it just didn't occur to me until this minute that it may have been Bobbie Jean. I figured it must have been Eda Mae behind me. Her and her old man were always a fightin'. Then makin' up, but when I think back to that night, they didn't come outta their trailer. Prolly 'cause they weren't home."

CHAPTER
14

Jase headed back to the sheriff's office. The good ol' boy looked up from the open file on his desk. Jase noticed it was the Gentry file. "I didn't figure you'd be back so soon, Detective."

"I just had an interesting conversation with Millie Saunders. She said she heard screams right before Ruby and her sister fled, then about an hour later more screams before the trailer went up in flames."

The sheriff sat back in his chair and pushed back his sweat-stained cowboy hat. "I suppose I'd scream if I was on fire."

"My point exactly. Bobbie Jean was alive and well an hour after Ruby left. I bet you a case of those cigars you like that Ruby didn't come back."

"Now, tell me why old Millie would tell you she heard screams, but didn't tell me?"

"She said she thought at the time it was Eda Mae behind

her fighting with her husband, like they did every other night. But it wasn't until later that she realized that Eda Mae and her hubby weren't even home. I took the liberty of asking Eda Mae, and she said they were up visiting her sister in Arkansas and didn't come home until the day after the fire."

The sheriff scratched his chin. "Well, that may be true, but all the evidence points to Ruby killing her mama."

"Where was the body?"

"It was in the bedroom, by what was left of the door."

"According to Ruby, she and her mother argued. She pushed her mother in the kitchen, where she hit her head on the Formica table. Not getting it bashed in from behind in the bedroom. Sheriff, would you mind letting me look at that file?" Jase asked, pointing to it.

Taylor gave him a narrowed glare.

"The life of a woman is at stake here. And you owe it to her to make this right."

"Either way, son, you need to bring that girl back here."

"I realize that, sir. I hope the next time she leaves Louisiana, she leaves a free woman."

Taylor looked long and hard at Jase, then slid the manila folder across his desk to him. "You got thirty minutes, boy. Then I want you outta here and I don't want to see you again unless you have Ruby Leigh Gentry with you."

Jase nodded and opened the file.

As she tossed the last of her cosmetics into her suitcase, Jade debated answering her cell phone. She looked at the LCD: *Private Caller.* What the hell, she was going to be history in a few hours.

"Hello," she answered as she crooked the phone between her ear and shoulder, continuing to toss products into her bag.

"Jade, it's Mac."

Jade tightened her grip on the phone. "Hello, Mac."

"I thought you might want to know, Genny is in the hospital. She tried to kill herself."

Jade dropped the bottle of Chanel No. 5 in her hand. "Oh my god! Is she going to be all right?"

"I'm not sure. Her brother called me. He's pretty upset. She's at Valley Memorial."

"I'll go by to see her, but she may not want to talk to me."

"I think you might be surprised. It may do her good."

"Thanks, Mac."

Jade hung up the phone, guilt riddling her thoughts. What had she done? Should she have given Genny another chance? She hurried and dressed, taking care not to move too fast. Who was she not to give Genny a second chance? Had Sam not given her a second chance, who knows where she and Tina would be? No, she owed it to Genny to at least stop by and see her, and to apologize. And to tell her she would recommend her for her job. It would be up to Genny and Jack Morton what happened then.

"Genny?"

Genny opened her eyes, the haze of drugs blurring her vision. She tried to smile. Her fingers wiggled and he took her hand. His warmth gave her strength.

"How do you feel, sis?"

Genny licked her dry lips and tried to focus. Her brother's red hair glowed molten under the shards of sunlight that managed to slip through the curtains in her room. He was a good brother.

"What happened, Dickie?"

"You took a lot of pills. Why'd you do that? Why'd you try to leave me?"

Genny closed her eyes for a moment, then slowly opened them, tears brimming. "I've failed us. I got fired."

"It's okay, Genny."

"No! It isn't! I can't support us, Dickie. All of Daddy's insurance money is gone. I—I didn't want to tell you." Great racking sobs crashed through her chest. Her world had come to such an abrupt halt. "I feel like such a failure." She looked up through her tear-filled eyes to her brother's solemn face. Even through the thick haze of tears, she saw anger spark in his eyes. He was blaming himself somehow. "I begged Jade for a second chance, but she told me no," Genny sobbed. "I don't know how I can take care of us."

Dickie's hand tightened around hers. "I never wanted you to work there. I told you those men only wanted one thing from you. I watched them lust after you every night. But I still have my job. I'll take care of us."

Genny tightened her grip on his hands. "Jade doesn't know you're my brother. We can't tell her, she'll fire you, too, for lying."

His voice took on the low measured tone of a man in control. "I'm not worried about Jade Devereaux. I fooled her, playing the poor pathetic Rusty. I'll continue to fool that bitch."

Genny stiffened and looked up at him. Her chest squeezed. She'd never heard that tone in his voice or seen anger in his eyes. Suddenly, she felt afraid for Jade. "Dickie, honey, don't be mad at Jade. She's a good person. I was stupid. I broke the biggest rule she had. When I feel better, I'm going to ask her for my job back."

"No, Genny. Those men will only force you again."

"But we need the money. And," she sighed, "the truth is, I really don't mind. I like the attention."

His eyes sparked like wildfire and he stepped away from her to the other side of the room. His hands clenched open and closed. He began to pace the small area of the room in slow jerky steps. "I've always given you attention. Isn't that enough?" he accused.

Genny strained to smile as pieces of her shattered life slowly fell into place. Did he mean . . . ? "You're—my brother, Dickie, and yes, you've given me lots of attention, and I love you for it. But I want a lover."

He moved closer to her, his shadow falling over her face. His big brown eyes were bright, his nostrils flared in excitement. His fingers stroked the back of her hand. "I love you, sweet sister. I'll take care of you now. You'll never have to let another man touch you again."

Genny's fingers flinched as his touch grew stronger. He hovered over her, his eyes intense. "No," she whispered, understanding. "Not like that, Dickie. It's wrong."

His eyes hardened, his lips drew taut. His fingers pressed harder into her skin. "You call what you did with Townsend in the back of the club right? And that Japanese guy? The one with the little prick? Sucking him for cash was right?"

Genny tried to pull away from him, but his fingers tightened around her wrist. Her blood pressure spiked. Bile rose in her throat. "And that piece of shit Otis? The things he made you do to him?"

"Dickie, how do you know about them?"

"I watched you and Townsend, the pig. The drunk didn't even have the decency to call you by your name! He called out Jade's name as he came in your mouth."

"Did—?"

"I couldn't let him live after disrespecting you that way. Then I thought maybe if the club got shut down, you wouldn't do that nasty stuff with any of those men. When that didn't slow down business, I went after Hiro. Jade had a turn with him before I got to him. She's a whore, Genny! She's whore, and she fired you for the same thing!"

Genny started to cry. "Dickie, you killed those men? Why?"

"I wanted you to stop! I don't want you fucking other men! You're mine!"

Genny yanked her hands from his grip and put them over her ears. "Stop this! It can't be that way. *Ever.* Even if you weren't my brother I wouldn't want you that way. I can't—I can't be with you now, even if I wanted to. You're a murderer!"

He pulled her hands down and leaned into her. "I did it for you! For us! I have money saved, we can go away."

She moved as far from the crazed look in his eyes as she could in the narrow bed.

"Jade did this," he whispered. He turned blank eyes to her. He began his agitated pacing again. Genny lay in the bed, terrified that if she argued with him he would hurt her. He mumbled to himself, his voice raging then lowering, as if he were arguing with another person in the room. Genny realized her brother was far more disturbed than the doctors ever suspected. "Dickie?" she softly called. As if he were alone in the room, he continued his pacing. Slowly, she

275

reached down the sheet to where the call button was. As she was about to grab it, he turned on her. His eyes had a far-away vacant look in them.

"Jade turned you against me." His tone was closed, clipped, leaving no room for argument. He slid the button from her hand and yanked it out of the wall. "Yes, she did." He nodded. "She made you like this."

"No, Dickie, Jade has nothing to do with me. She's worked hard for her sister, just like I've worked hard for you. It's what family does, not—what you want. It's not right. I could never be more to you than a sister."

His eyes glittered now. She could see the wheels turning. "Please, leave Jade out of this," she begged.

"I have no intention of going after Jade. I hurt her enough when I ran her off the road."

Genny gasped. "You did that? You—" Genny weakly pushed at him. He didn't budge. "Get out of here. Get out of here and never come back. I hate what you've done."

Dickie moved away, his eyes going blank again before they cleared. He smiled, sanity replacing the twisted, crazed look. "I will always love you, Genny. Never forget that."

He took her hand and kissed it. "Good-bye."

"What are you going to do, Dickie?"

"An eye for an eye, sweet sister, an eye for an eye."

He turned and ran from the room. Genny started to scream.

Jade's cell phone rang. "Hello?"

"Jade Devereaux?"

"Yes?"

"This is Dr. Hernandez at Valley Memorial. Miss Monroe requested I call you and ask you to get here posthaste. She's quite hysterical, we need to sedate her, but she insists on speaking to you first. Room two forty-five."

"I'm on my way now. I'll be there in ten minutes."

Jade rushed into the hospital. She wasn't sure what to expect, but it certainly wasn't Genny pacing her room. The minute Jade walked in, Genny cried out and threw her arms around her. Jade flinched, the pain of the embrace tweaking her sore ribs. Genny didn't notice and Jade endured it. "Oh my god, Jade. It's Dickie. He killed those men, and I think he's after Tina!"

"Who is Dickie?"

"Rusty!"

Jade's entire body went rigid. Her adrenaline spiked and she felt no pain. Her stomach twisted as bile shot through it.

"How does he know where she is?"

"Otis had the picture. He must have told Dickie before he was killed. I don't know if he is, but you have to warn her."

Jade shook Genny and pushed her to sit down on the edge of the bed. "Calm down and tell me what's going on. *Everything*, from the beginning."

When Genny finished her story, Jade called Tina. No answer. *Shit.* Then she called Jase. No answer. *Double shit.* She left a message telling him where she was going. Her flight was leaving in less than an hour. She would be on campus in less than three hours.

Jade called Tina again and got her voicemail. She left her a message instructing her to leave the dorm, go to a safe house, anywhere, and to stay put until she got down there and called her back.

Jade was nervous the entire flight down. She had the uncomfortable feeling that she was being watched, but when she looked around there were only passengers too busy with their own thoughts to pay her any mind.

She went to the rental car kiosk. As she was getting into her car, her alarm bells shrilled. Rusty slipped into the passenger seat and gone was the half-addled teenage boy. In his place, a cool menacing killer held a gun trained on her heart. Jade swallowed hard and forced her blood pressure to stabilize. In her injured condition, she could not hope to overpower the man beside her. Once again, she would have to outwit a man to survive.

"Hey, boss lady, let's go. I can't wait to meet your little sister."

When Jade didn't move, he jammed the gun into her chest and leaned into her. His breath stank, and his brown eyes burned bright with crazed glee. "Start the car, and drive normal. I have nothing left to lose, Jade, so if you try something, we both go down in flames."

Jade started the car, put it in gear, and slowly drove from the parking lot.

"The cops will be there, Rusty."

"No, they won't. You're public enemy number one." He leaned closer and softly said, "By the way, my name is Richard."

She looked straight ahead. "I guess you'll find out the hard way, then."

Richard settled back into the seat. "Nice try, Jade. Or should I call you 'Ruby Leigh Gentry'?"

He laughed when she stiffened and groaned in pain. "I knew you were a whore at heart. Otis showed me your video and told me about all the nasty things his daddy did to you.

Then you had the nerve to fire my sister for a blow job? Hypocritical bitch!"

"My past doesn't change the fact that the cops will be there."

"No, they won't. You didn't call them. You don't want to get arrested for killing your mama."

Touché. "I guess you don't know me that well, then. I'll go to jail for my crimes before I'll risk my sister's life."

"You're lying."

Jade's confidence built. Let him underestimate her. "I guess we'll just have to see about that, won't we?"

Richard settled back comfortably in the bucket seat and flashed a false smile. "In the meantime, sweet Jade, why don't you tell me more about yourself."

She kept her eyes focused on the highway ahead, refusing to be drawn in by him. "I think you know enough about me."

"Tell me how you killed your mother."

Jade pursed her lips and continued to look straight ahead.

Richard wasn't so easily put off. He dug the nose of the gun into her right temple. "Tell me."

Jade clenched her jaw and slowly exhaled. What did it matter? "I pushed her, she fell and hit her head on the corner of the kitchen table, and bled to death. I didn't stick around to help out."

"Otis told me you burned her up."

Jade looked at him perplexed. "I didn't start the fire."

"Cops think you did."

Jade shrugged and kept her eyes on the road. "It doesn't matter. I hit her, she fell and cracked her head open. There was lots of blood."

Richard snickered.

Jade glanced at him, then turned her attention back to the road.

"What?"

"It's amazing how perception can completely distort the truth."

Jade nodded. Perception was what kept her alive all these years. The perception that she was someone worlds away from who she really was.

"Why did you kill Townsend?" she asked.

"He called my sister your name as he was coming in her mouth. I think that was pretty rude. Then I watched him come on to you in the parking lot. You were slick stabbing him. I finished him. If anyone asked, well, you *had* threatened to cut off his balls and shove them down his throat. How could I resist such a superb ending for such a superb piece of shit?"

"So you killed Townsend because he disrespected Genny?"

"That was the trigger, but after I thought about it, I figured, what a great way to shut down the club. And if the club was shut down, then my sister wouldn't have to turn tricks to pay for tuition. I heard what Jack Morton told you to do with Hiro. And you proved you were the whore I knew you were. I didn't give my sister a chance to get dissed by that little prick. I went in right after you. The guy thought I was you coming back for more. I surprised him."

Jade's belly did several slow flops at Richard's confession. Would Jase know the truth about her in the end? Desperately, she wanted him to know she had no hand in the Callahan's murders. She swallowed hard and asked, "And Otis?"

"Well, now, Otis did the same thing to my Genny. He

fucked her and screamed out your name the entire time. Then he slapped her around. Imagine my anger." Richard laughed. "But Otis had a lot to say before he died. Some of it might interest you, but you'll never know. I want to see you burn."

"Why do you want to hurt my sister?"

"I don't want to hurt her, I want to take her away from you, permanently, just like you took Genny away from me. She thinks I'm a monster, you know." Richard's hand wavered and he coughed back a small sob. "All I ever did was love her. I soothed away her tears all those times Father hurt her, sticking that sweet little-girl body of hers with his big ugly cock. He was disgusting! She let me hold her and kiss away her tears. When she was twelve and cried in my arms that she was going to kill herself before she let him touch her again, I made sure she would never have to take her life."

"You killed your father?"

"I cut his balls off and shoved them down his throat, Jade. Just like you threatened to do to Townsend. Is that poetic justice or what?" He laughed, the sound high and grating. "I'd say great minds think alike, but you're a whore."

As Jade pulled onto the SDSU campus, Richard told her to slow down. "Don't try anything, I know which dorm is Crystal's. I also know you have a key to it."

"How did you know her real name?"

"As I said, Otis was quite talkative before I killed him."

"Crystal has a roommate."

Richard smiled and shook his head. "Come on now, Jade, I'm not a complete moron. I know you pay extra for a private suite."

As Jade parked the car, her cell phone rang. It was Jase.

She went to answer and Richard clamped his hand over hers. "Don't answer it."

Jade gritted her teeth, resisting the urge to break out of the car and make a run for it. Although it was evening, there were plenty of students on campus. The last thing she wanted was more blood on her hands. They walked to Tina's suite. When she said she had no key, Richard grabbed her purse and pulled out her key chain. He thrust it at her. "Open the door."

Jade prayed Tina had gotten her message, but if she were in her room, Jade would become a human shield and kill Richard Monroe herself.

The room was empty. Jade breathed a huge sigh of relief. Richard shoved her inside and locked the door behind them. For a dorm suite it was small: the requisite single bed, desk, closet, and bathroom. But the room smelled like her sister, sweet and innocent. Pictures of her and Jade littered the walls and her desk. Her laptop was gone and Jade noticed the room was in some disarray. Hopefully, Tina had gotten her message, grabbed her things, then took off.

Was it too much to hope Jase was on his way?

They had sat for two hours in the room, neither speaking, when it occurred to Richard that maybe Tina was not coming back. He looked in her bathroom and cursed. Her toiletries were gone. His eyes swept the desktop, then landed on Jade's gaze. "You warned her."

"What else would you have had me do?"

Richard stepped toward her, his arm raised. She didn't flinch. She sat erect, her eyes challenging. "Just go ahead and kill me, Richard, get it over with."

He moved closer and ran the nose of the barrel down the side of her face. "That would be too easy. I want you to feel my pain. Everything I did, I did for Genny. Like you did for Tina. How come you get to keep your sister when you took mine away from me?"

"Rus—Richard, I didn't make Genny's choices for her."

He laughed. "How can you say that? You encouraged all of those girls to put out. And you led by prime example!" His face twisted in ugly anger. "Now you're going to know how it feels to lose the only person in the world who matters to you."

"Genny is alive!"

"I'm dead to her. You did that, Jade. All I wanted was for her to love me, to let me take care of her. I took out all of the people who hurt her, and now *she hates me for it*."

"It wasn't my fault."

"*It is!* You fired her! She almost died because of you!"

"I didn't make Genny's choices, Richard. She did."

"That's right. I forgot you're better than everyone because you pulled yourself out of the whorehouse! Well, you're the same as us. Now you pay!"

He looked wildly around the room. "Call your sister."

"I—"

"Call her! I want her here, in twenty minutes!"

Reluctantly, Jade dialed Tina's number. When her sister answered, Jade screamed, "Stay where you are!" Richard ripped the phone from her, the Glock trained on her head. "Hey, Crystal, my name is Richard Monroe, and I want to meet you. I'm at your dorm room. Come over now or Big Sister dies. And don't bring any friends." He hung up.

A minute later, Jade's phone rang. It was Tina. Her captor answered, "Yes, Crystal?"

"I'll come, but meet me across the quad in the music lobby," the girl shakily said.

"You aren't in any position to be making demands, little girl."

Jade heard the fear in her sister's voice, but also the steel that bound them together.

"I—I don't want any of my dormmates to get hurt. The music building is quiet this time of night. No one will see you."

"Who knows I'm talking to you?"

"No one," she cried. "I did what Jade told me, I went somewhere with no one around. Please, just let my sister go. I can give you money, I can give you whatever you want."

"I want you, Crystal. Just you, an even trade."

Through her tears, Crystal said, "I'll meet you there in ten minutes."

When Tina closed her cell phone, she looked up at the detective, her big green eyes as expressive as her sister's. "Promise me you won't let him hurt Jade."

Jase smiled slowly and squeezed her shoulder. "I promise." He turned to the gathered group of campus police and said, "Let's go."

The sergeant in charge nodded, then said, "If it goes to shit, we're going in."

"I appreciate the professional courtesy, Sergeant. If you ever need it up my way, consider the favor returned."

Luckily for Jase, he'd worked with Sergeant Munson on a UC drug case a few years ago at a nearby campus. Under normal circumstance, the locals would have told him to take a backseat, but Jase had explained the facts of life and had been given the green light to proceed on his own.

Quickly, Jase went over the plan with Tina. She was to get Monroe as close to the large window as possible and to stand sideways and as far away from him as she could for the sniper to get a clear shot. She was also miked. Jase would come in the rear and try to take Monroe out if the sniper couldn't get a clear shot. If that failed? Munson would step in.

Jade prayed for rescue as Richard used her as a human shied, ducking and moving her in tight circles while keeping to the darker shadows as they worked their way the short distance to the auditorium lobby.

As he shoved Jade inside, her hopes of rescue crashed. Her adrenaline spiked so high as she watched her baby sister—the one she had spent her life protecting—walk right into death's jaws, she heaved. Richard quickly tied her hands with curtain cord he'd ripped from the wall as spasms racked her body, then pushed her down to the floor. Jade felt completely helpless.

As Tina walked closer to the large glass door, Jade's adrenaline came around and spiked again, and she rolled on her ass with as sweep of her outstretched legs, kicking Richard in the back of the calves, causing him to lose his balance. He screamed and hit the floor hard. When he put his hands out to break his fall, his gun skittered across the linoleum floor. He rolled over and moved to his hands and feet, scurrying across the floor like a crab. He grabbed the gun, rolled over, aimed at her, and pulled the trigger.

The loud crack of the gun discharging sounded hollow and somehow far away in the big empty room. Jade heard screams and realized they were coming from her. Her chest constricted as her lungs compressed, expelling air. The velocity of the bullet when it struck sent her flying back onto the floor.

In a slow-motion haze, Jade heard her sister's scream. As

her body skidded, she watched, wide-eyed, as her sister ran toward her. Richard was up. He clotheslined Tina around the throat, her body jerking suddenly as the velocity of her actions were stopped. Jade blinked and the next frame horrified her. Richard had her sister in a half nelson. The nine-mil dug into her temple.

"Jade!" Tina screamed, twisting and kicking at Richard.

No! Stop, Tina, Stop! He'll kill you! Jade opened her mouth to scream the words, but none came out. For several long seconds, she could hear nothing nor feeling anything. Shock infiltrated her body. Haziness engulfed her senses. She was going to faint and then Richard would kill them both. Another round of adrenaline spiked. She took a deep breath.

Still reeling from the shock of being shot, Jade managed to scoot back on her butt and lean up against the wall. Her vision cleared and sound was restored. Her body throbbed, one huge mass of bruises. Her shoulder burned like hell. Her chest screamed. She couldn't take a deep breath without her damaged ribs jabbing into her. With her hands tied behind her back, she couldn't apply pressure. The warm flow of blood covered her arm. She looked at Tina, who had finally quieted and who watched her as big sobs racked her chest, her face tearstained.

The room spun twice more in one direction before it changed and settled back to almost normal. Jade shook her head and carefully focused. Fire flared from her arm. She glanced at it. Yep, she'd been shot, a nice hole in the fleshy part of her upper arm. It hurt like a son of a bitch.

She attempted to take several deep, cleansing breaths. The pain was unbearable. Jade looked up at her stricken sister. "I'm okay, Tina."

Richard laughed. "Excellent! I want you alive to watch

me fuck your sister while I slowly strangle her." With Tina as a shield, he moved to the front doors and turned the lock. The light switches were on the other side of the door; he reached over and dimmed the light of the room. Now any passersby would have difficulty seeing inside. Jade's heart pounded, blood raced through her arteries, and panic rose. How the hell was she going to get them out of this?

She'd been tugging at the frayed cord. With her slick blood acting as a lubricant, she almost had one hand out.

Richard pushed Tina toward her, careful to keep the gun trained on her temple. Jade knew with the slightest provocation he would pull the trigger. He stopped ten feet away.

He grabbed Tina's ass with his free hand and squeezed. Tina cried out and it was all Jade could do not to lunge at the bastard. "Is that how it is for you, Richard? Molesting sisters?"

"Shut up! I loved Genny! I protected her!"

He slid his hand up Tina's waist. She squirmed and screamed out. He dug the end of the barrel deep into her skin. "Stop moving, little sister, or you die." Tina immediately stopped. Her wild eyes pleaded with Jade to save her.

"I protected my sister, too, Richard. I killed for her. I'll kill for her again."

Richard laughed momentarily, halting his groping. "You think you're all bad because you think you killed your mama to keep her from turning this sweet thing out?"

"There was no thinking about it. I killed her just as sure as you're standing there."

"What if I told you all you did was give her a good bump on the head?"

Jade's heart stopped. "How would you know what happened?"

"I told you, Otis talked a lot before he died. That boy sure hated you, Ruby Leigh. You can add him to your fan club. It was him who your mama was gonna sell Crystal here to. He was gonna get you through this little thing. Kind of like what I'm doing right now. But you were too smart for him. He didn't expect you would rebel. He came looking for the girl, found your mama sitting at the kitchen table with an ice pack on her head and a bottle of whiskey in her hand."

Jade gasped. "I saw the blood!"

"Head wounds bleed like a stuck pig, especially when you're full of alcohol like your drunk mama. Did you bother to check for a pulse?"

Jade shook her head. She hadn't wasted a minute after her mother had hit her head. She'd grabbed Crystal and run as far and fast as she could. She knew about the fire, she'd seen it erupt while she and Crystal hid in the thick shrubs surrounding the park. She'd read in the paper the next day that they were looking for her.

"Otis was furious when that hag told him you'd done run off. He took the pot of lard sizzling off the stove and threw it in her face. To cover it up, he bashed her head and locked her in the bedroom and set the place on fire."

"Why would Otis tell you that?"

"When I told him what I did to Townsend and that I had a way to give you to him, he became my best buddy." Richard chuckled, enjoying his story. "He told me he killed his mama just to hurry getting you up the hill. But his daddy got to you first. That made Otis real mad. His daddy didn't care. He killed him, too."

Tina started sobbing uncontrollably. And in a slow, unhurried surreal montage the chaotic pieces of Jade's life fell into place. And while she felt the burden of the world lifted from her shoulders with Richard's confession, flashes of Jase's sexy smile flashed before her face, and she felt a stab of pain so deep and so profound it was unbearable. She smiled then, despite it, thinking how she would have given it a shot. Being part of a couple. A *them*. Something good, something clean, something wholesome . . . but that would not be. Because for her sister to live, Jade knew she would pay the ultimate price for it, and knowing that, an unexpected calm filled her.

She looked at her sister, Crystal Blue—Tina, as she had been for the last eleven years. Such a sweet girl. A good girl who deserved everything. They had run all of those years because she thought she'd killed their mother. It was time for it all to stop. Here. Now. Jade shook her head and caught Richard's crazed stare. Slowly she stood, then walked toward him, never once breaking eye contact. "Kill me, Richard. Kill me and let her go."

"No!" Tina screamed. She twisted in the maniac's arms, trying in vain to get clear of him. Jade flung the cord from her wrists as she continued to walk toward him. She reached for a nearby chair to throw at Richard, and as she brought it up in front of her, Tina dropped to the floor. A single shot rang out and Jade's screams mingled with her sister's.

Richard stood rigid, his hands out at his sides, his palms open, a stunned look freezing his face. Jade caught his shocked stare and felt no pity for him. A dark stain seeped into his white T-shirt, spreading to cover the middle of his chest. He looked down and touched his hand to it, then looked up to Jade in disbelief. He sank to his knees, then fell face-first onto the hard linoleum tile.

In the split second before the room swarmed with cops, she looked up to see Jase standing twenty feet away in the shadowed corner of the room, the gun in his hands still aimed at Richard's heart. Jade nearly fainted with relief. She dropped the chair. Instinct drove her into the arms of the man she loved more than her own life. As Jase's strong arms wrapped around her, pressing her into his hard strength, Tina hugged Jade from behind and the three of them stood in the center of the room, one big hugging mass of relief.

As the cops swarmed around them, and time stood still, a hard wave of emotion overcame Jade, and this time, instead of trying to keep it locked up deep inside of her, she let it out. Her body trembled, then racked as great sobs shuttered through her. Tina hugged her tighter. Jase whispered comforting words against her ear, and had she not been sandwiched between the two people on earth that she loved, Jade would not have been able to stand.

Jase led her over to a chair, and when he moved to set her down in it she clung tighter to him. So he sat down and brought her into his lap. Tina sat down beside her on the floor, wrapping her arms around Jade's legs and resting her head against her thigh, and for several more long moments Jade let her emotions run unchecked. She didn't feel the pain in her arm or her ribs, or the pain of what she had endured at the colonel's hand or even Donny's. All she felt was an incredible sense of relief, and a deep, burgeoning love for the man who held her and the sister who clung to her for dear life.

As she hiccoughed back a sob, Jade looked up into Jase's ocean blue eyes and to her astonishment found them shiny with tears of his own. She reached a fingertip up to him and caught one on his lash, then brought it to her lips and kissed it.

Jase pulled her up to his lips. In a slow demonstration of love and hope he parted her lips; their tears mingled, the saltiness of them sweet on her tongue. And at that very moment Jade knew her knight in shining armor had not only awoken her emotions from a long, dormant freeze but had cleared the path for her to live as normal a life as humanly possible.

She didn't ask what he learned in Sykesville or how he found Tina or how he got to her in time. She didn't care. All that mattered was that he came for her, that he was here, and that he would not leave her.

Six weeks later
Avoyelles Parish Municipal Court, Room C

"Miss Gentry," the judge began.

Jade raised her hand, halting him. "Judge Fevre, legally my name is Jade Devereaux."

He cleared his throat. "Miss Jade Devereaux, also known as Ruby Leigh Gentry in these parts, with the new evidence presented to this court, I hereby drop the charge of murder in the first degree. You are free to go, young lady."

Jade smiled and squeezed the hand in hers. She looked up into Jase's happy ocean blue eyes and let out a huge sigh of relief. He pressed a kiss to her lips. "Are you ready to start a new life, Jade?"

She nodded, nervous. "I think so. But I have no idea where to start."

He pulled her along through the courthouse and out into

the sunshine. He looked up at the blue sky, then back down to her. "How about one step at a time. With me?"

Jade laughed, the sound carefree, honest, full of happy promise. She brought his hand to her lips and kissed it. "I'll keep you in mind."

He pulled her into the circle of his arms and kissed her like he would never let her go. "You'll do more than that."

Jade's eyes darkened and she spoke, a serious tone to her words. "Jase, I don't do much well. Especially the relationship thing. I might drive you crazy."

He kissed the tip of her nose. "One step at a time, sweetheart. One step at a time."

Hands intertwined, they looked at each other. Then, in sync, they took one step forward.